THE
MEDICI
RING

Nicole St. John

RANDOM HOUSE NEW YORK

Library of Congress Cataloging in Publication Data

The Medici ring.
  I. Title.
PZ4.J7233Me [PS3560.03897]   813'.5'4   74-26795
ISBN 0-394-49342-7

Manufactured in the United States of America
98765432
First Edition

Pavane for Two Sisters

There were two sisters, dark and fair,
The one was skilled in subtle art,
The other pure in garb and heart,
And she wore lilies in her hair.

Still through the dark pavane they move,
A dark pavane of death and love.

One sister loved with virgin truth
A stranger gallant, strong and sure.
The other, with her wiles impure,
Stole off the heart of that same youth.

One sister wore with brazen pride
The favor once to t'other shown;
And she, forsaken, mourned alone,
Till in her bosom love had died.

A man of craft came passing by,
He saw a woman seemed so fair,
A-wearing lilies in her hair,
And oh, she caught the craftsman's eye.

Alas for faithful love once scorned,
And for false love that seemeth true;
For failing old and choosing new,
Death came upon a grey-eyed morn.

"Oh sister, you have loved well,
I die of love that is not true,
But who chose better, I or you,
Is secret time alone will tell."

THE MEDICI RING

I

I sat straight and still in the high-backed Florentine chair, my hands clasped quietly in my lap, while outside the narrow windows the dull rain beat down on the cobbled pavements of Minetta Street. The little parlor, crammed with Uncle Eustace's collections, was chill, but I had not bothered to light the lamp or stoke the frail fire behind its screen of Galápagos tortoise shell. A few fingers of flame licked fitfully at the coals, and the great ruby on my right hand winked quietly in the dying light.

Across from me the Hon. Mr. Blyden, Esquire, and his partner sat on the edge of their chairs with a kind of neat primness, like two elderly gnomes from a Cruikshank drawing, trying to make everything perfectly clear.

"I trust I am making this perfectly clear, Miss Stanton," Mr. Blyden even said, and pursed his lips. "Mmm, yes. Perfectly clear."

Indeed he had, but I was not about to give him the satisfaction of acknowledgment. He and his partner, in an exchange of glances between watery old eyes, had already summed me up—young, impecunious, overeducated, orphan —and concluded that since I was female and not ugly, I naturally had no brains. They were, I knew, disconcerted by the quietness with which I heard them out. A proper lady probably would have swooned. A proper lady would have been prostrate at the melancholy drama of the funeral concluded a scarce hour and a half before. By many standards of this Year of Our Lord 1874, in New York City, I was not a proper lady. But my grief was private, and when Mr. Blyden had approached me in the dripping wetness of Trinity Churchyard to request an immediate interview to discuss "Mmm, yes. Business," I had acquiesced with an abrupt, silent nod. He did not know that my stony façade concealed not only grief but anger.

That was another thing for which I could not forgive them, their intrusion into my private moment of farewell to Uncle Eustace. No, not my uncle—never my uncle; that was one of the things Mr. Blyden had been making perfectly clear.

I understood that now. Although I had not known the truth before, not known that I had been lied to all these years that I'd been told he was my dead father's uncle. That most of my life we had lived, my mother and I, on the beneficence of a man who was no blood kin. For my father had died before I was born, killed in an accident and leaving no estate. I had been four when Uncle Eustace found us living in genteel poverty, and gathered us in, and I had loved him ever since. My mother was a proud woman who would accept no charity, but this was different, for Eustace Robinson was supposed to be her husband's kin. Only he hadn't been, I was now for the first time learning. Mr. Blyden did not know that, nor did he know the shock almost did knock me senseless, that I was sustained only by my own ramrod pride and even more rigid corsets inside the mourning basque of tight black faille. That, and the Medici ring.

I had caught Mr. Blyden gazing at that ring with something like covetousness in his pale old eyes. But that he would not have the disposition of. Uncle Eustace had given it to me for my twenty-first birthday a year ago, and had made my ownership of it "perfectly clear." Unfortunately, though he had for years made clear to me that he took for granted I would maintain his antiquarian collections by judicious buying and selling, after he was gone, he had neglected to make it clear to his solicitors or to make legal provisions for the same. So here was the honorable Mr. Blyden, this bleak wet October teatime, telling me that the house on Minetta Street was no more my home, that he was taking possession as executor and would, "Mmm, naturally," distribute its antiques and oddities, its tortoise shell and tapestries and Chinese jade to Uncle Eustace's legal heirs, whoever and wherever they might be.

I had never heard Uncle Eustace mention any heir other than me. It seemed I knew very little about his family. It was rapidly being impressed upon me that I knew very little, as well, about my own. Somehow that had never seemed important. We had been a tight, self-sufficient little circle, my mother, Uncle Eustace and I.

Perhaps, had my life been less secure, I would have sought to know more about my background. As it was, I had never felt the need. My mother had been an orphan; I remembered her as a quiet, intelligent and gracious lady. She had been widowed young; very early in life I realized it caused her grief to speak about my father, and so I never did. Anyway, Uncle Eustace had seemed a whole family in himself. When I was a child I saw him as a fairy godfather, a plump, cherubic elf, a collector of the unusual, the precious and the rare. It seemed somehow incongruous to realize, as I grew older, that he was an expert's expert, an acknowledged authority on Renaissance tapestries and jewels. He cared little for public notice, being of a retiring nature, so he was known only among a select circle of collectors whose expertise was almost as fine-honed as his own. I seldom saw any of this side of his professional life. "Uncle Eustace" to me meant elderly eyes twinkling over rimless glasses, and tea beside the fire with Uncle reading aloud from loved leather volumes and Leonardo, our huge orange Persian, settled like a purring kettle on my lap. It meant a gentle old voice rumbling on a steady stream of odd and fascinating facts, plump fingers teaching a child's awkward ones to mend old lace and tapestries with the care of a cloistered nun and call it fun.

When Mother died, when I was seventeen, I came home from Miss Milbrook's Female Academy to keep house for Uncle in her place, and gradually my childhood interest in Uncle's rarities had changed to adult appreciation and, slowly, to shared knowledge. I was on my way, Uncle said, to becoming as expert as himself. I was fortunate that Uncle was more attuned to Renaissance respect for such legendary women as Lucrezia Borgia, Elizabetta Gonzaga and Isabella d'Este than he was to nineteenth-century New York's small opinion of female knowledge. And now Uncle was dead. Uncle was dead, Mother was dead, and I was all alone.

"You have no contacts with your father's family? Or knowledge of them? Mmm, yes. Your mother was Mr. Robinson's housekeeper, I understand. Exactly so." Already, in their prissy, old-maid way, they were reading something scandalous into the association, and anger flamed within me. Don't let it show, a voice warned silently, but I knew my eyes were blazing. Instinctively I sat taller, and the dull faille of my mourning rustled with my movement.

With exquisite timing, Leonardo chose this moment to make his own entrance and allegiance known. He stalked in from the hall, stopped on the Chinese hearthrug to glare at the solicitors, then with a disdainful twitch of his tail came over to leap upon my lap, where he settled among the folds of my overskirt, kneading bread and rumbling balefully. Mr. Blyden's papery old face relaxed and became almost human.

"A handsome animal. Mmm. We must consider, of course, what will become of him."

"He will come with me. Naturally," I said coldly.

"Naturally. That is, if you can—" Mr. Blyden seemed at a loss as to how to proceed. A corner of my mind took malicious satisfaction in that, even while the rest of my thoughts grasped what he was too discreet to say. Where would I go? Where *could* I go? And how could I know Leonardo would be welcome? There were few roads open to a young woman without fortune and too genteel and independent to enter service.

A cold draft seemed to eddy the faded brocades at the window, and my hand, stroking Leonardo's shoulders, pressed down too firmly. He shrieked, spat a feline curse at me, and batted at the ruby ring.

"Of course," Mr. Blyden said, "you can always, if necessary, redeem the value of that ring. Unless I am mistaken, it is a singularly perfect stone."

"It is." I lifted my chin. "And unless you *should* be mistaken, it is my own. You will find the insurance is carried in my name."

That jibe was unworthy of me, but it made me feel much better. He spoke so easily of parting with it, as if the worth of such objects lay in their financial value. Uncle Eustace had taught me better than that.

"The music box is yours. You're going to sell it?" I remembered my long-ago self saying of some particular childhood favorite. And I could almost still hear Uncle's gentle voice. *"No, child. It has been my privilege to have the pleasure of it for a time. Now I shall pass it on to another who will appreciate and care for it."*

What I had told Mr. Blyden was true, but not the whole

truth. Like Leonardo, the great ruby winking at me with its quiet fire had a life of its own, beyond and apart from mine. I was merely the curator. But I would never relinquish that. Not if I starved first.

Mr. Blyden glanced at his silent partner and cleared his throat. "Miss Stanton, ah, forgive me, but I must inquire. Have you any ready funds of your own?"

I looked at him blankly. "No, of course not. As I told you, we had a familial rather than business arrangement. Uncle— Mr. Robinson turned over the housekeeping money and my personal allowance on the first of the month."

"Which is slightly more than a week away. And you will, of course, need—er, to be able to take care of financial responsibilities attendant to your changing situations." He cocked his head at the other man, who produced a cheque-book. "It would be entirely proper for us to reimburse you from the estate for your caretaking of the collections till your departure. And also, if you will be so kind, for your assistance in cataloguing and sorting the wheat from the chaff."

He crooked his lips to indicate this was a little joke, but I was not amused. There is no chaff here, I wanted to say. I also wanted to say, keep your conscience money, this is a labor of love you cannot buy. But a small voice within me whispered that pride was a luxury I could not afford. It was a voice that was new to me, and shaming.

"And of course, you are under no necessity for haste. I think a month between now and your departure would not be out of order."

"You are very kind. I shall leave within the week." A clean cut would be best, not a prolonged leave-taking as with a loved but dying invalid. No, I must be honest with myself; that had not been logic speaking, it had been pride, escaping from its bonds, and I did not regret it.

The light outside the windows had been steadily waning, and now the French clock on the mantel chimed the half-hour. Mr. Blyden looked as though he was longing for his tea. So was I, but I was in no mood to share it. I tilted my head and looked at the two men, waiting. Behind their shoulders I could glimpse my reflection in the pier-glass—a young woman framed by a Florentine chair that gave her the look of a Renaissance portrait, a look enhanced by a black basque cut like a grandee's doublet; perhaps too slender, and too haughty; the black gown and the weight of auburn hair, braid-coiled, drawing the color from her face. They did not know what to make of me, and the malicious satisfaction I derived from this sustained me through dignified, brief good-byes. Then I shut and locked the door behind them and all at once, like a house of cards collapsing, felt myself go limp.

Leonardo rubbed against my ankles and then sat down with determination on my train. It was his way of saying, All right, I've given you sympathy, now I want attention. I went to the kitchen, with Leo promenading conversationally at my heels, filled and lit the teakettle, crumbled bread, poured milk over it and divided it between us. It was a routine I had followed on a hundred evenings, but this was the first time I had done it for Leo and me alone, and when Leonardo jumped up into my lap I hugged him harder than his dignity preferred.

It was my intention to commence directly upon the task of cataloguing, but as it happened both Leonardo and I retired early. He leapt, as was his custom, onto Uncle Eustace's bed. I do not know how he found his slumbers.

An ironic fact impressed itself upon me during the ensuing days: time was money. I arose the morning after the funeral hardened into adamantine determination—I would, I must, find a suitable situation and begin my new life as rapidly as I could. I discovered that, having obligated myself to cataloguing the estate, in order to finance such beginning, I had no time to search out what it was to be. I only hoped I would be able to do so before my means ran out.

I had been a fool to announce so blithely that I would be leaving in a week. But I did not regret it. There was healing in hard labor, comfort in not having time to think as I handled the jade and crystal, the silver boxes and cloisonné for the last time. Leonardo kept me company, a companionship for which I was not always grateful, since he considered that my prime responsibility was his entertainment. I would be hard at businesslike accounts, or deep in polishing brasses, when I would hear an imperious trill, there would be a soft *plopp*, and Leonardo would land in the midst thereof, demanding notice. Too well brought up to break anything, he nonetheless considered many of the smaller objects admirably suited as rolling toys.

"Leo, *no!*" I rescued a cloisonné snuffbox, looked at his indignant amber eyes, and relented. "Poor gentleman, you don't understand what's happening, do you?" I endeavored to scratch his ears, but Leonardo would have none of that. He spat, stalked over to the marquetry cabinet and strode back and forth before it, yowling insistently. I dropped my pen, my throat catching.

It had been the nightly routine, Uncle Eustace sitting in his Morris chair saying, "Well, sir, what shall our evening's occupation be?" Leonardo, padding back and forth before the cabinet, voicing a demand until at last Uncle would laugh, throw open the cupboard doors and allow Leonardo to leap upon the ledge and poke about in the cupboards to find a favorite toy. The cabinet, a really fine inlaid piece, was treasure-house for each of us and we had our own domains among its cubbyholes and drawers. It occurred to me that I was going to miss this cabinet most of all.

It was my responsibility to empty it, too; I would not care to have Mr. Blyden uncovering any lingering schoolgirl treasures. I opened the doors, allowed Leonardo to jump up, and began a turning-out of my own section. A lock of my mother's hair; I had always meant to put that in a locket. Seashells, collected on a Jersey beach long ago. A packet of letters from Mother and Uncle when I was attending Miss Milbrook's Select Female Academy. Another, thinner packet of envelopes addressed to me in a childish, spidery hand. They still gave off a faint scent of cinnamon. I turned away from the cabinet, half smiling at the recollection.

Damaris . . . what was her name? Something outlandish. *Damaris Culhaine.* She had come to the Academy when she was eleven and I was seventeen, and she had clung to me as many lost little souls in such situations cling to any older girl who shows them kindness. If I had been a bewilderment to our schoolmates, Damaris had been more so. At Miss Milbrook's, among the many ways in which we aped our elders, we were snobs, and Damaris committed the double sin of being new rich and Irish. I had earned my place in the company by being able to brazen others down with the sort of look I had turned on Mr. Blyden. But Damaris was frail as a frightened mouse and she had no chance.

I first became aware of her when I found her in a cubbyhole after someone had called her "shanty Irish." She had cried so hard that she had become very sick indeed. Her violent gasps for breath alarmed me, but she would send for no one; all she would say afterwards, besides thanking me for staying with her, was, "Please, Miss Stanton, don't tell them that I cried." The dignity and stern pride had struck a chord in my own heart; her constant bouts of illness won my compassion, and as the winter progressed we had become sisters, after a fashion.

Then, at the end of winter, Damaris had gone home one weekend and she had not returned. We learned, some days later, that her mother had died. That was when the letters began, almost hysterical at first with grief and fear. I replied at once, of course, and for a time we corresponded regularly. But Damaris had not the knack of sounding like herself in letters, she grew guarded and distant, not the frail and vulnerable child I'd come to love. Gradually the letters grew intermittent. Then, that spring, my mother fell ill with typhoid, and I went home to nurse her till her death. I did not return to school. Vaguely I recalled Damaris writing that she was being taken to live abroad, but that letter had been lost in the upheaval of my mother's dying, and after that there had been no further word.

That had been five years ago. Damaris must be a young lady now. But I had neither time nor place for sentiment in my present situation. Resolutely I went over and tossed the packet of letters into the fireplace grate.

Leonardo, hearing the tantalizing sound of paper, pounced over, and I picked him off firmly. "*No*, sir! Stay with your own possessions!" I turned to deposit him back among his toys. Then I froze, clasping the marmalade cat tightly to me, as the first real consciousness of Uncle's death crashed over me like a drowning wave.

Uncle was gone forever. Uncle was gone, and Leonardo knew it. He had not been playing with his own toys, he had transgressed where he had never dared before, into Uncle's private drawers. On the floor in a tangle lay Uncle's old pipe, his personal snuffbox with its contents scattered, the tobacco pouch my mother had embroidered one long-gone Christmas, the quill pens he still persisted in using. Leonardo had also upset the silver inkwell and the shot had spilled like fallen stars across the Chinese rug, while the scant remaining liquid dripped with a kind of slow insistent inevitability on the little book lying back-broken on the floor. One of Uncle's journals . . . year in, year out, on good nights and bad, I had seen him scratching away at them like a kind of genial Pepys. I knelt down, like a dutiful caretaker, to blot the ink off the priceless rug, and instead found myself holding the disfigured journal, gazing at it through stinging eyes.

Leonardo had been playing with the paper, and the pages were rumpled. I blotted them carefully and smoothed the pages. *April 17, 1873* . . . That had been my twenty-first birthday. Scarcely conscious I was trespassing, I read beneath the date the familiar disjointed writing. *Lavinia's natal date. I have had Marianne's ruby made into a ring for her, and she seems most pleased.* He had never told me the stone had been my mother's, nor had I known she owned it; how odd. And I could have sworn not just the stone but the gold snake that coiled around it as setting was very old. My brow furrowed, I read on, trespassing forgotten.

I have determined that I shall write to Boston. Lavinia is of age now, and she has a right to know the truth. Marianne wished to live without restitution, and we have abided by her wishes, but it is time now Lavinia should make her own decision.

My mother had known. That was the first chill pain which registered through my numbness. My mother, that lady of integrity and honor, had known all along that Eustace Robinson was not my uncle, had collaborated in a lie which had brought me ultimately to the agony of today. My mother, my uncle, the two lodestars of my existence, could not be trusted, and so all life, all values now were false.

Why had they lied? Had they told themselves they did it out of love? But love cannot have basis in deception. Those we deceive are those we don't respect, else we would know them able to bear truth.

Eustace Robinson must have known that, for his spidery writing ran on in agitation. *I must confess to feeling uneasy at having played this game with Lavinia all these years.*

What game? my nerves shrieked within me. What game, other than pretending to be my uncle when you were not? What game, other than leading me to believe you were leaving treasures and title in my keeping? Other than teaching me to care for this life, these living things as if they were flesh of my flesh, bone of my bone, until life at any lesser level seemed unbearable? What game, other than raising me to be a lady—no, a *Renaissance* lady—and then leaving me a dependent female ill-equipped for the modern world? Without warning the knife that had been in my heart twisted to its opposite face of anger and almost hate.

The ink, Leonardo, time itself was forgotten. In an unaccustomed frenzy I tumbled drawers and cupboard contents onto the floor about me. I searched like one driven through letters, notes, cheque-stubs, all the fat old journals. I scarcely even knew for what I was searching . . . some clue pointing to Boston, to my mother, the ruby; some key to the tie that had bound us, some explanation of the game. The hope-raising, disillusioning, heartless game.

When I arose hours later, black night had fallen. My back was stiff and aching, my eyes were red with strain, and my heart was cold. Leonardo had given up and gone to bed without me, and I might as well have done the same, for I had not found what I was seeking, a sense of identity or a reason *why*.

A few pieces of *what* stood out with painful sharpness. Eustace Robinson, I would not call him uncle, had known something about my father. He had deliberately, hiding that knowledge, come searching for my mother, introducing himself with the lie of being her dead husband's kin. At some point my mother must have learned the truth, whatever it was, but she had changed nothing. She had continued as his housekeeper, and all the while we had gone on living together, the man who was not my uncle acting out a charade of kindness and family love. Masking what? I did not know, and I had to learn.

I had but two things to go on. *Boston*. Eustace Robinson had come from Boston, and had apparently been in correspondence with someone there eighteen months ago. And my mother's ruby, winking at me inscrutably with its timeless sense of human folly and intrigues past.

One day, I did not know when or how, I would make those pieces fit together.

I tottered to bed. I did not expect to sleep, but such was my brain's exhaustion that I knew no more until cold light flooded my window and Leonardo yowled in annoyance for late breakfast.

School, and my mother's training, have disciplined me well. I did not descend until my hair was piled back in its accustomed braid and I had donned clean linen and dressed for public view. I started automatically to put on my black mourning, then stopped abruptly. No; I would not wear it. I buttoned myself into one of my ordinary day-dresses, a brown sprigged challis, with a modest polonaise drape, and went downstairs.

The post had already come, and a little heap of mail lay beneath the brass mail-slot in the door. An antiquarian periodical; a flock of what appeared to be condolences—I would deal with those another time. I looked at the last, a lavender-white envelope addressed in feminine script to Miss Lavinia Stanton. The writing was strange, and for a moment I wondered what had caused the sudden sense of familiarity. Then I recognized it. The faint, foreign scent of cinnamon.

I tore the envelope open.

"My dear Vinnie . . ."

How long since I had been called that name. I scanned the thin sheets swiftly.

My father has told me of your uncle's death. You will recall Papa also is a collector, so this is how he discovered the sad news. I never knew your uncle, but from how you spoke of him I know you must be crushed with grief.

Oh, Damaris, I thought, there is a great deal that you do not know.

. . . have just returned from several years abroad, and have opened the house on Marlborough Street for the season, indeed we hope to make it our permanent home. "We" being my dear father, my Aunt Marina, who has been like a mother to me, and myself. This is the first we have all been reunited since my mother's death. I was not well after she died—you remember how ill I used to get sometimes at school—and it was thought I would be better off abroad.

Dear Vinnie, we have been out of touch for so long, and I do not know your future plans, but may old friendship justify intrusion in your grief? I am longing to see you, and would so like to have you come as soon as possible for a long visit. You know I always felt better when you were near. Father is thinking of permitting the house to be opened for a charity Gala, to exhibit his Renaissance art, and your specialized knowledge would be an invaluable help. Aunt Marina also has quantities of antique laces she is hoping to restore, and I have told her how clever you always were at that sort of thing. Do write, or better, cable, and say you will come soon to stay as long as you wish. Papa says to say that you're most welcome, and I'm looking forward to returning a little of all you've done for me.

Your loving "little sister,"
Damaris.

I crumbled the pages in my hand, and my eyes stung with angry tears. Oh, Damaris, I thought, you are a young lady and much more polished of phrase, but as transparent as ever in your thoughts. I know what this letter is, a carefully phrased employment offer to an indigent friend who is too genteel to be offered charity. Sharp pride bade me tear the letter to bits and throw them in the fire.

Two things stopped me. One was a single line, added beneath the signature in what seemed haste and obvious disturbance. "I have not been well again. Sometimes I fear—" No more. I knew Damaris' own uncomplaining pride, and it had cost her something to say that much.

The other was the address. Marlborough Street. Damaris lived in Boston, one of the two clues I had found while searching Eustace Robinson's things.

I would begin my search for my true identity on Marlborough Street.

II

The few days of my leave-taking, and my journey to Boston, I will pass over in the belief that the less remembered the better. I had few things of my own to pack, and prolonged farewell to the house on Minetta Street was more than I felt my fine-strung senses could sustain. Better to cut the ties quickly, with no looking back. I did run my hand once over the old marquetry cabinet. Then I picked up my reticule and Leonardo's basket and went down the narrow stone steps for the last time.

The train ride to Boston was a matter of crowded, chilly cars, scant meals and self-absorbed, overconfident traveling salesmen. I rode in the general coach, fearing to expend my scant money on the luxury of the parlour car. By the time we arrived in Boston station my limbs were stiff from the jouncing journey, Leonardo was muttering imprecations beneath his breath, and the chill seemed to have permeated my very bones. When I descended into the dim bleakness of the station, dusk had fallen. Around me on the platform salesmen were bidding each other jovial farewells, family groups were being reunited. I stood alone, and for the first moment since this all began, loneliness assailed me and my courage almost failed. I must not allow it. Pulling my shawl closer about me, I lifted my chin and set forth to find a hansom cab.

I had never before ventured into one of these alone and I was surveying the row, searching for a likely looking driver, when a coachman in impeccable livery presented himself before me.

"Miss Stanton, ma'am?" Beneath the correctly tipped hat, eyes twinkled at me from a shining Irish face. "Marchesa Orsini has sent me to meet you, ma'am, if you'll step this way." I must have looked at him blankly, for he added, as a confidential afterthought, "The Culhaine carriage, ma'am."

"Oh. Yes, of course." I followed him to the handsome equipage with some discomfiture. Marchesa Orsini . . . that must be the aunt. I did not recall Damaris' mentioning that her relative was titled. Come to think of it, I did not remember her ever speaking much of an aunt at all. Ridiculously, I felt I had been placed at a disadvantage.

"If you'll give me your baggage ticket, ma'am, I'll be seeing to your trunks." I surrendered them silently and the man assisted me into the carriage and vanished. He seemed pleasant enough, and kindly. How stupid of me to have assumed, as I had not been aware I did till now, that Damaris, and perhaps her aunt and father too, had come to meet me. I had come not as a guest but as a quasi-employee, and should remember it. I sat stiffly against the dark velour upholstery, and waited. Presently the man returned, superintended the loading of my single trunk, and climbed to the outside box. We moved off through the purple mist.

In this excellent carriage the jolting of the cobblestones was hardly noticeable. I wiped the mist from a square of window pane with my handkerchief and peered out, but could see little except the looming black bulk of houses set close to the curb, and here and there the flickering lights of fog-shrouded streetlamps. We rattled past an expanse of iron fence and high, lowering trees. The public gardens?. How little I know of Boston, I thought. Against this background, my expectation of setting forth on a quest seemed little short of quixotic. I smoothed my kid gloves firmly and felt, beneath my fingertips, the twisted straining bulk of the ruby ring.

The carriage had stopped. The coachman opened the door and held out his hand and I stepped down to carriage block and curb. Before me, four-square on its corner and framed by a wrought-iron fence, rose a gracious house. I could not say why, for I could not discern its features, but even through the dark it held out to me a sense of stability and Georgian symmetry. The center door was framed with fan and side lights of leaded glass. On either side, and on both floors, were window bays, perfect in proportion. Lamplight streamed through them, and I caught my breath. For the square panes were not smooth, but rounded, old bullet glass, and they were not clear. They were an odd, exquisite lavender-pink.

The gate at the cobbled center path stood open and now, at the top of the stone steps, the black door opened also, sending out a fan of light. Behind me the coachman was already lifting down my trunk. He stood deferentially at my elbow, and his rich brogue came to me so low that for a moment I was not sure I heard.

"It's welcome ye are, ma'am. Miss Damaris 'ud have ye know it."

What a heartwarming gesture, I thought. But when I turned to thank him, he was already back busy at his work. In the doorway an austere elderly figure waited. I lifted my chin, feeling the plume of my tilted hat flutter at my nape in the night air, and went up the steps into the house of Culhaine.

If the coachman was Irish, the butler was pure Oliver Goldsmith and not a decade later. He seated me on a straight striped satin chair in the central hall and left me despising myself for my own sense of gaucherie. In the moment of solitude my first impressions were a series of shimmering images: bareness, a polished parquet floor, gilt-framed old paintings hanging high on walls that rose three stories to darkness that would prove by day to be a skylight. On each of the upper levels the halls circled like galleries with dark carved railings, joined together by a sweeping stair. All this I saw in a single flashing moment. Then on one side of the hall a door opened silently, and a woman entered, and I was aware of nothing more.

Once, when I was a child, I had seen a moth moving with no seeming motion before a light. Its wings chrome-yellow velvet, marked with purple-brown, it had seemed to dim the light itself with its own splendor. It was that moment which the Marchesa Orsini made me remember now.

"Miss Stanton? I am Marina Orsini. How very good that you could come to us." Her voice had an organ's resonance and richness, and it was very kind. Subtly, indefinably, I was conscious of myself and of my status. A shadow seemed to fall across me, as if a pair of great wings had fluttered slowly before the light.

Marchesa Orsini was a golden woman, the gold of silks and velvets in old Italian portraits. Her red-gold hair was drawn back from a classic brow into the currently fashionable cascade of curls. Her gold-brown velvet costume was exquisitely tailored, and her earbobs matched the dark topaz which fastened the fine lace ruffles at her throat. I rose, fighting back a ridiculous impulse to curtsy the way I had been taught in school.

"You must be tired from your journey and will want to

rest. The man will send your trunks up to you directly. *Madonna santa!*" Her face blanched, and she recoiled as if she had been struck.

In the parlance of sentimental novelists, I should have liked to die.

Leonardo had liberated himself from his traveling basket and had seated himself firmly, as was his wont, on the marchesa's velvet train. He had been through an ordeal, he proceeded to make plain; he was being ignored; as a good hostess she should be comforting him with bread and milk, perhaps laced with brandy, which he adored. He looked magnificent against the brown velvet, and he doubtless knew it. Even in my embarrassment the farcical aspect of the situation struck me, and I was puzzled that the marchesa's reaction, rather than being the annoyance to which she richly was entitled, was sheer horror.

I picked Leonardo up, forcibly restraining his swinging paws, and explained his presence with some incoherence. "I am sorry if he frightened you," I finished.

"I am not frightened. It is not good for Damaris to be exposed to cats; they make her ill." Marchesa Orsini made a gesture of dismissal. "You will, of course, keep him confined to your own quarters. I have put you in the blue bedroom on the third floor. The sewing room is right next door, you see, so it will be most convenient."

Ah yes, indeed, my position well defined. Too high for servant, not quite a lady guest. My bosom rose and fell with the effort I was making to control my tongue. Then from somewhere in the upper reaches of the house a light beamed down warm and golden, and a breathless voice called, "Vinnie, dear!"

Damaris was hurrying toward me down the stairs, clinging to the banister with both hands in her haste, the soft white of her wrapper billowing out behind her. She was still small and slight, and the pale hair tumbling to her shoulders made the years fall away. It seemed we were back in boarding school again, and when she flew at me with arms outstretched I took her into my embrace without restraint. It was not until I held her off at arm's length that I noted the too-finely-chiseled features, and knew she was no more a child. Her dark eyes had the look of one too early old. Tears starred her lashes, but her face was alight, and she was laughing with a little catch in her breath that I remembered.

"Vinnie, Vinnie, it is so good to see you! Do forgive me for not coming to the station—I was not well! What a handsome cat. Will he let me pet him?" Leonardo not only permitted it, he promptly started to purr. "You must be weary. Let me take you up. You shall have the front room next to mine. There is a door between, so we can talk in the night the way we used to!"

"I have put Miss Stanton in the blue room," Marchesa Orsini said pleasantly.

Damaris grew still. I touched her hand with my fingertips, but she paid no heed. She stepped up onto the lower steps so that her eyes were on a level with her aunt's, and she looked straight at them.

"Lavinia will be next to me, Aunt Marina." Her voice fell into the silence like chiming silver bells, and it was the marchesa who gave way.

"Very well, if you wish it," she said indifferently, and turned aside.

"But I do, of course! We have so much to talk of. Come, Vinnie, I have ordered tea sent up. Then you must dress, for we dine at seven. I hope Papa will join us, since it is your first night." Damaris' foreign travels had given her a patina of poise. I allowed her to lead me up the stairs and around the gallery to our left, talking thirteen to the dozen all the way.

"My room is at the end, by the stairs, and my dressing room next. And here is your room. It looks out on Marlborough Street, you see." Damaris crossed to pull open the heavy purple drapes as I shut the door and set Leonardo down on the flowered rug. He at once began to investigate the handsome room done in plum and olive and gilt, and it was not until I turned from taking off my hat at the walnut Italian bureau that I saw Damaris had gone pale, her whole body shaking.

I hurried to her. "Damaris! Are you ill?"

Damaris gave an abrupt shake of her head, and her fingernails dug into her palms. "No. So very, very angry. Lavinia, I am *so* sorry."

"About what?" Then I understood, and my own face flamed. I took her thin hands in mine. "Dear, it's all right. Don't distress yourself."

"It is not all right. It was insufferably rude, and an insult to you, my guest. But I must ask you to forgive it, for my sake."

"You know I do." I could not say that harsh necessity, and self-interest, forced me to swallow such slights and more. Damaris would hear my story, or at least part of it. But not yet, not now.

Damaris dropped down on the green velvet chaise as if the strength was leaving her with her draining anger. "Aunt Marina is good. But she is European. She—sees things differently. In Europe, everything is old family, and money, and she has had both. Here, what matters is having a Mayflower ancestor. Since we opened the house two months ago, some of the first families have come calling. Out of curiosity, and because they want Papa to endow an art museum! Some of them are poor as church mice, and their families were peasants when we were earls and dukes, but in their eyes we are shanty Irish and Italian immigrants."

Damaris stopped, not looking at me, her fingers carefully smoothing out the tassels on a satin cushion. "We'd been in Italy. We'd forgotten. Aunt Marina—it has given her pain.

You know, Lavinia." Our eyes met, then skittered apart. Yes, I knew.

Leonardo jumped up and settled himself in a round orange ball between us, purring lustily, and I think we were both grateful for this interruption. Damaris scratched his ears. "Definitely, he does not have to stay in your room. My father will agree. My father likes cats. He gave me one for my eleventh birthday, but it died." Her fingers slowed, and her voice petered away.

"But if cats make you ill . . ."

"They don't," Damaris said firmly. "Aunt Marina is afraid of them, but she won't admit it. Anyway, there is no reason for it, and my father says one must face one's fears down and conquer them. So we will speak no more about it. Vinnie, I am so glad that you have come."

"It was good of you to ask me."

"I've thought about you so often since we've returned. But I didn't know how to reach you. When Papa learned of your uncle's death, it seemed providential." Damaris' fingers laced and unlaced themselves, and she seemed on the verge of some confidence from which she shied away. "Forgive me; that sounded dreadful! But now you are here, you must stay for a long, long visit. Papa says so. You must make allowances for Aunt Marina."

But Marina was the honest one. As a visitor I was masquerading under false pretenses, and all at once Damaris' delicate diplomacy was suffocating.

"Damaris," I said gently, "let's not play games. I've had enough of that. I know why you asked me here."

I was not prepared for the violence of her reaction. Her head jerked up and her eyes flared with a look I knew because I had seen it in my own, short days before. Blind panic. Then the rasping harsh breathing struggled in her chest, and I pushed Leonardo off, to his great annoyance, and put my arms around her, bending her forward in the way I remembered learning in the old days. Fortunately the attack was a mild one, and in a few moments she lay quiet and exhausted.

"Your aunt was right. Leonardo should not be here."

Damaris shook her head firmly. "It's not that. It was—oh, here's tea!" She sat up with evident relief as a trim maid entered carrying a laden tray. Damaris busied herself playing hostess with the silver pot as I laid aside my wraps and stripped off my gloves. Her eyes fell on the ruby ring, and her brow furrowed.

"Did you have that in school? It seems familiar, but I can't remember."

I shook my head. "My—it was given to me for a recent birthday. It's a family piece." I looked at Damaris, snuggled like a little girl among the cushions of the chaise, and for a moment the old relationship was there. I was on the edge of opening to her my quixotic quest. Then the door opened, and the moment was gone.

The woman who stood on the threshold wore a maid's uniform on her ample bulk, but it was obvious from her speech that she was on more familiar terms. Grey-haired and red-complectioned, with a hearty Irish face, she represented the finest type of old family retainer. "Miss Damaris, the clock's more'n struck six and you not started dressing! What'll your pa say if you're to keep him waiting?"

Damaris jumped up. "Is Papa coming home to dinner, Maggie?"

The woman sniffed. "And how should I know? The *markaysey* ordered the table set for four, so it's pick and choose whether it's himself or that Mr. Sloane again, third time this week. But you'd best get moving, Missy, either way." She left, after setting a steaming jug of water on the washstand. Damaris departed through the connecting door, and in a moment a footman brought in my trunk and I was able to commence my own toilette.

The marchesa had not been pleased, I felt quite sure, with

the way Damaris had made plain I was to sit with them at dinner. Let her! I could hold my own. An imp of pride provoked me to take from my trunk my favorite gown of aubergine silk. The color was sober enough for governess-companion, but not the style. The overskirt was draped back into a cascade of extravagant pleats, and the low square neck and long tight sleeves were edged with flounces of rare old lace. I had woven it together with invisible stitches from hundreds of scraps Uncle Eustace had found in some old chest.

Maggie, coming in to hook me up, approved my choice. "The *markaysey* can't wear that color. Makes her look too sallow. You keep your sails up, miss, and don't let her draw the wind from them. You're welcome here." It was an echo of what the coachman had said. The servants, at any rate, were behind me—or behind Damaris.

I had been right in thinking Maggie an old retainer. She had been Damaris' nurse and had been pensioned off, apparently, while the family was overseas. This I learned among a constant soft babbling that accompanied her hooking and buttoning, brushing my hair and assisting me in pinning it up. By some instinct, remembering Marina Orsini's waterfall curls, I styled my own hair in its familiar coil of braids. It was not the fashion, but it became me. Then I dismissed her and sat down by the fire to compose myself until the dinner bell should ring. My heart was pounding, and I could feel my pulse throbbing in my wrists.

To still myself, I picked up a book lying on a low table at my side. It was an old one, of vellum and fine morocco, and I was more interested at first in binding than in contents. Then I let it fall open at random in my hands.

> . . . . His form had not yet lost
> All her original brightness, nor appeared
> Less than Archangel ruined. . . .

                               . . . . but his face
        Deep scars of thunder had intrenched, and care
        Sat on his faded cheek, but under brows
        Of dauntless courage, and considerate pride. . . .

I had stumbled into Milton's *Paradise Lost*.

A meditation on the sin of pride was not amiss, but it was lost on me in my present state. I sat gazing unseeingly at the yellowed page.

Somewhere in the lower reaches of the house a bronze gong clanged, and Damaris came through the connecting door. "Vinnie! Are you ready? How fine you look." She held out her hands to pull me to my feet and we went out into the hall together. Damaris was wearing an elaborate dinner gown in the latest debutante mode, but its magnificence overpowered her. She looked smaller, frailer and paler than ever, and as we went downstairs together and voices came to us through the open library door, I felt her shrinking behind me. Her dependency strengthened my own backbone, and I stepped across the threshold with my head held high.

As we entered, the conversation ceased and it seemed that everything grew still. I know I did. It was not the occupants, but the room itself, which caused my quietness and slowly spreading joy. It was a room such as I had always dreamed of owning, a room lifted whole from fifteenth-century Florence or Verona. High, square and dark, its effect was one of emptiness and peace. Here and there stood high-backed chairs and settles in dull old Venetian reds and blues and golds. The walls were lined with books, save where old paintings looked down from their heavy frames. Set in the paneling of the mantel was a portrait of a young woman garbed in white. Her hair, done in the same loops and coiled braiding as my own, was butter-pale, with lilies intertwined. Dark eyes gazed off into the distance as if observing things others could not see. Round her neck was a curious necklace, a twisted collar of reticulated gold.

It was with some difficulty that I detached my gaze from the old portrait to observe the human occupants of the room. Marina Orsini, exquisite in amber silk, was seated in a low chair, her jewels winking in the candlelight from the gold wall sconces. But my eyes were caught by the tall, slender masculine figure standing before the fire, bending carelessly toward the flames. He was examining a piece of crystal which he was turning carefully with his long fingers, and it sent forth rainbow fingers of light which dazzled my eyes.

"Papa!" Damaris said with evident delight.

Ross Culhaine straightened and turned toward her, and I was able to observe, unmarked, the fine cut of black broadcloth and white pleated linen. It was the man himself who interested me more, interested and for some odd reason also alarmed me. His hair was blue-black, and his skin of that odd sallow hue which always seems both pale and dark. And his face—my eyes traveled to it and I almost gasped. My suggestibility, no doubt, was due to the nature of my recent reading, for there before me, I could have almost sworn, stood Milton's fallen angel. The chiseled bones were so fine-honed, the black-fringed eyes so deeply set, that for a moment it seemed as if I stared upon a head of death.

It was not until, at Damaris' prompting, he turned full towards me, that I saw his eyes were as green as emeralds. And as cold.

III

I was to remember that first strange dinner for some time to come. Even as it was going on, a corner of my mind was recording it, analyzing, seeking to find a pattern in crosscurrents and contradictions.

I wonder why I thought of it as a dinner party, although it consisted only of the four of us resident in the house. Perhaps it was because I was not accustomed to dining in such splendor. Perhaps because I caught no sense of family, and perceived the lack was not due to my own strangeness.

Mr. Culhaine offered me his arm to escort me in. I was not sure whether this was because I was a guest or because he happened to be speaking to me when the meal was announced. I was sure of one thing; the marchesa was not overpleased.

The dining room was on the other side of the hall and to the rear, a long narrow room reminiscent of an Italian abbey. The walls were dark and glazed, with a painted border; a tapestry hung above the sideboard. Tall chairs up-holstered in cut velvet were drawn up to a refectory table, the wood of which was bare. Down its center ran a brocade runner, set with a gold pedestal bowl of hothouse fruit and tall altar candelabra. The candles in these, and the wall sconces, provided the room's sole illumination. Mr. Culhaine seated me at the side, where I could just look into Damaris' eyes across the high bowl of fruit, and took his own place at the end near the tapestry. The marchesa had already assumed her own seat at the head and at her imperceptible signal the parade of service began.

After a few moments I found myself listening crazily for the sounds of hidden viol, recorder and flute; a private orchestra seemed all that was missing. There was a footman to stand behind each chair, possibly needed at that, for we were separated by so long an expanse of table that we could not possibly have passed things one to another.. The food was exquisite, deceptively simple, and like nothing I had ever eaten. The flickering candlelight, falling from high above our heads, made our faces into gargoyle masks. I glanced across at Damaris, but she was eating quietly, not looking up. Her aunt ate in the European manner, the fork in her left hand. The service was accompanied by the liquid flow of her charming voice.

"Mrs. Cabot and her committee are coming to tea tomorrow, Ross. Can you be here?"

Ross Culhaine made an impatient gesture. "I'm in the middle of merger negotiations. You know that, Marina. I can't promise to interrupt them for frivolity."

"It is not frivolity. The ladies have asked you repeatedly to set a definite date for the Gala. You cannot put them off forever with generalities."

"I am not putting them off forever. And I warn you, Marina, if they press any further they run the risk of receiving a flat no. I will not have your Boston biddies pawing over the collections until they have been properly inventoried and displayed."

"You know Warren Sloane is most anxious to help. Besides, I thought tending to all that was the reason that Miss Stanton is here." Marina Orsini's voice was soft as silk but a draft seemed to creep into the room, and I felt my ears flatten the way Leonardo's do when he scents a rodent. Ross Culhaine fastened his death's-head gaze upon her coolly.

"Miss Stanton is here by reason of being Damaris' friend. I hope she will stay long to give her companionship and perhaps some comfort." An odd choice of word, I noted, alert. "And I scarce think such a pretty young woman will be wanting the heavy responsibility for a Medici treasure trove of breakables and easily lost objects."

The compliment did nothing to counteract the chill that instantly ran up my spine. I said, "I would not think of it without proper bonding. Which should be easily obtained. I catalogued the Rensselaer collection in New York last winter, under personal insurance, with no loss nor breakage. I am not, after all, unfamiliar with Renaissance artifacts."

It was ostentatious of me, I confess it; I put my hand up casually to my face so that the stone of my ring glittered in the candlelight. To my right I heard a faintly audible sound from Marina Orsini. But I was not concerned with her. I gazed coolly down the table at Ross Culhaine, and had the satisfaction of seeing him react as if a fluffy kitten had suddenly shown its fangs.

Ross Culhaine did not like being caught off-guard, or challenged, I was sure of that already. Damaris had presented him to me as if he were a king, her voice awe struck and breathless. King he might be in her eyes, or in his own; he was not in mine. My pride ran up against the realities of needing to earn a living, and was struck with the blunt fact that if my work was not respected, I might as well not hope to have the chance to do it.

To my astonishment, I perceived after a second that his flexible mouth was hard put not to curve into a smile. "And is it a second feline we have in the house, in addition to the handsome creature I've already heard of? I look forward to meeting your leonine friend at an early occasion, Miss Stanton, and contrary to what you may be thinking, he's welcome among us. And if you be wishing to assist in unpacking of the Culhaine Collection, you're more than welcome. 'Twas not my meaning to be implying you'd not be appreciative and careful, only that the finer points of evaluation for cataloguing might be beyond your ken."

"Lavinia's more than just appreciative and careful," Damaris' soft voice put in. "She knows a great deal about antiquities. I've told you, Papa."

"Aye, from Eustace Robinson. He was a rare man indeed for recognizing the genuine from the counterfeit, and knowing its true value, even if none else did. And glad I am to hear if some of it's rubbed off by association."

I could not help myself. "A rare man indeed," I said, "and able to tell the counterfeit from the genuine in people and in voices, too, as in antiques. Aye, and even if concealing the true worth with ever such art."

Stillness fell upon the table with the weight of a crystal falling into a pool. I felt Damaris hold her breath.

"And just what," Mr. Culhaine inquired with sardonic precision, "might be the meaning of that ambiguous remark?"

"That it strikes me the brogue in the House of Culhaine, however charming, may be not quite so authentic as its Florentine chairs. I've seen rare furniture at times covered with coarse cloth to conceal its fineness from the Philistines."

There was another second's stillness, then Ross Culhaine put back his head and roared. Damaris clapped her hands.

"Good for you, Vinnie! You're the first to find him out. Papa does love to tease by talking Irish."

"He loves the excuse it gives him for eloquent rudeness," Marina corrected. "Ross, how can you!"

Ross Culhaine flashed a singularly charming smile. "I love the way it excuses me from talking to the Philistines, you mean. That was an excellent diagnosis, Miss Stanton. Accept my apologies. You are a worthy adversary, and I'll not—I mean, I won't, try that particular gambit with you again. So you noticed my Florentine chairs, did you? Would you care to put a date on them?"

"Late fifteenth century. But the upholstery's later. That particular weave did not come in until the fifteen-twenties." I was in luck there, for Eustace Robinson had owned similar chairs, but I was on thin ice and hastened to get off it with my banners flying. "What particularly interested me was the portrait above your mantel. It looked like a del Sarto. Is it?"

"Of his school, certainly, though its actual source has never been authenticated. But I believe, like you, that it may well be from his own hand. You saw the look about the eyes?"

I nodded.

"She's called la Bianca," Damaris put in eagerly. "There's a legend about her. Papa has another picture of her, too, only I haven't seen it since we came home. She's wearing the collar in that one also, but with a pendant—"

"Damaris," Ross said coldly, "you are babbling. Please desist."

It was the most cruel, and off hand, dismissal I had ever heard a parent give a child. Damaris subsided as if a light had been blown out within her. She addressed herself to the dessert before her but could not eat; she raised the fork to her lips, then let it fall, untouched. I was so angry I could scarcely trust myself to speak, but yet I did.

"I noticed a harp on the table also. Do you play, Damaris?" I was trying to give her a chance to reassert herself, and I pointedly ignored her father, but it was he who answered.

"She does. If you ladies have finished, we will have our coffee in the library and Damaris will play for you."

"Only if she wishes to."

"Oh, she will," Culhaine said carelessly. "Damaris likes having a chance to contribute something, and she plays quite well technically, although without passion."

Had it been my harp, and he my father, I knew precisely what I would have done with it at that moment. Then I checked myself. It was easy for me to talk, never having known a father. Perhaps I had been more fortunate than some.

We withdrew to the library again, and coffee was brought in, thick and bitter in small fragile cups. It was not to my liking, and I was discomfited that Culhaine knew it; his eyes were amused. Damaris made no pretense of taking more than a sip or two. She shrank into a corner of the settee beside me and stared at her hands. But when Culhaine turned to her and said, "Music, Damaris," she rose obediently.

I put out my hand. "Pray don't, if you don't feel like it."

"I will be happy to sing for you, Vinnie," Damaris said quietly. She fetched the little harp and sat down with it on a low seat before the fire, and ran her fingers once or twice across the strings.

I watched her with some disturbance as she adjusted the tension and bowed her head forward a moment, lost in her own thoughts. This was not the Damaris I remembered, whose strength might be feeble but whose spirit was not. Something had happened during the missing years, something that had killed her courage and even—no, I was not being too fanciful—had marked her with the frosty finger of fear. I could see its pale touch as she threw back her head and closed her eyes.

Ross Culhaine had been right. The music did have no

passion. But I had been wrong. Damaris' spirit might be shadowed, but it was not destroyed.

> "There were two sisters, dark and fair,
> The one was skilled in subtle art,
> The other pure in garb and heart,
> And she wore lilies in her hair.
>
> "Still through the dark pavane they move,
> A dark pavane of death and love . . . "

She was singing a ballad about the woman in the portrait. And I had a pretty shrewd idea of why. Mentally I applauded. I wished I dared look blandly at her father, but I did not. Instead I watched Damaris' fingers run up and down the strings as she curved over her instrument, like a lady in a medieval tapestry. After a while her eyes opened and she gazed off into the shadows with the same look as their painted counterpart's. Her voice, though untrained, was sweet, and it rang like clear bells in the stillness. There was no sign from the other listeners, but presently, in mid-verse, she struck a false note and stopped, her head dropping forward. "I'm tired," she said childishly.

"Enough of that, anyway." Marina shrugged her silk shoulders restlessly. "How you can like that thing so. It's morbid. Ross, will you play for us? Play something gay!"

"Not tonight," Culhaine said shortly. He was looking at Damaris with something like displeasure, and I observed that she had commenced to tremble. I rose.

"I am weary also. It has been a long day. If you will forgive me."

"I'll come with you." Damaris seized gratefully at the straw I'd offered. She kissed her aunt good night with real affection and then, hesitantly, her father, and followed me out.

As we started together up the stairs, I caught a glimpse back through the open doorway and had an odd sensation of looking back through time. The two figures, seated so still, facing each other directly across the old portrait and framed in their turn by the room's carved double doors, had the look of a medieval triptych. And the same sense of waiting.

Damaris' head was high but she went upstairs slowly, her hand gripping tight the banister. After we were out of sight of the doorway she stopped and leaned against the wall a moment and grasped my wrist.

"Damaris! Are you ill?"

Damaris shook her head. "I have trouble . . . breathing on the stairs. I'll be all right in a moment." She started up again determinedly.

I would have pressed her further but when we reached the top the elderly maid materialized in Damaris' doorway and took over firmly.

"You've got yourself in a state again. I knew you would. I heard you playing that tune again, though you know you oughtn't."

"It's my own song. I've a right to sing it," Damaris murmured with tired obstinacy.

"Aye, and fiddle for the devil's own dancing, like your pa playing on the edge of the pit. I know you, missy. Say good night to your friend, now, there's a new day tomorrow." She marshaled Damaris off as if she were no more than six.

I went on to my own room, feeling weariness descend on me like a heavy cloak as soon as I had latched the door that shielded me into a private world. The bed had been turned down and the lamps were lit, casting a rosy glow that was echoed by the coal fire on the hearth.

Leonardo was curled in luxurious content on the cushions of the velvet chaise. Judging from the saucers on the hearth, he had dined exceeding well. I sat down beside him, scratching his stomach abstractedly as I took down my hair. He stretched and rumbled. Obviously he had taken the measure of his surroundings and approved.

It was my intention to sit up a while writing in my journal, in an attempt to sort out my tangled impressions. But almost immediately I knew it was no use. I blew out the lamps and crept between the cinnamon-scented sheets. Contrary to my expectations I fell asleep almost at once.

It may have been hours later, it may have been minutes, when I heard a faint mouse-tapping at my door. I sat up, fully awake. A few coals glowed fitfully on the grate and the house was still. Down by my feet I could feel the warm humming bulk of Leonardo like a great tea-cozy. The tapping was repeated, then the door of the dressing room opened silently and Damaris slipped inside.

"Vinnie! Are you awake?"

"Yes. What is it? Are you ill?"

Damaris shrugged. "I couldn't sleep," she said airily. Even in the darkness I could see her eyes were very big, and I wondered if she'd been taking some sort of draught for her nerves. "Can I come in with you the way I used to?"

I held the bedcovers open and she snuggled in like a little girl, pulling the coverlets tight up against her chin. "Mmmm. Lovely! Even a footwarmer for our toes. I'm glad you're here, Vinnie. I hate the cold."

"I'm surprised, then, you left Italy."

"Papa thought it was time I learned to live here," Damaris said vaguely and was silent for a time. "I lived with Aunt Marina, you know. On a lake, in a little town between Milan and Venice. It was very beautiful. Papa—Papa mostly traveled. This is the first we've really been together, you see. He can't seem to settle down, he's—restless. Maggie says ever since the accident he's been mad at God."

She was trying to justify her father's rudeness, and my heart ached with impatient pity. I longed to ask the circumstances of her mother's death, but checked my curiosity, for

Damaris had grown cold and had begun to tremble. I searched for a change of subject to divert her. "Tell me about the portrait," I suggested. "You started to before. You said there's another picture of her also?"

"Did I? I don't remember," Damaris said blankly. "There must be many pictures. It's a famous legend, you know, in Northern Italy. And it's about my ancestors! That's why I wrote the song about it, you see?" She laughed, too brightly. "I sang that song at a musicale, right after we came back from Italy, and somehow the story of the song and the legend and the Culhaine Collar got printed in *Town Topics*. Papa was furious, and he's forbidden me to sing the song in public since. But I will sing it, when we're alone, because it's mine! There were two sisters, it seems, one good, one bad, and the bad one stole the other's lover, and then one died, they say of unfaithful love . . . That's how my parents met, did I ever tell you? Papa owned the collar, and that painting, and he was trying to trace down the legend. He heard there was a tapestry that showed the story, in our old palazzo on Lake Garda . . . He was sitting in the belvedere—our little summerhouse—beside the lake, talking to my Aunt Marina, who was just a girl, when he looked up and saw my mother coming up the path, all in white with her gold hair flowing . . . like Venus rising from the sea . . ."

Her voice had taken on a rapid singsong quality, and her breath was coming in those jerking gasps I recognized with alarm. What was new, and terrifying, was the way she suddenly, with a cry of pain, clung to me like a frightened animal. Instinctively I held her tight, soothing her as one would a child, masking my own panic in quiet reassurance. After a while the shuddering stilled, and I knew that she was weeping.

"Damaris," I said as calmly as I could, "what in the name of God is going on?"

"Why, nothing," Damaris said in that false child's voice. "I'm just being foolish."

"That explanation means nothing to me, and you know it," I retorted. "Tell me. You know you tried to, in your letter."

"I've been—ill," Damaris said slowly. "The way I've always been. You remember, Vinnie. Everyone said I'd get better as I grew older, and I was better while we were away, but it's come back again, ever since we've been home, and worse than ever. Different, too. I've had such pains."

"What kind of pains?" She didn't answer. "Have you seen a doctor?"

Damaris flashed me that curiously dispassionate, ruthless look she sometimes had. "You know the doctors! They say it's nerves, and I oughtn't to get worked up. They've been saying that for years."

"Have you told your father?"

Damaris shrugged. "Papa believes the doctors. Papa hates weakness. He thinks, if I'd just use will power—Marina understands, I think. She did try to make Papa take me back to Italy. But Papa's told her if folks make a fuss over me, I'll never try . . ."

"But there's more to it than that, isn't there?" Again she didn't answer, and I had an odd feeling she wanted me to force the truth. "Damaris, why did you write me that you were afraid?"

"You won't believe me," Damaris said dully.

"Try me."

"I think," Damaris said after a silence, "that I'm being poisoned."

She said it exactly as if she were saying it was starting to rain.

I wet my lips, maintaining my careful calm. "Do you think you know who's doing it?" No answer, but I felt her assent. "Then tell me."

"I can't."

"Yes, you can." I had always had the power to compel Damaris, and I used it mercilessly now. Her eyes opened and stared off into the darkness and her voice, when it came, was scarcely more than a cat's breath.

"She comes to me in the night . . . ever since we came home. My mother."

IV

When I awoke in the morning, Damaris had vanished. A pale sunlight filtered through the window curtains, and the house was close and warm, a heavy steam heat to which I was unaccustomed. I wondered whether what I was remembering was but an odd, disturbing dream.

The household sounds were muffled by the thick luxury of draperies and carpets. I dressed and went out onto the gallery, a well of light now streaming from the glass panes in the roof high overhead. Damaris' door was shut. The trim maid was passing in the hall below, and she bobbed a curtsy to me as I descended.

"Morning, miss. Breakfast is set up on the sideboard in the dining room, if you'll please to help yourself."

"Miss Damaris?"

"She'll not be down till noon, not usual. She don't sleep well, miss."

The girl seemed predisposed to linger, and I should like to

have heard her confidences, but it was not seemly to interview a servant concerning her young mistress, so I dismissed her and proceeded thoughtfully to the dining room. On the sideboard beneath the tapestry a sumptuous spread was set forth in the English fashion. Steam emanated from a silver coffee urn, and chafing dishes jostled cheek by jowl with silver warmers in what struck me as a prodigal display for so few persons. A masculine figure stood with his back to me, filling a laden plate. At first I thought it was Ross Culhaine, and felt an unaccustomed and annoying wave of shyness. Then, as he straightened, turned, and smiled, I wondered how I could have been even momentarily deceived, for the man gave an immediate impression of being both smaller and less severe.

"Good morning! I recommend the sausages. The morning coffee's American, and good, but don't risk the tea unless you've a cast-iron digestion. It's Irish style, which means English boiled three times over."

He seated himself at the table and commenced eating with gusto, obviously much at home, while I served myself in silence and berated myself for not drawing Damaris out further about the household. He was no member of the family, that I knew; Damaris had no relations save her father and her aunt. I am not the sort who makes casual acquaintances easily and I wished heartily that Damaris were there to perform the necessary introductions. My companion evidently suffered no such handicap. As soon as I turned from the buffet he was on his feet, holding out the chair beside his in such a manner that I could not avoid it without rudeness.

"Those of us who rise at civilized hours must make shift for ourselves. Awkward for a newcomer, but one gets used to it. Marina never stirs from her boudoir till the clock strikes noon, and I suppose the little one's had another bad night. And how did you find your first night in Castle Culhaine, Miss Stanton?"

I gazed at him in frank astonishment. "You have the advantage of me, sir."

"Forgive me." Eyes twinkling, he swept off an imaginary hat. "Warren Sloane, very definitely at your service. I would present my card, were it not bad taste to have a business card in the House of Midas."

"Are you a—relative, Mr. Sloane?"

"Perish the thought, tempting as it may be. No, I am what is known in the haunts of the rich as the Deserving Poor, otherwise meaning self-supporting. Actually I'm an art curator, attached to the New York Museum, but currently on loan to assist in cataloguing the Culhaine Collection. Which, since you are here for the same purpose, means we should be great and good friends, don't you think? More sausage, Miss Stanton? No? Coffee? Allow me." He refilled my cup before I could answer. "Have you seen the famous necklace yet? You must get Culhaine to show it to you. It's right in your line."

"You seem," I said faintly, "to know a great deal about me."

"I know a great deal about everything," Sloane said calmly. "At least about everything pertaining to Renaissance art on Marlborough Street. And since you do not look exactly a fool, I wonder how long it will take you to know all about it, too."

I did not bother to answer. Warren Sloane was definitely, I thought with annoyance, a most presumptuous young man. It was odd that I automatically thought of him as young, for he could have been anywhere in the vicinity of thirty. He had, however, the sort of face and form that would eternally be thought youthful. There was a pixyish quality about him, a ready and familiar smile, crinkling brown eyes, and a thatch of gold-brown hair that fell over one eye in an engaging and no doubt deliberate fashion. Since I am not normally given to prejudice, I wondered why I should so instantly feel myself withdraw.

"You don't like me," Sloane said cheerfully. "No need to worry. I grow on people, so I'm told. Finished already? Take the cream jug with you and give the cat a treat. Marina won't mind so long as no one tells her."

"Miss." It was the little maid, curtsying. "If you're quite through, Miss Damaris says will you come up to her room."

I escaped, feeling decidedly topsy-turvy.

Damaris' room, swathed in opalescent silks and laces, resembled the interior of some luminous shell. Damaris herself was sitting up in the great bed against a pile of embroidered pillows. There were circles underneath her eyes, but she held her arms out gaily. "Will you forgive me? My head ached, but it's better now, and the pains behave themselves so long as I stay still. But I am sorry you had to have your first breakfast here alone. I know Papa wasn't there. He always rises with the birds and goes off to his office three hours before his clerks come in. He says he's still a laborer at heart, which makes Aunt Marina simply furious!"

She pulled me down beside her, laughing breathlessly, and her eyes were dancing. I smiled back, feeling myself relax from a tension I had not recognized was there. Yet it had been present, somewhere beyond the edge of thought, an uneasy embarrassment at recalling our strange nocturnal conversation. But Damaris made no reference to it; she seemed indeed to have forgotten it entirely. Naturally, I made no mention of it either.

"You needn't have worried," I said, "about breakfast. I was not alone."

"Warren," Damaris said. There was an odd note in her voice, and I looked at her sharply.

"Damaris, who is he?"

Damaris gave me that look of starry innocence. "Mr. Sloane? He's an art expert. Italian Renaissance, same as you, Vinnie, so you shall have a lot in common."

"That's what he said," I retorted, "but I doubt it."

"Mr. Sloane is very clever. He has a faculty for making things work out."

"But what's he doing here? He's not—" I stopped. It was not tactful to say he was not quite her kind, and after all I was in no position myself to be a snob.

"He's here to help Papa get the Collection catalogued and displayed," Damaris said. "That is, if Papa will ever let him. Papa is not much taken with him, either. Aunt Marina arranged his coming through a museum in New York. She's trying to force Papa to go through with this Renaissance Gala for the Arts Museum."

"But why, if he doesn't want—"

"Because she needs the leverage for social acceptance." There was a hard edge to Damaris' voice. "She's determined to make me the debutante of the season, God help us all, and don't ask me why I don't fight her on it, Vinnie, because I can't."

"Why not?" I looked at the violet shadows around Damaris' eyes and felt a wave of annoyance at the ambitious marchesa. Throwing Damaris into the social sea was roughly equivalent to tossing a lamb into a pack of wolves. "If you don't want it, why go through with it? Certainly your father wouldn't care."

"Papa," Damaris said grimly, "is at war with Boston. He has nothing but contempt for these people. He goes out of his way to be obnoxious to them, and yet when they snub him, it hurts him with a deep hurt. And that is why Aunt Marina and I are going through with this, no matter what the cost. They cannot treat my father in that fashion."

This was the Damaris I had known of old.

"All right," I said. "I see your point. But you won't accomplish much if you allow it to make you ill."

"I won't. Or at least I won't let it show, if you will help me. Fortunately, Papa and Aunt Marina are easily deceived. They've never believed in my pains much anyway. And

Warren—" Damaris colored slightly. "Mr. Sloane has been very good to me," she said carefully. "He—understands these stupid spells of mine. Like you do, Vinnie. He's looked after me, when I've needed someone. But of course, at the parties—" She stopped and flushed.

"You mean he's socially acceptable as an employee," I said brutally, "but not in public."

Damaris would not look at me and her voice trembled slightly. "I do think," she said carefully, "that Aunt Marina has not been very kind."

"I wonder that she has allowed me, then. You had better not count on my support in society, Damaris, because by that yardstick I am not more acceptable than he."

Damaris sat bolt upright, her face very white. "Don't you ever say that! Don't even think it. With Mr. Sloane, it's different. It would not be proper for me to . . . But you are my guest. You are my friend. I will not allow you to be patronized. Do you understand me?"

"All right, all right! Don't fight with me. You'll make yourself ill for nothing!" I said hastily. Damaris alarmed me with her passion, and when she saw the expression on my face she laughed and relaxed against the pillows.

"I'm sorry. I didn't mean to startle you. But I'm Irish too, you know, and I understand also related to the Borgias. Most of the time I take it all into myself, but when I'm crossed too far, watch out!"

I laughed also. "I'd hate to be the ladies at your aunt's tea party, if that is the way you propose to act towards them!"

"My soul, I forgot that." Damaris' eyes darkened. "Vinnie, be a love and help me dress. We'll go for a walk. It will help us brace ourselves before we beard the lionesses, or vice versa."

I was not sure if this was advisable, for Damaris looked alarmingly frail. Fortunately, Maggie materialized and took matters out of my hands.

"That's right, lamb, go for a nice walk and get some appetite for lunch. Cook has some lovely chops. You see to it she gets some real exercise, miss, will do her good." And presently we were strolling down the flagged paths of Marlborough Street between the gracious houses and tall trees. The sky was grey as slate and against it the treetops glowed like strange jewels, orange, red and gold. Damaris shivered and pulled her dolman tighter around her.

"In Italy it would still be summer."

I deemed it not advisable to encourage Damaris' longing for the past, so I did not answer, and we walked in companionable silence to the Public Garden. The round dome of the State House gleamed golden through the trees. Plump pigeons huddled in our way, and the chill breeze sent dry leaves scudding across the paths. It blew the cobweb shadows from my brain, and I felt my spirits lifting.

Apparently such strolling was the fashion. From time to time a handsome carriage rattled by, and Damaris exchanged formal bows with well-dressed walkers. Street urchins raced by, intent on their own games, and the children of the rich, supervised by starchy Nannies, rolled hoops or aired their dolls in carriages. I was glad to see the color returning to Damaris' cheeks.

"Tell me about this tea party this afternoon."

Damaris laughed ruefully. "The current slang is tea-fight, and it may be apt. The Ladies' Committee from the art museum sponsors are coming to lay plans for the Gala, which, since Papa obstinately refuses to be specific about cooperation, is rather hard on poor Aunt Marina."

"But what precisely *is* a Gala?"

"That," Damaris said, "is what at this point the ladies would like to know!" Her eyes twinkled. "As I understand it, it will be a cross between a ball, a reception, and the fête that greeted Lucrezia Borgia at her third marriage. Very rich and rare, with the emphasis on outdoing one's dearest friends.

And the star entertainer is supposed to be the Culhaine Collection."

"Your father doesn't agree?"

"Father thinks exploiting works of art is akin to exploiting human beings."

It was an attitude I could understand, and I felt some sympathy toward the intractable Ross Culhaine.

The tea that afternoon was everything that I expected—exquisite, exotic and enervating. It was held in the double drawing-room, which like the other public rooms was perfect in its simplicity and accurate in its recreation of the Renaissance. It was also, despite its cream walls, blazing fire and, to me, oppressive warmth, surprisingly bleak. That sensation may have been caused, however, more by the company than the surroundings. I wore my best black silk, sat in an unobtrusive chair and felt decidedly superfluous.

These half-dozen ladies were Old Family and Old Wealth, which meant they were expensively behind the fashion and made a virtue out of dowdiness and too much jet. Marina's gossamer cashmere of prune and cream was wasted on them, although the heavy silver tea service was not. I caught one of the dowagers casting covetous eyes upon it. A Mr. Blyden in side-curls and petticoats. Her co-lioness was an imposing matron with iron-grey hair whose bulging bustle was matched by her rigidly corseted bosom. They had three objectives: to see the Culhaine Collection, set the date for the Gala, and depart. I was impressed with the skill with which Marina, who was in no position to negotiate, parried to protect her weakness.

"More tea? Allow me; you must try our special blend. And my dear Mrs. Cabot, you must have one of these little honey cakes."

Boston's disdain for foreigners, I noticed, did not extend to its appetites.

Marina, I perceived, was stalling, preventing their departure. In the hopes of Ross Culhaine's appearing? I doubted that he would, and I could not blame him. Presently she sent Damaris for her harp.

"She sings charmingly. She shall sing some Italian ballads at the Gala. Wearing authentic costume, of course, from the Collection. And your daughter, also, Mrs. Cabot? I understand she has a delightful voice."

The daughter, a faded middle-aged miss, simpered, and Mrs. Cabot looked a trifle less iron-clad. Damaris was pale, but she fetched the harp obediently. After the first Italian song, however, she lifted her chin and closed her eyes.

"One sister loved with virgin truth
A stranger, gallant, strong and sure.
The other, with her wiles impure,
Stole off the heart of that same youth.

"Still through the slow pavane they move,
A dark pavane of death and love."

It was the "Pavane for Two Sisters." And I made no mistake about it; Damaris was asserting her independence. Marina knew it too, and knew as well as I did that the older ladies found the tale a bit too frank for Boston prudery. The moment was saved by the heretofore-silent Miss Cabot bursting into excited speech.

"It's the legend, isn't it? The one *Town Topics* told about! The Legend of the Two Sisters? And is it true that Mr. Culhaine owns the actual portrait and the favor? Everyone's whispering of it all over Boston. My dear Marchesa, you must allow us one private peep!"

Miss Cabot was decidedly too arch, but I blessed her all the same. Marina said graciously, "Why, of course," and led the way across the hall. We all stood in a decently respectful row, gazing at the portrait above the library mantel.

"The collar," Mrs. Cabot said decisively. "There is an actual collar, I believe? We are counting on it to be the rara avis of the exhibition. Or is the collar as nonexistent as the date for the Gala still seems to be?"

I admired Marina's discipline. The flash of anger in her eyes was quickly veiled, and in a tone of perfectly serene command she said calmly, "Damaris. Show Mrs. Cabot your mother's necklace, if you please."

Damaris' eyes flared. "Aunt Marina—"

"Get it, Damaris. It will be yours one day, so you have a right to show it. Your father will understand."

I had an idea he would, at that. Ross Culhaine looked like a man who would also call a bluff.

Silently Damaris went to the wood paneling beside the fireplace, pressed a hidden spring, and a cupboard door swung open. She reached within and took out a dark blue velvet-covered case. She was just moving towards Mrs. Cabot when she stopped abruptly, gazing across the dowager's head. She looked as though she had been struck. I turned.

Ross Culhaine was standing in the doorway. He said just one word, "Damaris," very quietly, and held out his hand. Damaris' eyes dropped. Like a chastized nun she crossed to place the jewel box in his hand and he, as silently, returned it to the cupboard and shut the door.

"When you make your debut, Damaris," he said curtly, "if you insist on going through with that charade, you may wear the collar. Meanwhile, it is not an object for Philistine display." Without bothering to bow, he left the room.

"You must understand," Marina said presently, gently, "the necklace belonged to my sister, who is dead."

All in a moment, by what was unsaid more than what was spoken, she had thrown a softening veil of romantic sorrow over what had just occurred and my admiration for her increased. The women were responding, Marina was suggesting the refreshment of more tea and leading them with quiet firmness back to the drawing room.

"If you will excuse us," Damaris said faintly. Her hand fluttered toward her bodice, then was rigidly controlled, but I had seen the spasm of pain momentarily twist her face. I bowed our farewells and accompanied her up the stairs, but she would not permit my help until she had reached her own room and the door was shut. Then she collapsed on the sofa, her face contorted.

I knelt beside her quickly. "What can I do?"

"Nothing. It will pass." Damaris gripped my wrist tightly, and beads of perspiration stood out upon her forehead, but presently she relaxed and lay back against the cushions, her eyes closed.

"Those women upset you. Would it help to talk about it?"

"No. Just stay with me, please." Leonardo came padding in through the connecting doors and leaped up to arch against her, and Damaris wiped her eyes on his fur, half laughing. "You," she told him, "are a comfort."

Leonardo, gratified, settled against her like a hot-water bottle and commenced a loud purring.

"Those bitches," Damaris said slowly.

I was genuinely shocked, as much by her passion as her language, for I had not known her capable of either. Her hand went on stroking Leonardo gently, but I could sense the tension beneath her tremor. "They were beastly to my mother. I told you, Vinnie. Now they think it's all so romantic and fascinating, because she's dead."

She reached inside her bodice and brought out an ivory miniature on a slender golden chain. I did not have to be told who the woman was, and gazed with interest. What did astonish me was how much the woman resembled the picture in the library downstairs.

"When I was little," Damaris said, reading my mind, "I used to think she sat for Bianca's portrait. I didn't realize the painting was an Old Master. Bianca *was* an ancestor, of course. Perhaps that explains . . . Oh, God, Vinnie! Hold

: 51 :

me—!" The pain was back again. I held her, and the old nurse Maggie materialized from somewhere. Fortunately she sensed my authority over Damaris and allied herself with me. Between us we got Damaris undressed and into bed and persuaded her to swallow a little brandy. I sat beside her and held her wrists until I had made her pulse slow and the pains abated.

"She'll sleep now," Maggie said. "Those doctors! Plenty the master spent on them in the old days, and they saying there's nothing to be done! But you have a touch with her, miss, no doubt about it." I had won my first real ally in the house.

Damaris did not come to dinner and neither, to my secret relief, did Ross Culhaine. Warren Sloane was present, though. The dinner conversation became a spirited sparring repartee between him and the marchesa to which I, relieved of necessity for participation, was a fascinated listener. After coffee in the library I excused myself, offering a desire to look in on Damaris as my reason. But Damaris was already sleeping, so I had the luxury of a solitary evening in my room with Leonardo as my sole companion. Being a house guest was more wearing than I had expected.

I filled several pages in my journal, recording my initial Boston impressions, and this assisted me in sorting out my thoughts. I was astonished at how emotional and apprehensive I sensed myself becoming; it was no doubt due partly to the strain I had been under, that last week in New York. Partly, as well, to the great tension I perceived in Damaris. Whether this was cause, or result, of the pains she suffered, I had yet to learn.

I completed my journal entry, read for a time in the Milton volume, and went to bed rested and refreshed.

Some hours later, as on the night before, I was brought suddenly awake. No mouse-tapping now. Damaris swayed in the connecting doorway, clinging for support and doubled up with pain. I got her into bed quickly and piled the comforts round her. "Shall I call Maggie?"

"No! Nobody. Just hold me. It's the only thing that helps."

"Perhaps some hot milk—"

"Marina brought me some hours ago. It does no good," Damaris said violently. "Nothing does. Oh, God, Vinnie . . ." She was rigid and trembling with cold and panic, as she had been the night before. I was afraid to excite her further by insisting.

So I held her, and rubbed her limbs where she told me the pain was spreading, until by sheer force of my own will I was able to make her grow relaxed and still.

It was to become a regular unspoken pattern, these nighttime attacks which in the morning were ignored as if they had never been.

V

The next morning I breakfasted alone, as I was frequently to do in the days to come. I peeped into Damaris' room on my way downstairs, but she did not stir. Some time in the hours before I woke she had crept back to her own bed and lay curled in sleep among the opalescent draperies like a lost child strayed into the enchanted bower of a fairy queen. When I was young those North European fairy tales with their shadows and bewitchments and malignant spells had always touched me with a nameless terror, and their memory did so now. I rebuked myself sternly for the fancy, and went downstairs through the pale silent house. Whatever ailed Damaris, it was real and not bewitchment, and my entering into her hysteria and panic would be of no help to her.

Breakfast was again set forth lavishly on the sideboard, and the pert maid came in to assist me, bobbing a cheerful curtsy and gazing upon me with bright curious eyes. I found it disconcerting to be a solitary eater beneath such attentive concentration.

"The marchesa has not come down?"

"Oh, no, miss. She always has hers sent to her boo-door. Is Miss Damaris all right this morning, miss? Seems like we heard her walking about again like, in the small hours."

Although her tone was respectful enough, her eyes were bold. Obviously she was not yet sure where to place me in the hierarchy of the house, and it seemed best to take a firm line with her at once.

"You may give me some more coffee and that will be all, Sarah," I said decisively.

Sarah dropped her eyes. "Yes, miss. And I was to give you a message, miss, when you came down. When you've finished, you're please to come to the conservatory. That's where the work on the Collection is going on."

Apparently everyone even remotely connected with the Culhaine Collection instinctively thought of it in capital letters. Despite a flicker of affronted pride at the peremptory nature of the summons, I must confess the eagerness that flared within me, the difficulty with which I forced a leisurely drinking of the second cup of coffee beneath Sarah's half-veiled inquisitive gaze. To my annoyance, my pulse was pounding and I found myself nervous as a schoolgirl at the prospect of this first professional encounter with Ross Culhaine.

He was only Damaris' father, I told myself sternly; and an arrogant upstart, if one came down to it, despite his wealth. It was Damaris, not the Culhaine Collection, which was my main concern. Yet such is human greed and folly that I well knew, as I followed Sarah down the hall, that it was the upstart's treasure, not my little friend, which occupied my thoughts.

Sarah led me through an L-shaped corridor to a part of the house which apparently, some time in the past twenty years, had been added to the house's whole back width. It had been designed in the most fashionable pseudo-antique style, and the wan sunlight of early winter flooded through the curving-glass-arched roof. She stood aside for me to enter, and a wave of hothouse fragrance, heavy and moist and enervating in its sweetness, assailed me. The great plant-dominated room was furnished as a garden bower in southern climes, and I was at once reminded of the family's long Italian stay. Iron furniture, and wicker chairs, invited one to linger in silken dalliance, and low tables of Roman and Chinese ceramic suggested leisurely, rose- and lemon-scented teas. The place had at once a strange exoticism and an odd familiarity. As I passed down a narrow aisle between plant boxes and the tendrils of a spider plant reached out to brush my neck, with a little chill of recognition I understood. Rappacini's garden, the poison garden of the Hawthorne story where lush plants grew that poisoned all who breathed their air, all but the frail and lovely girl who grew among them and could not survive in the healthful oxygen of the world outside.

I must not allow myself to be seduced by such distorted fancies. I moved with determination down the narrow aisle, and turned a corner to be confronted with a broad masculine back. And my own back stiffened, for the shoulders were clothed in tweed, not broadcloth, and they belonged not to Mr. Culhaine but to Warren Sloane.

"Good morning!" he greeted me, turning cheerfully. "I was wondering how long it would take for you to appear."

"I came as soon as I could," I said acidly. "I did not know it was you who sent for me."

Sloane grinned. "Sorry if you're disappointed. Or annoyed. Probably quite rightly; knowing Sarah, I have no doubt my message lost something in translation. Plainly put, I have at last received permission to get on with the cataloguing, and to be blunt, I wanted a witness, as well as having an expert's eagerness to share the goodies with a colleague. So I asked if you would join me."

He waited courteously for me to precede him and I passed, slightly mollified, down the aisle he indicated. Then I emerged from the greenery into an open space, and looked, and the pettiness of my anger drained away.

"Magnificent, isn't it?" Sloane said quietly behind my shoulder.

Magnificent, for the first time in my experience, was a meager word. The pretension of my sophistication, my complacency at having been for a few years an assistant antiquaire—yes, and the gaps in that experience—for the first time struck me. I felt, as one always does in the presence of great art, both awed and humble. For these products of unknown Renaissance craftsmen were, in their own way, the equals of the work of Michelangelo or da Vinci. Goblets and bowls and trenchers, reliquaries and altar candlesticks, they spread in careless profusion across the potting benches of the conservatory, and they dazzled the eyes. It was the treasure trove of a magpie—a very cultivated magpie of infinite learning and exquisite taste. It was a sight to drive even Midas mad.

"Can you understand my meaning," Sloane said, "when I say even the air gives one a sort of psychic indigestion? As if too long exposure could make one unfit for the outside world."

His voice had exactly the tone of what I myself was feeling, and I found it both surprising and disarming. I would have expected from him either a businesslike matter-of-factness or a kind of oily greed; I had been jumping to conclusions again, with the usual results, and I did not like it.

"Cuts one down to size, doesn't it?" Sloane's voice said knowingly.

"You said something about commencing on a catalogue."

"Yes. It will probably facilitate matters if we do some kind of sorting first. Which would you suggest, categories or place of origin or chronology?"

"Categories, with chronological subdivisions, would be most efficient."

And so it happened, to my utter astonishment, that I found myself spending a long and pleasant morning of companionable professional activity with Warren Sloane. Apparently he accepted my equality as a colleague without question, and I will not deny that this was a tonic to my bruised ego. Too, there was a bond in our mutual appreciation of the artifacts we handled. By the time the luncheon gong sounded we had the objects lined up in neat gleaming rows, were wrangling pleasantly over relative datings, and we both realized with a start of surprise how much time had flown.

"We've made a good beginning," Sloane said with satisfaction. "Of course, all the really precious items in the Collection are still under lock and key. Would you make any wager on whether Marina pries them loose?"

I did not respond. I disliked the familiarity with which Sloane spoke of the marchesa, and the easy assumption of rights to this magical stuff with which we worked. Annoyingly, he interpreted my silence quite correctly.

"I shock you, don't I? Come, Miss Stanton, you're not one of the milk-faced Boston Puritans, you're a businesswoman, and I assure you I'm only making business shoptalk with a colleague. I may not be a Mayflower descendant, but do you really think I have so little breeding as to indulge in idle gossip about my employers with outsiders?"

My face burned. I swept with some austerity into the corridor leading to the front of the house. Alas, my hopes of a dignified escape were blocked by our encountering of Marina in the passage, an elegantly gowned Marina radiating an aura of European charm, who linked her arm through my companion's and made it quite, quite clear that not only was he to be our tablemate at the midday meal, but that his company was preferred to mine. It occurred to me that taking meals with the family, although confirming my status as a gentlewoman, would also be a strain. Perhaps, if Damaris continued feeling poorly, I would be able to lunch upstairs with her.

To my surprise and relief, Damaris herself was in the dining room when we arrived. She was wearing a blue-grey house gown that accentuated her pallor, and two pink spots burned on her cheekbones, but her manner was very bright.

"Vinnie! Sarah tells me you have been bewitched into slaving away on Papa's precious loot! How exciting for you, but you must not allow yourself to be overworked. I felt quite lonely in my tower without you."

"Why did you not send for me?" I felt not only compunction, but also perplexity as to where in this household my first duty lay. Then I looked at the hectic shine in her eyes, and felt something more. "Damaris, are you quite well?"

"Perfectly! I feel newborn! And pray do not feel any guilt on my behalf; I spent a most delightful morning. Leonardo came in to offer his company!" Damaris' voice was brittle bright, but her eyes, meeting mine when the others were not looking, held a sober sanity at odds with her gaiety of demeanor.

Ought I to have spoken out boldly then, before the others, of her illness? I will never know. What I did was respond to the implicit appeal in those somber eyes, and hold my tongue.

The meal passed pleasantly enough, in the mesh of sparkling parry and thrust, advances and defenses which seemed to serve for small talk here in Boston, and for me at least illumined more and more the intricate interrelationships of the three who sat with me at table. A pattern was here, a complex pattern I did not understand but whose shape showed ever clearer, and encompassed not only the debutante, the marchesa and the curator but also the empty chair that stood at the table end in place for the head of the Clan Culhaine.

After the meal was over, Damaris excused herself, saying

she wished to rest and then practice in private on her harp. "I may have a new song for you later. Come up and have tea by the fire with me and Leonardo," she said, departing. Marina disappeared without explanation and Sloane and I, as if by unspoken agreement, returned to the conservatory and the Culhaine Collection.

The Culhaine Collection. What can I write of it that will make those who have not looked upon it understand? Damaris' term, *bewitched*, had been the proper word. Perhaps seduced was even better. I think back to that afternoon, and those that followed, and my senses dissolve into a blurred montage of oppressive hothouse scents, the sweetness of tuberoses and hyacinth, the warm moist air, the touch of heavy embossed silver, cool beneath my fingertips, the gleam of exquisitely wrought gold. And I am, again, as I was then, not in the house on Marlborough Street but in the long-gone Italy of the Medicis and Isabella d'Este. In a world which, contrary to what logic and history had taught me, brought to my turbulent spirits a sense of quietude and peace. I forgot my irritation with Warren Sloane. The Prince of Darkness himself could have been my companion and I would not have cared. An hour passed, and more. Then I heard a voice, breathless and excited, calling, "Vinnie, come!"

"I'm in the conservatory," I answered, and when Damaris did not appear I went through the narrow aisles between the planting beds in search.

I found Damaris coming towards me, running down the corridor from the hall. When she reached the conservatory entrance she stopped as though she had run into an invisible wall. Her face went from that sallow pallor to a burning brightness and back again, but her voice had the hectic gaiety it had held at luncheon, and her eyes matched it.

"Vinnie, come quickly. Papa's come home, he's brought tickets. He's taking us all to the afternoon musicale at the concert hall. Aunt Marina says to hurry!"

Hastily I took off the gardener's apron Sloane had handed me to protect my gown. "Take a moment and come see what we've done."

"No!" Damaris said swiftly. At once, as if her sensitive ears had caught her own discordant tone, she slipped her arm through mine cajolingly. "Do come, you've barely time to change your gown." I noticed now, as I had not before, that Damaris herself was splendid in overpowering silk. She marched me off, talking a mile a minute, and sat on the chaise with Leonardo in her lap while I obediently changed into my aubergine silk and recombed my hair.

We hurried downstairs to find Ross Culhaine waiting. He handed us into the carriage and said little as we rattled off along the cobblestones of Beacon Hill. I wondered what had prompted him, unsociable as he was, to offer this excursion. Marina of course took no notice of his silence. She was exquisite as always, and paid me little mind. When we reached the brightly illumined hall I saw the other concertgoers were equally well dressed and was glad Damaris had made me don the aubergine. Indeed, I felt quite out of place and ridiculously like a country mouse for one who had lived most of her life in New York City. Ross Culhaine had secured a box in an excellent location for seeing and being seen, and Marina, bringing her opera glasses into play, was serenely conscious of being the cynosure of many eyes. Then the music began, and I thought of little else.

I have sometimes wondered whether my unknown father had music in his make-up, for I am passionately fond of it, although on the intuitive rather than tutored level. The group today was a chamber quartet playing Italian airs, and they carried me with unconscious association back to the Renaissance dream world where I had spent my afternoon. It was with difficulty that I returned to the reality of bright lights and laughter when the first part of the programme ended.

Civilized Boston visited back and forth during the interval, and it was the matter of only a few moments to realize that although our box was the object of much notice, it was not so of calls. From across the way Mrs. Cabot and her daughters bowed in response to Marina's bow, but they neither beckoned nor came. I saw Ross Culhaine's eyes follow Marina's narrowed glance, and his lips tightened. He immersed himself in the programme notes.

Marina and her opera glass were surveying the other tiers of seats and her voice, coolly amused, said, "Well, fancy that."

Among an upper bank of seats a familiar figure in rough tweeds was pushing toward an aisle, obviously bound in our direction. Beside me Damaris made a faint ejaculation, quickly hushed.

Warren Sloane arrived at our box, brisk and cheerful, unconcerned over being ill-attired for the occasion, bowing politely over the ladies' hands. "Marchesa. Mr. Culhaine. What a delightful coincidence."

Perhaps it was because my mind had been steeped in thoughts of Florentine intrigue that I remembered Warren Sloane had been in the conservatory when Damaris had come running up in search of me.

Marina was rustling to her feet, tucking her arm through his, accepting the invitation for a promenade and an ice which the rest of us declined. Damaris' pallor seemed to increase slightly as she watched them go, and almost as soon as they were out of sight she rose.

"I think I will step out to the anteroom, where the air is fresher. No, Vinnie, please stay. Really I would prefer to be alone."

So I remained in my seat, reading my programme, thinking of Damaris and longing for the music to again begin.

I looked up presently to find Ross Culhaine's eyes upon me.

"You really enjoy this, don't you?"

His voice was genuinely cordial, and I responded. "The music is—beyond words."

I gave unconscious emphasis, and his quick ear caught it. "But not this?" he nodded toward the social circus going on in the aisles below. "You have good taste. And sense. My daughter, thank the Lord, has too. Or had, until she allowed her aunt to lure her into this nonsensical debut."

Since my agreement with this sentiment was a thing I could certainly not reveal, I strove for a change of subject. "I'm afraid for me music works a Merlin's spell. Tea and ices seem so—anticlimactic."

"An intrusion into Avalon of a discordant time?"

"I fear it is I who am discordant. I know too little to properly understand, and too much to be a contented Philistine."

Ross Culhaine gave me a rueful smile. "I assure you that more such appreciation, however untutored, would be a refreshing change." He glanced sardonically at a neighboring box, where an amply endowed, overdressed female was flashing diamonds and chattering shrilly, and we both laughed. Then our eyes met, and it was I who looked away.

"I am not familiar with the next selection. Do tell me of it." I spoke quickly, for to my astonishment my pulse was pounding and I felt slightly giddy. Damaris had been right. The air in the confines of this velvet-swathed box was very close. I picked up the fan she had left on her seat and fanned myself, hoping the flush I felt in my cheeks would escape my companion's notice as he bent towards me and commenced a scholarly and interesting dissertation on the piece we were about to hear.

Damaris slipped back in, saw her father and myself engrossed, and sat down quietly, looking gratified. There was a stir below; the musicians had returned and were tuning their instruments. The lights dimmed and the sublime contrapuntal melodies began. The piece was well begun when the door behind us opened and closed and Marina appeared, still accompanied by Warren Sloane. He took the empty seat beside her quite as a matter of course.

Ross Culhaine had ceased speaking the moment the first music notes began. Not so Marina; she leaned forward on the box's padded rail, the hand with the yellow diamond dangling negligently, and kept up a spirited whispered conversation with Warren Sloane for the balance of the afternoon. Her eyes were bright; she looked magnificent; remembering the snubs she had earlier received, I had to admire her for having all banners flying. Then I caught sight of Damaris, shrunk back in her velvet chair. She was glancing from Warren to Marina and back again, and I could not bear to identify the naked emotion I saw brimming in her eyes. Oh, Damaris, I thought, and turned away, and let the great majestic chords of music blot out all other sense and sight.

After the concert, Culhaine invited us all to stop at a hotel for tea. Sloane excused himself, perhaps feeling out of place, for when we arrived I saw that all the men present were in black or pearl grey broadcloth and looked very grand. I gave little thought to him, however, or to the tea and ices and little cakes which presently arrived. My mind was engrossed in the memory of the music, and in Damaris, who only picked at her plate, looking pale and tired.

When we reached home she went straight to her room, begging to be excused from dinner, and I went with her. I helped her undress, and spoke lightly and soothingly of unessential matters, and was glad to see, after a while, some of her liveliness return. Presently Sarah brought up a fine tray, and we dined in my room before the fire, with Leonardo bridging the gap between our feet and purring lustily.

The night passed much as had the ones before. Damaris retired early; I read for some hours before I disposed myself for sleep; sometime in the midnight hours Damaris came in to me again for comfort, though whether for emotional or physical suffering I could not be sure. This time I got her quiet fairly quickly, and soon fell asleep again myself.

Fell asleep to dream, most disconcertingly. For the images that rose from my unconscious were neither of Renaissance masterpieces of music or of art, nor of my troubled little friend. They were of two figures, one roughly tweeded with ginger hair, the other a death's head magnificently carved, with green and piercing eyes.

VI

My life in Boston was beginning to take on a pattern which, though strange, was no longer unfamiliar. I awoke early, often even before Maggie tiptoed in to open the draperies and admit a pale grey light. Damaris, if she had been there during the night, would have already left; I never knew when she slipped away to her own boudoir, not to emerge till noon. She still came to my room nearly every night, more for a friendly visit than because she was having "spells"; although she still complained of pains in her chest and legs, she was nowhere near so distraught as on those first few nights.

Thanks to Maggie, I had obtained a little spirit-lamp on which I was able to brew us both some after-midnight tea, for Damaris had developed a distaste for the hot beverage which always appeared punctually at her own bedside. This meant I was also able to make myself a solitary early-morning cup of tea in the English fashion, and I enjoyed the luxury of these quiet periods to myself when the house was still, with the pearly morning light filtering through the lavender window-panes and Leonardo purring contentedly on my knees. I would read, or sew, or merely dream, until I heard sounds of life stirring on the floor below. Then I would dress in businesslike apparel and go down to the breakfast table, where I presided.

Often Sloane, arriving early, joined me; we were developing an easy, casual camaraderie. Occasionally Ross Culhaine would be there as well, and these times were strained, although I could not put my finger on the cause. Generally he would have breakfasted earlier still and gone about his business. I had not known that gentlemen of wealth were so occupied with their affairs of business, but Ross was no dilettante at anything; from early morning he was off at his downtown office, or closeted in the library, and often he did not even emerge at lunch.

My own morning was spent in the conservatory, at times working side by side with Warren Sloane; at times, although he was in the room with me, working in some curious sense alone. Even then I sensed the spell that was to hold me in its thrall in after years—how at mention of the Culhaine Collection, or the sight of a goblet gleaming gold, the scent of tuberoses would assail my nostrils, the plash of water in a fountain would sound in my ears like silver bells, and time and memory would dissolve. I would be back again in the conservatory, back in an enchanted world. The Culhaine Collection. I had heard that great wealth, great art, could work a kind of hypnotism on those exposed; I had thought myself too sophisticated to succumb. I had been wrong. Those mornings in the conservatory left me in a sort of ecstatic intoxication from which I would emerge, when the gong for luncheon rang, with senses dazed and my temples throbbing.

If Damaris was occupied with her own affairs—as she often

was, for Marina kept her busy with preparations for her debut—I would return to the conservatory to continue cataloguing in the early afternoon. Outside those glass walls, early winter was settling on Beacon Hill; inside was endless summer. It was strangely cloying.

One grey afternoon, when I had been working in the conservatory alone after Sloane had gone, I looked up with a dull ache spreading through my head behind my eyes, and a stiffness in my spine, and saw the skeletal branches of the great tree in the back garden bowing before the wind. It brought back memories of grey November with the dead leaves scudding before the wind in Washington Square. How often on such afternoons, with the shop still and Eustace Robinson dozing contentedly before the small fire, I had slipped out for a brisk walk around the park, to return for tea with cheeks glowing and spirits all restored. Unexpectedly my eyes filled, and an ache I had thought forgotten rose in my breast.

Impulsively I pulled off my working apron. "I'll go out now. It's exactly what I need." I did not know my way round Boston yet, but the Public Garden was a scant five blocks away, and I knew it was quite the custom for gentlefolk to walk or ride there on fine days. Today was not fine, but so much the better!

I am ashamed to say I tiptoed past the closed door of Damaris' room; I was in no mood for solicitude, confidences, or even her companionship on my way. I pulled on my outer wraps, took up my muff, and slipped unnoticed out the great front door. A cold wind stung my face and there was raw dampness in the air. On Commonwealth Avenue the Palladian windows and shallow black iron balconies wore traceries of frost, and black birds sought nooks for shelter in turreted rooflines. The fanciful rooftops reminded me of the parapets of French Châteaux, and in the public Garden the twisted limbs of gnarled dark trees seemed figures from an even earlier time. Or from Dürer etchings. Oddly enough, these darksome images did not depress me; they seemed to put my own thoughts in perspective. The dome of the State-house gleamed good cheer against a leaden sky, and round the outer bank of the Common, ragged children played. At last, my spirits lifted, I turned back towards home.

Hopkins, the butler, admitting me, looked more than a bit askance at my ruffled hair, but I didn't care. "Here you are, Hopkins," I said pleasantly, allowing him to take my wraps. "Am I late for tea?"

Apparently the assumption of authority was the proper decision; Hopkins' demeanor thawed to merely a gentle chill. "Not at all, miss. I'll send Sarah with a fresh pot at once. And Miss Damaris says will you join her in her bou-doir."

I went upstairs to find Damaris also glowing. "You stole out on me, you naughty thing! What have you been up to, Vinnie, secret intrigue? I can see the sparkle in your eye!"

"You look as if you've had a fascinating afternoon, your-self."

"I have! Warren—Mr. Sloane—came by. It must have been just after you'd gone out, he had the designs for the floral decorations for my debut to show Aunt and me. He's mar-velously clever at such things. It's going to be simply splen-did." The glow in her eyes diminished. "Poor Aunt Marina!" she said ruefully. "She has such high hopes for the occasion, and she is bound to be so disappointed."

"What nonsense," I said strongly.

"Vinnie, be honest. You of all people see things the way they are, and you needn't pretend." Damaris looked at me squarely. "It's supposed to be my debut into fashionable so-ciety, a stepping stone to the Gala, and to be vulgar, one in the eye of the whole Back Bay. Tell me true, Vinnie, can you see me carrying that off? My mother could have, or you. You're made of stronger stuff."

"Why don't you tell your aunt the way you feel?"

Damaris ignored this preposterous suggestion. "The one saving grace is that no one hereabouts expects me to have any colors flying. If I fade into the woodwork they will not even notice the loss. Ironic, isn't it? Someday you must hear the stories of my ancestors, or of Papa's younger days. Apparently the bloodstream's been watered down by the time it got to me. Poor Papa!"

I was about to change the subject when the door opened and Damaris herself broke off with evident relief. "Here's our tea!" She fluttered over the silver service with a proprietary air until Sarah departed with evident reluctance, shutting the door behind her.

Damaris gave something suspiciously like a snort. "That girl! She's a good enough worker, all right, but too curious by half. *And* her older sister's in service to Mrs. Cabot. Maggie told me. What do you wager, Vinnie, those old cats on Louisburg Square know every time we change our linen?"

"Does your aunt know?"

"No, and she won't from me. Marina has enough to trouble her. Anyway, what does it matter? The Culhaines have nothing to hide—and certainly not from Beacon Street." Her head was up in that proud way, but the hands on the eggshell cups had commenced to tremble, and I hastened with diversion.

"When are you coming out to the conservatory to see what I've been up to? Oh, Damaris, I confess I break the tenth commandment every time I cross that threshold. I'm drunk on your father's treasures!"

Damaris laughed. "You haven't seen the half. After the gold and silver there's still the softwares. Tapestries—there's one somewhere, I told you, that shows the Legend of the Two Sisters. I haven't seen it around since our return. Old ecclesiastical vestments, and embroideries. And then the laces. Vinnie, you'll go wild over them!" Her voice shadowed. "I remember, when I was very small, Mama wearing that lace. She had a ball gown of corded white silk, with enormous hoops; it had a deep bertha of Venetian lace with silver threads. She came into my room to show me before she went out with my father, and I thought she was a fairy queen."

She fell silent.

There were times when I wondered whether there was any subject safe to bring up with Damaris. I decided to settle for the lesser of the available evils.

"Tell me about the designs Mr. Sloane brought to show you."

Damaris brightened at once. "They will be a sort of dress rehearsal for the Gala—if Papa ever really gets around to allowing that to take place. Between you and me, Vinnie, I have my doubts! Papa's a Machiavelli when he puts his mind to it. Oh, Vinnie, wait until you see Warren's sketches. He's done an enormous amount of research, the dear thing, just on the chance it might strike my fancy! Lilies and ivy, and hyacinths and white violets—he's had the pretty conceit of using the Language of Flowers, from the old tapestries, and of course all has to be white and innocent for a debut."

"You have lilies and hyacinths right at hand, which is fortunate," I said drily. If Sloane really intended fidelity to the Language of the Flowers appropriate for a young girl's debut, he would be leaning heavily on spring flowers in November, as well as shy and humble plants not usual at the entertainments of the great. "Damaris! Why not open the conservatory and hold the party there?"

"No!" Damaris sat up very straight, and her color came and went. Seeing my start of astonishment she checked herself, rubbing her hand across her brow. "I don't like the conservatory," she said vaguely. "The scent gives me headaches. So many flowers are overpowering."

"How will you be able to tolerate them at the ball?"

"They could be convenient," Damaris said with a spark of malice. "Won't they provide me with a lovely excuse for ducking out? Don't look so disapproving, Vinnie, I'll carry through. You'll be there to give me moral support. And Warren. Marina's decided to overlook the fact that he's an 'employee,' thank God. At least I'll have one masculine cavalier at court." Her eyes caught mine and she colored, and looked away quickly. "Mr. Sloane," she said carefully, "is very kind."

For what reason? I wondered. I sternly buried the disloyal thought.

I tried to be austere with Warren Sloane the next day, but I did not succeed. For one thing, he was too casually matter-of-fact. For another, we were of necessity thrown together. And he did not, after all, have anything of the adventurer, or lounge-lizard fortune hunter, about him. He was merely an intelligent, middle-class young man, who worked quite hard at a skill he knew and loved. But my uneasiness persisted all the same.

After that day, I began making solitary afternoon walks in the Public Garden a regular routine. They blew the cobwebs from my brain, blew too the overpowering scent of tuberoses and gardenias. The cold wind of winter brought me to myself, Lavinia Stanton, working gentlewoman now of Boston, and nipped the fancies that bred and bloomed in the hothouse air. Perhaps that air *was* poisonous. Oh, not in any botanical or metaphysical sense, but in its artificiality. Fancies were magnified there, as well as flowers. My mind, already steeped in ancient literature and Renaissance intrigue, overran its bounds the way the great sprawling spider plants overflowed their hanging pots. The grey cold reality of Boston cut my thoughts quite sensibly back to size.

The air was cold, for November was well upon us now, and the six-block trot down the cobblestones of Marlborough Street, followed by a brisk pace round the perimeter of the

Garden left me not only cheerful and invigorated but also chilled. Quite early on I took to stopping in the new museum as a regular thing. Although it was still raw in its newness, the lovely outlines of what was to be were plain. Sitting on a velvet bench, gazing around the healing openness of the tall bare rooms with their Old Masters dark and glowing in their great gold frames, I envisioned one or another of the Culhaine treasures displayed like jewels, and I could understand why Mrs. Cabot's beringed fingers were so covetous.

Mrs. Cabot was the chairman of the Ladies' Guild for the museum, a title which she wore like a tiara. I encountered her there one afternoon, coming through an archway with the mousy daughter in tow, just as I turned refreshed from contemplation of the Tintoretto which always drew me like a magnet. I commenced to bow, then stopped. Mrs. Cabot had passed me by, not snubbing me, simply not seeing me any more than if I had been part of the furnishings, a humble but necessary bell pull on the wall. The daughter's eyes, which had met mine, skittered off, and she trailed on in her mother's wake, like a dinghy after a majestic liner.

My face burned. This is ridiculous, I told myself sternly. Face reality; I am a paid companion and as such invisible to that woman's eyes, but that in no way diminishes the person I am inside. I turned back to the Tintoretto and strove for calm.

A voice behind my shoulder said, "Lovely, isn't she?"

I whirled.

Warren Sloane was standing with hands clasped behind his back, smiling blandly. "The madonna," he said. There was a hidden edge of irony to his voice. I wondered whether he had observed the snub, but I was not about to ask.

Damaris was right, he could be kind. He continued talking pleasantly, looking tactfully at the painting on the wall while I composed my face. "She is one of my favorites. I often come here; it restores the soul. And the head size."

What an uncanny echo of my own recent thoughts. "Have you seen the Titian in the next room? It's quite splendid." He offered me his arm, and I found myself taking it quite as a matter of course.

We had a delightful promenade through the galleries. Sloane, by way of his museum connections, had access to some of the exhibits not yet completed. However satisfying was a solitary contemplation of great art, there was a stimulation in being able to discuss it with an expert. When, presently, Sloane said, "Speaking of restorations, why do we not go restore our bodies with some cakes and chocolate?" it took me only a moment to reply, "Why not?"

Sloane ushered me to a little confectionery on a nearby street. He was known there; the little mustachioed Viennese proprietor came bouncing forward to usher us with a flourish to a choice table. The little man was just pushing in my chair when I looked up and beheld the Cabot party at a table by the wall. The daughter, sensing my gaze, dropped her eyes and looked embarrassed.

For a moment I felt a hot flush growing within me, then my head came up. This was my world, the world of art and afternoon walks—yes, and of afternoon tête-à-têtes with a masculine colleague in the arts. I knew already that the Cabots, for all their wealth and patronization of culture, were inept beginners. In this world, Sloane and I were their superiors.

Besides, a spark of malice whispered, he's an attractive man, and well they know it.

I probably ought to be ashamed of what I did thereafter. At the moment I didn't spare a thought to the fact that I was using Warren Sloane; he had it coming. I pulled my hand from its kid sheath and rested it negligently on the table, the great ruby sparkling. And I leaned forward, angling carefully so the Cabots could observe our faces, and began a most deliberate flirtation.

For a second Sloane's eyes looked puzzled, then he shot a glance in the direction of the wall and lifted an eyebrow wickedly. And promptly commenced to respond to me in kind. Our laughter cascaded lightly around the little table, and our glances sparked and flashed, and the little waiters danced attention, and the mustachioed proprietor beamed. He even, under the delusion that what he saw was real, sent a gypsy violinist to serenade our table. When the piece was finished, Sloane tipped the fellow ostentatiously, then lifted my ringed hand and kissed my fingers.

"I think that makes a good curtain scene," he murmured. "Shall we leave?" He helped me into my dolman, handed me my muff, and we swept out grandly.

We maintained our society air until we were well out of sight of the shop, halfway across the Common. There, secure in the unfashionable section, we looked at one another and burst into gales of laughter. Sloane tucked his hat under his arm.

"After that performance I need reviving!" He held out his hand for mine and we ran down the length of the walk like scholars released from school, while our audience of ragged children clapped their hands. At length, breathless, we collapsed on a convenient bench.

"Oh, my!" I wiped my eyes on my glove. "We ought to be ashamed, but for the life of me, I'm not! I must tell you, sir, you played your part splendidly."

"I must say, madam, that it was not hard, not with such a provocative partner to play opposite." He looked at me. "You were, you know. Quite charming."

"I must go. It's long past time for tea. Damaris will be worried."

Sloane rose also. "I'll see you back. No, I insist, at least to the Culhaine corner. It's growing dark."

He saw me, not to the corner, but to the black iron gate itself. There he bowed, hesitated, and with a wickedly lifted

VII

First and foremost of those questions, which I struggled with as I dressed for dinner, having first paused to report to Damaris that I was home, was what imp of perversity had possessed me to behave that way. But I was glad I had. I am not cut out to be a saint, and the self-effacing humility of a paid companion was very wearing.

The second question was, What possessed Warren Sloane? I could see his entering into the byplay in the chocolate shop, but why that parting comment at the gate? He had nothing to gain by turning his charm on me. Unless, which scarcely seemed likely, he had meant what he had said. That would mean he was interested in me as a woman, and I am engaging in no false modesty when I say I did not credit that at all.

Where did Damaris and his attentions to her fit in? Either he sincerely cared for her (the best tonic she could have, albeit dangerous), or he was, as I suspected, using her. In which case, why me? Unless he wanted the cake of the Culhaine Collection, with a little extra sauce upon the side.

The thought angered me, the more so because, if true, I had encouraged and catered to his efforts.

Oh, be honest, Vinnie, you had reveled in it!

I jerked my corset strings viciously, pulled on a governessy gown, and went down to my dinner with poor grace.

Fortunately, Damaris neither had missed me in my absence nor observed my agitation now. She and Marina were locked in a hen-scratching over the debut, and Damaris looked tired.

"Really, darling," Marina said with some asperity, "this party is for you. If you can't manage some enthusiasm, I don't know why I try!"

"I'm sorry, Aunt." Damaris stirred herself with effort. "Whatever you plan will be quite splendid. I do appreciate it. It's only . . ."

"Only what? We spent the whole afternoon with the dressmaker, trying to develop a pattern for your gown, and you displayed no more interest in it than a sick kitten. If the order is not placed soon, there will be no time."

"Let Papa pick the style," Damaris said in a quiet voice.

Ross looked bored. "Now, really, Marina, if this whole house is to be upset for a fête the child doesn't even want, what is the point? I am perfectly willing that you give the party, since you seem to feel it would be good for her, but pray do not expect me to become involved."

"I am not trying to involve you, *caro*. But I want Damaris to be a credit to you. Mrs. O'Shaugnessy and I spent the entire afternoon trying silks and patterns on her, and the child wouldn't even make an effort. How any girl who has spent six years on the Continent can carry herself with so little confidence, I do not understand."

"Aunt Marina," Damaris said evenly, "the styles you suggested would look magnificent on you. Unfortunately, I cannot be you. Or Mama. I have tried until my very bones ache, and I can't try any more. Forgive me, Papa, I know I am a terrible disappointment, but I have tried. I can't try any more." Uncharacteristically she stood up, although dessert was just being served. "Please, will you excuse me."

She stumbled out of the room while I sat wooden, not knowing what my proper role should be. A moment later we heard harp music coming from across the hall, and I knew that she was better left alone.

Marina gave an eloquent Italian shrug. "Ross, *caro*, I am sorry. But I too have tried. She has no *brio*, no flair. Sometimes I wonder how the blood of you and Isabella could produce such a pale copy."

I felt quite angry. "Why must she be a copy?" I found myself saying. "Why can not Damaris simply be herself?"

It seemed to startle the other two to realize I was there. Marina turned with an ironic *moue*. "But that is just the point, my dear. What self? The poor *bambina*'s like an unfledged chick. Ross, I told you she needed another year or so in Italy."

"The family has been separated long enough. Italy is not our native land, Marina. I understood Miss Stanton's presence was supposed to make Damaris feel more secure. Now, may I have my coffee, please?"

Marina's eyes flashed as she bent over the tray of cups. I would have liked to walk out myself, but Damaris needed a champion in the field.

"Damaris is right, you know," I said boldly. "Modern clothes do not become her. Mr. Culhaine, with your eye for art, surely you agree."

"Unfortunately," Marina said drily, passing coffee, "this is 1874. Damaris cannot appear like a Primavera, however much it might suit her pallid style."

"But why not?" I was growing quite excited. "Not Botticelli fantasy, but in a gown from some Renaissance painting.

Many New York women have done so for ceremonial affairs."
I had read of such in the society papers. "It's part of the
new appreciation of the artworks of the past."

Ross looked sardonic. In the library the strains of the harp
went on, and we could hear her plaintive voice in that obsessive ballad.

> "A man of craft came passing by,
> He saw a woman seemed so fair,
> A-wearing lilies in her hair,
> And oh, she caught the craftsman's eye.
>
> "Still through the dark pavane they move . . . "

The melody caused me to leap where angels feared to
tread. "Why cannot Damaris wear a gown patterned on that
of la Bianca?"

"It would be a pretty touch," Marina said, in a tone I
could not discern. I saw quite clearly, however, the glance
with which she held Ross's eyes across the bare expanse of
polished table. Challenging? Threatening? I would not try to
put a name. Some sort of gauntlet had been thrown down, I
knew quite well.

"Not that portrait," Ross said tersely. "Any other. You can
rummage through the paintings in storage if you like. I'll
give orders for the attics to be unlocked. It would be, as
Marina says, a pretty touch."

And that is how I came to spend the next morning in the
Ali Baba's cave beneath the eaves. Damaris, I was happy to
find, exhibited some interest in the plan. "We must ask Warren to help. He has such an artistic eye."

Marina declined with a faint shudder to be a member of
our party. "Have the footman bring down what you find. I'll
look it over to see if it's suitable." She pulled her skirts away
in a faint involuntary movement, as though shrinking from
dust.

So it was Damaris, Sloane and I who climbed the steep winding stairs to the fourth level, accompanied by Leonardo, with his orange tail fluffed high. One side of the narrow corridor was occupied by servants' rooms, but on the other a door stood ajar—Ross had remembered his pledge to have it opened. Leonardo disappeared immediately to his own pursuits, probably in hope of mice, while the rest of us, following Damaris' lead, ducked through the low doorway into a long, open, slant-walled space. Sloane stopped with an ejaculation of awe.

"I knew you'd be impressed," Damaris said drily.

"My dear child, I'm overpowered." The room was stocked with paintings—paintings jostling one another for space on the one full-height wall. Paintings still in canvas wrappings with foreign markings or in wooden crates. Paintings leaning one against the other in upright holders, like blank canvases in an artists' shop. Paintings framed and unframed, restored or cracked with age, satiating the senses in an embarrassment of riches. I caught a glimpse of a Veronese I had seen reproduced in art books, a Titian, one I thought might be a Rembrandt. Most, however, were of the Italian school.

Already Sloane had forgotten our mission, forgotten even that we were there, reverting to his museum curator's role. He strolled about, studying the works with professionally narrowed eyes, occasionally whipping out a magnifying glass to study brush stroke or skin tone at close range. As for myself, I found the quantity too overwhelming. I began working my way methodically through the piles, intent upon our purpose, noting or rejecting on the basis of whether female figures bore any similarity to Damaris. Occasionally we caught a glimpse of the flag of Leo's tail and knew he too was parading through the rows. Damaris hurried ahead of me, giving each painting an even more cursory glance. Presently she sat back on her heels in disappointment.

"It isn't here."

"What isn't?"

"The portrait I told you of, the picture of Bianca with the different necklace. You remember, Vinnie. I haven't seen it since we returned, and thought it must be here. Papa would never sell it." She began humming the tune of her ballad underneath her breath. It was beginning to get on my nerves, that song.

"What does it matter? You aren't to dress as Bianca anyway. Your father said so."

"My mother did once. He dislikes to be reminded of her." Damaris wandered off again, singing softly. " 'Still through the dark pavane they move, A dark pavane of death and love.' "

In my opinion it was high time to change the subject.

I rummaged through the small stack of paintings I had deemed suitable. "How about this one, dear?" It was a small painting from the Veronese school, of a girl in a white dress— white was, as Damaris had said, required for debutantes— carrying a spray of flowers. The simplicity of the dress, with its square-cut neck and ribbon-tied sleeves, would suit Damaris. What a pity that it was not the custom to make debuts in summer. Damaris belonged in chiffons and filmy muslin.

"If you like. Papa picked that up in Milan." Damaris glanced at the portrait indifferently.

Fortunately Warren Sloane heard us and came over. "Excellent," he said immediately, sizing up the figure and Damaris with a connoisseur's eye. "With a few minor adjustments it would be most suitable." He too had noticed that Damaris was growing tired. "Let us take it at once to *la marchesa* and see if she approves."

We trooped out of the storeroom and Damaris locked the door carefully behind us. "I promised Papa I would return the key to him myself." She picked up Leonardo, who was twisting around her ankles, purring loudly, and we descended. I surprised a look of—anger? annoyance?—on

Sloane's face. Apparently he had had hopes of returning to study the paintings later at his leisure?

Marina luckily approved our choice, and with her customary decisiveness put the work in train at once. "We will go this afternoon to purchase silks. Tomorrow—no, tomorrow your father is taking us to a concert. Thursday Mrs. O'Shaugnessy will come to cut the pattern." She glanced at Sloane. "You will please be here to advise on cutting. She will need information from someone familiar with the period."

It was an order, however casual. Behind Marina's back Sloane raised his eyebrows at me with a satiric look; the queen had spoken.

We spent that afternoon, Damaris, her aunt and I, in Slattery's and the other downtown shops where the clerks scurried with attentions. A length of silk was purchased, ivory pale with opalescent lights, and we carried it home in triumph to late tea.

"No need to look for laces," Marina said carelessly. "Ross can open the trunks where Isabella's things are stored. I'll see to it. Miss Stanton can mend what's needed some time next week."

"I have the key," Damaris said quietly. "I'll take care of it myself, Aunt. If Vinnie is kind enough to help, I will be very grateful."

Damaris' firm reply made me wonder, not for the first time, what her mother had been like. Isabella Culhaine. I knew little about her, other than her name. Other than that her husband had adored her. What manner of woman was it whom the young Ross Culhaine had chosen, had brought across the sea from Italy to Boston, had cherished so that even now the memory of slights she'd suffered there could fill him with a seemingly implacable hate? For I made no mistake about it; even as I myself was haunted by the past, as much and far far more was Ross Culhaine.

I was thinking of this as I worked in the conservatory next day, after Warren Sloane had left. Thinking, I fear, of Isabella to avoid the disturbing awareness of how very much Ross Culhaine himself was present in my thoughts. I was holding a golden goblet, caressing with my palm its lovely curve and wondering whether the bygone Isabella had ever done so, when I felt an odd prickling sensation as one does when one is being watched. I lifted my eyes and stared into the face of Ross Culhaine.

He had come so softly on the tanbark path I had not heard him. And he stood motionless, in frozen movement, as though his approach had suddenly been checked by something. Some ghost; he was staring at me as through veils of time. No, not at me. His eyes met mine with no spark of recognition. Then I moved, and his eyes focused, and the moment was gone. He was again himself, speaking to me with courteous detachment.

"I have tickets for a concert again this afternoon. Since you appreciate music, I thought you might enjoy it. The marchesa and my daughter are coming also."

In the face of his austerity I dressed myself not only in good black silk but in most stern resolve. But it was no use; my reserve and his both dissolved wordlessly before the magic of the music. During the intermission, I almost nerved myself to ask him about that moment in the conservatory, but just as I was about to do so, he fell silent. My eyes, following his gaze, saw that he was staring at my ruby ring. For an instant, my secret purpose in coming here to Boston sprang to my mind. Here was my opening; almost, I spoke of it. But all at once Ross was eons away, wrapped in remoteness, beyond my reach. I looked at him in troubled wonder, and suddenly a strange thing happened. Suddenly, as a violinist feels the vibrations of the strings, I felt in my own person what Ross Culhaine was feeling, although I could not know his thoughts. I shook with the intensity of a bewildering anguish. Only a moment, then the experience passed, leaving me spent and considerably disturbed.

Try as I would, when the afternoon was over, to think of it in rational perspective, I could not do so. I dreamed of Ross Culhaine that night, and the next afternoon, when I was working alone in the conservatory, it was not the concert music which ran through my mind, but a certain voice.

I was working there deliberately, long past the time for my customary walk, for I wanted to be too busy to have time to think. Warren Sloane was elsewhere, lending expert advice on Damaris' gown, for which I was very glad. I itemized, evaluated and recorded, and the sweet moist air of the conservatory enfolded me. Presently I caught myself singing the words of Damaris' haunting song.

> "Alas for faithful love once scorned,
> And for false love that seemeth true;
> For failing old and choosing new,
> Death came upon a grey-eyed morn."

This would never do.

Diligently I applied myself to the task at hand, which happened to be the dating and placing of a flock of small silver boxes. Eustace Robinson had had many such; I could see him again in the lamplight of the cozy cluttered shop, see his plump fingers turning over the delicate things, pointing out the workmanship while the tea kettle hummed a counterpoint to Leo's purring.

"See this hallmark, Vinnie? Some clumsy apprentice put the center symbol backward on this piece." Eustace Robinson had had a little box, almost the twin and image of the one which I now held. He had sold it, shortly before my mother died. To Ross Culhaine? That seemed too much coincidence even for poor fiction. Culhaine, though, had been familiar with Robinson's work and reputation.

I felt quite faint, which was absurd. *"I have determined I shall write to Boston. Lavinia has a right to know the truth." I will begin my search for identity on Marlborough Street.* I had come to Boston determined to discover who I was; then I had become so seduced by the aura of the House of Culhaine that that other mystery had receded in my mind.

The so-familiar feel of the silver bas-relief beneath my fingers brought back past memories of Washington Square, memories whose reliving I did not want.

Absently I turned the box to its reverse, as though seeking confirmation of my own folly. The box in Eustace Robinson's shop had been scarred with a deep arrow-shaped scratch, a scratch for which my own childhood had been responsible and for which I had been soundly scolded.

The box I held now bore on its back a deep arrow-shaped scratch.

It was not so remarkable a coincidence, really. The collectors' world, on this rarefied level, was very small. I held the little box closer to see the hallmark, and heard again that patient old voice, and my eyes stung. I wiped my eyes and looked again. There was no backward symbol on the hallmark.

Dazed as I was with memories, it took a while for the implication to penetrate. It was improbable that two identical boxes, if they existed, should carry the same arrow scar. But the box I had damaged had borne a backward hallmark.

I wished Warren Sloane had been there for consultation, but he was not. I don't know why I did not wait. Perhaps I do now; perhaps it was for reasons I was not ready then to face. Be that as it may, I pulled off my gardener's apron, took the box, and went down the L-shaped corridor to knock on the library door.

Ross Culhaine's cool voice asked what was wanted.

"It's Lavinia Stanton," I said. "I have something here I think that you should see."

Ross himself came to the door to let me in. "You seem quite wrought up," he murmured, smiling faintly. "What is it, another crisis in the *couture* line?"

For answer I placed the silver box upon his desk. There was a faint drumming in my ears, and I was uncertain where I should begin.

"Please tell me. Did you purchase this box from my—from Eustace Robinson?"

"As it happens, yes, I did. If you're concerned about it, I assure you the acquisition was quite legitimate."

"I did not mean—" I stopped. He was baiting me, and I had allowed myself to be pulled into the trap. "I am not questioning the authenticity of the transaction," I said with dignity, "but of the box itself. As a matter of fact, I myself as a child was responsible for that scar. But the box I damaged had a backward hallmark; this does not. That means—"

"A forgery? My dear Miss Stanton!" Ross's eyebrows lifted. "I appreciate your concern, but I assure you it is quite wasted. The box has been in storage from my wife's death until a few weeks past. The conservatory, unless you and Sloane are in it, is under lock and key."

"But the hallmark—"

"You were how old, Miss Stanton, eight or nine? And doubtless being punished by Robinson for carelessness? Is not this reverse hallmark business just the sort of thing a child that age would imagine, to make the whole thing more dramatic?" The sardonic smile in his eyes had deepened. He moved around his desk and picked up the catalogue he had been perusing. It was a faint but definite gesture of dismissal.

I went back to the conservatory with as much dignity as I could muster, but inside I was seething. A child would imagine, yes. But I had not been just any child. I was Eustace Robinson's foster niece, and he had taught me well. I was an expert in my field.

If Ross Culhaine did not accept me as that expert, my

employment on the collection was an act of charity, no more, and I could not tolerate it. At least Damaris was feeling better now. If her father did not recognize my professional qualifications, then once her debut was over I would no longer stay.

VIII

Midway to the conservatory I changed my mind. I had already put in a hard day's labor, as my aching temples proved. If my work was not appreciated, why waste my time?

I turned about and went up the stairs to my own room. The house was still, but the sound of voices drifting down from the sewing room showed that the conference on Damaris' gown was still in session. Good! I was in no mood to see anyone at all.

In my bedroom I discovered Maggie had laid out a plush-bodiced dress for me to wear to dinner, and Leo had chosen to take his afternoon nap upon it, embroidering it liberally with orange hairs. I chased him off and he departed in a huff. For a few moments I devoted myself meticulously to repairing damages, then I slammed it down. The servants could do that. I was going out. Fresh air was what I needed.

Not bothering with gloves and muff, I slapped on hat and dolman and hurried out into the lowering clouds of Marlborough Street. Today I did not take my customary stroll around the Garden but headed straight for the museum. Hopefully the serene majesty of the paintings would calm me down to size.

The museum was nearly empty, for which I was most grateful, and I had the bare peaceful chamber to myself. Almost at once, though, I heard footsteps hurrying towards me across the polished floor. I rose with some annoyance, preparing to move on, when I heard a voice call, "Lavinia, wait!"

Warren Sloane was coming towards me, his hair disheveled and his greatcoat only slung about his shoulders.

"You look like the Goddess of War," he greeted me. "I saw you from the window when you flew off, but I couldn't catch you."

"Is your stint at the galleys completed for the day?"

"So that's it," Sloane said obscurely, surveying me. "Do sit down before you overflow with fire. Have a peppermint drop." He produced a shabby candy bag from his pocket. "All I have to offer at the moment, but it may be soothing. It appears some sweetening is in order, or am I wrong?"

"You are not wrong," I said grimly. Despite myself, I found myself laughing at his nonsense.

"That's better," Sloane said approvingly. "Very therapeutic things, peppermint drops. Have another. Then count to ten and tell the oracle what it was aroused your wrath."

"*Men!*" I said with vigor.

"Yes, indeed. Present company excepted, I do hope. Or are you referring specifically to millionaires? The *genus* robber baron can be exceptionally hard to take. In which case I might also add, 'And *women!*' "

I grinned. "Your day, I gather, has been edifying too?"

"Amen! And may I never have to witness another dressmaking session for the rest of my natural days. It does violence to the masculine constitution."

"How goes the debut creation?"

"Appallingly. The marchesa and Mrs. O'Shaugnessy are at the peak of fighting fit, and I tell you the Irish widow is able to hold her own."

"And Damaris?"

"Half collapsed into the woodwork and looking as though she longed to complete the vanishing act." Sloane grimaced. "Poor thing, she's like a plucked chicken being raised by eagles."

"You ought not to speak of her that way."

Sloane looked at me. "I did not speak to be insulting, or facetious. You know that, don't you?"

"There is a good deal more to Damaris than anyone gives credit for."

"I know that. The question is whether Damaris herself will realize it before she's smothered. And whether she'll have enough strength to fight, if she does discover. She's not well, you know. And her family has no patience with any kind of weakness."

I had already learned that fact. And I knew, too, how Ross and Marina both had the diabolic knack of draining one's spiritual strength with a careless word. I turned away, my lips tightening.

"But it was not the matter of Damaris which drove you today into the wilds of the Public Garden," Sloane said, uncannily following my thoughts. "What happened, Lavinia?"

We seemed to have slipped, easily and naturally, into first-name terms.

"I was working in the conservatory after luncheon. With the silver objects, you know, that we commenced on yesterday." I stopped. "I'm not sure whether I should speak of it or not."

Warren waited a moment, and when I did not continue he rose and put my dolman round my shoulders. "Come have a chocolate at Franz Joseph's. Then you can decide."

Whether it was the little chocolate shop's cozy warmth, the delighted attentions showered on us by the major domo, or the equally concerned sympathy turned upon me by my escort, I do not know, but I shortly found myself pouring out the whole story.

"I am absolutely certain of my facts," I finished. "And my conclusions."

"You would be. Naturally."

"I assure you, Ross Culhaine was none so sure!"

Now it was Warren Sloane's turn to fall silent. "You said you were not sure if you should speak," he said at last. "I find myself in somewhat the same position. But I must tell you this. You are not alone in your suspicions."

"You, also?"

"I am, in a small way, considered somewhat of an expert in this field. You are aware, of course, of my connection with the museum in New York? What you may not know is that there is a possibility of my museum's obtaining part of the Culhaine Collection—either outright or on a sort of perpetual loan. There have been talks regarding possible exchange arrangements with the Boston museum in which, as you know, Marina Orsini has taken interest. None of this, naturally, is spoken of at all. In point of fact—and you understand this is strictly confidential—my employment on the Culhaine Collection is in part, shall we say, a blind? My real mission in Boston is to determine the authenticity of certain pieces in the Collection, and their authenticity of title as well."

"For whom, your museum?"

"That is one of the things I'm not supposed to say."

The ethics of all this disturbed me slightly, but I was well aware that such secret appraisals and verifications were common practice when important collectors or museums were the principals. Major art transactions involved all the intrigue and secrecy of the world of Machiavelli. It did seem deceitful for me to remain silent about Warren's dual loyalty when Ross Culhaine was both my host and my employer, but certainly Culhaine himself was not naïve. And I had, after all, tried to warn him.

Warren signaled the waiter to bring another pot of chocolate and a plate of cakes. "You understand, Lavinia," he said earnestly, "it is not a matter of my not trusting your confidence. Professional ethics hold me to a pledge I have already made, otherwise I would gladly tell you the whole story."

"I understand."

"Then will you consider me unbearably presumptuous if I ask you this? If you observe any further—er—discrepancies, details not in order, will you come to me?"

I hesitated, then nodded. Ross Culhaine obviously did not wish to hear, and if, later, either museum did obtain items from the Collection and their authenticity should be questioned, it would be best for my own professional reputation if I had reported anything I had noticed to another expert.

It was only afterwards I realized that my acquiescence was predicated upon my continuing residence in Boston.

The waiter arrived at this juncture with a laden tray. When he had set it on the table, Warren waved him off. "Thank you, we'll serve ourselves. Will you do the honors, madame?"

The chocolate pot was flowery Viennese china, and there was a crystal bowl heaped with piles of stiff-whipped cream. I poured, feeling self-conscious about having forgotten gloves, and on my finger the great ruby gleamed.

"That's a very handsome stone," Warren said. "I've noticed it before." I'll wager you have, I thought drily. "The setting's a remarkable piece of workmanship. Italian, of course."

"Florentine, I believe."

"I would have said Milanese." Warren laughed. "Judging from your face when I encountered you outside, you must have been tempted today to employ its hidden assets." I gazed at him blankly, and he looked puzzled. "Surely I am right. That is one of the famous Medici poison rings?"

Now it was I who stared. "Surely you're joking."

"Not at all. I have seen one or two, and yours is very close to type. The high setting, higher than necessary for the design, and the gold very solid round the base. You don't mean the possibility has never crossed your mind?"

Obviously my expertise had just gone down in his estimation. In my own, also. "I have reason to believe the setting is a recent reproduction," I said faintly.

"The ring proper, quite likely, but I'd stake my reputation on the authenticity of the serpent head itself." Warren seemed quite excited. "There may be indications in the gold itself, you know, and I warrant anything, a secret spring. Let me take a look at it, Lavinia, and I'll show you."

"I never take it off, except in my room at night." It was a precaution Eustace Robinson had impressed upon me.

"Do you suspect me of attempting a switch in a crowded restaurant? Give me your hand. I'll screw my jeweler's glass into my eye, if you like, so you won't appear to be being compromised."

"Don't be ridiculous." I held out my hand, and he turned my fingers over, examining the ring professionally. "See here, a barely perceptible difference in gold between ring and setting, minute but definite variance in color and in sheen. We haven't yet succeeded in duplicating that exact antique patina, although the difference is unrecognizable except when as here, the two are side by side." He produced his glass and offered it to me, that I might see it also.

"No wonder I was always so sure the piece was old. I never doubted until I came on recent records. I had always looked at the setting, not the ring itself."

"Your instincts were sound. How did it happen that the serpent head never suggested that you employ the curiosity of Eve?" Warren reclaimed the glass and began to scan the setting closely, turning my finger back and forth beneath his eye. Suddenly he gave a soft ejaculation. "Look, Lavinia, here." With his fingernail he pressed delicately on the tiny forked tongue that protruded from the serpent's mouth. The ruby sprang upward on a hidden spring, revealing a shallow well beneath.

"I was right," Warren said with satisfaction. "Truly, Lavinia, did you never guess?"

I was disproportionately embarrassed. Yes, and resentful of Eustace Robinson, who surely must have known and had not told.

"I'm being unfair," Warren said kindly, seeing my face. "There are few of these poison receptacles in circulation, and I had the advantage of you, since I've encountered some before. Besides, I seem to have poison on my brain of late. It must be the atmosphere we are working in."

Out of the recesses of my unconscious flashed the memory of my first night in Boston. Damaris stumbling into my room, doubled up with pain; her stark whispered belief that she was being poisoned. I had written it off as nightmare or sick delusion, for Damaris had never mentioned it again. Perhaps she had, to Warren Sloane?

There was a faint white residue in the corners of the hidden well. "What is your guess, Lavinia? Arsenic, or belladonna, or some unnamed poison? Shall we test it, as the Medicis are rumored to have, on some poor unfortunate passer-by?"

"It's more likely a residue of jeweler's paste from when the ring was mounted." I needed that demythologizing common sense to dispel the mood that had enveloped us. I snapped the ruby shut, but Warren did not release my hand. He had returned the jeweler's glass to his pocket, but he continued to concentrate on the ring, bending over it closely.

I was beginning to feel self-conscious. "We must be going.

What are you doing, sir, memorizing the pattern so you can make a counterfeit some day?"

Warren, not taking his eyes from the ruby, shook his head. "I have the oddest feeling I've seen this serpent's head before."

"You could not have. It's a family piece. I believe my— father gave it to my mother, before I was born."

"The Stanton family jewel?"

I did not respond. Warren, with that intuitiveness which I had discerned before, asked gently, "Lavinia, have I said something wrong?"

I looked up, involuntarily, into his eyes, very close to mine across our locking hands. I saw his eyes, which had been gentle, narrow, lift beyond my head to gaze at something I could not see. The warmth left his face, to be replaced by something I could not identify, and he let go my hand.

"What is it?" Instinctively I straightened.

"Don't turn around." Warren's voice, though low, was sharp, and I reacted. After a moment he relaxed, grinning wryly. "If this were a melodrama we ought now to receive a message, 'Flee! All is discovered!'"

"Don't be so clever. What was it you saw?"

"La Marchesa Orsini. You needn't look, she's left. Apparently she did not wish to mix with the plebians."

"Most likely she did not see us." I rose. "I really must be getting back. No, Warren, today most definitely I will escort myself."

I got rid of him with some difficulty and hurried back towards Marlborough Street, my gloveless hands thrust deep in the pockets of my dolman, bending against the wind. The house was quiet; Damaris' door was shut, but in my bedroom a fire burned cheerfully and someone had removed all traces of Leo's nap from the plush-bodiced gown. I knew I must dress quickly, for it was late, but I found myself sitting for some minutes before the fire, gazing blankly at the ruby ring.

Dinner was strained, for to my own annoyance I felt both diffident and awkward, and took defense in being brusque. One cause was my still-rankling anger towards Ross Culhaine, which made me in no mood for trivia. In my brain I was cursing Warren Sloane for telling me Marina had seen us in the chocolate shop; I kept imagining she was watching me with calculating eyes. Damaris' presence might have helped, but Damaris was not there. She felt poorly, Marina said, and had sent word she would dine upstairs from a tray.

"Perhaps I should join her." I fairly leapt at the excuse.

Marina shook her head. "She made it quite clear she wished to be alone. It is by far best to humor her when she takes these fancies."

I longed to answer that this was not quite the policy she maintained herself at times, but I held my tongue. If Marina or Mr. Culhaine thought I was moodish or sullen, that was just too bad.

I disciplined myself to endure the meal for propriety's sake, but as soon afterwards as was decent I made my escape, and no doubt both the others were relieved to see me go. I went to the firelit sanctuary of my own room, locked the door, and changed the stiff silk for a comfortable wrapper. After a time I went to the connecting door and knocked. There was no answer, but discreet investigation proved that the latch on Damaris' side had not been thrown.

"Damaris?" I called softly, and when she again did not respond I opened the door and went through the connecting boudoir into her room. The place was suffocatingly hot, and Damaris, in a padded robe, was standing by the back window overlooking the conservatory, her head against the wall.

"What do you want?" she asked, not turning.

"To see how you were feeling. Your aunt said you were ill."

"I am fine. I merely wished to be let alone. So you need not trouble yourself, Lavinia."

"It is no trouble. I haven't seen you all day, and I was concerned."

"Not too concerned to slip out for an assignation in a public restaurant."

So that was it. "I had chocolate with Warren Sloane," I said quite bluntly, "after what was, if you must know, an extremely trying day. Your father, Damaris, is not the easiest person in the world for whom to work. But I did think even the hired hands were entitled to a few hours off without accounting."

"Oh, nonsense, Vinnie! You are no hired hand, and never think it." Damaris swung round, and two pink spots burned in her cheeks. "No doubt you will think me amusingly naïve, but it did—shock me, that you would take refreshment unchaperoned in a public place."

"Obviously taking refreshment in public is not so scandalous that your aunt, not to mention the Cabots, don't indulge. Or is it the fact, Damaris, that I was with a gentleman?"

"He is not a gentleman, he's a—" Damaris stopped.

"A common tradesman? I never knew," I said deliberately, "that you were such a snob. Or for that matter, that you found anything objectionable in his presence."

I was prepared for anger, but not for the changes that came over Damaris' face. She seemed to crumble inside; the color drained from her face and she gazed at me like a stricken deer. My own wrath vanished as quickly as it had come. "Damaris," I said baldly, "are you in love with him?"

Damaris recoiled. "You have no right to ask that."

"I know. But I need to know, Damaris. Tell me."

"I cannot tell you." But looking at the face she turned away, the flush that came and went, and her too-rapid breath, I knew the answer, even if she did not.

"Aunt was right," she whispered after a moment. "I could not credit it, but she was right." Her voice had the stunned tone of a disillusioned child.

I felt a surge of anger. "Did it ever occur to you that Marina might be—"

"What? Jealous?" Damaris swung upon me harshly.

"I did not say that."

"No. You wouldn't. You're so fastidious, Vinnie. So kind, not wanting to hurt people's feelings. But you hurt them all the same. I know all about Marina and Warren Sloane."

"But why—"

"Marina needs a cavalier. And so, God help us all, do I. I'm human, too, you know." She turned away, leaning her face against the window pane, and I could not watch. "*Why*, Vinnie?" she said at last. "You're strong, you're independent, you're brilliant, you're *well*. Why, of all the ones in the world, must you choose him?"

"I didn't," I said, and knew this was the unkindest part of all. "We have a—a camaraderie. We work together." I could not explain the sort of bond that results from the common indignity of being employed in a great house. "As for the rest . . . He has met me by chance, now and again, at the museum. He has taken me for chocolate. Nothing more."

"He held your hand in a public place," Damaris said, as if repeating a litany. "He kissed your hand."

"Did your Aunt Marina neglect to tell you he was examining my ring?" I looked at her, and my anger drained away. "It may have been indiscreet, but nothing more. It's been— hard at times for me here, Damaris. My whole life's changed. I've felt quite alone sometimes. Sloane saw that, and he's shown me kindness."

"He has been kind to me too," Damaris said.

"Doesn't that tell you something?"

"About Warren, or myself, or both?" Damaris demanded. "I may be deficient in many respects, Vinnie, but I am not a fool." Before I could divine her intent she had grasped my wrist and swung me round so that we stood side by side before the mirror. My eyes were still bright with anger, and my color came and went. Beside me Damaris looked frail and haggard, like a child too early old. "Do you think I do not know which any normal man in his right senses would prefer? I'm a disappointment to my father, to Marina, to myself. But I have one advantage, Lavinia, I know myself. And I know what Warren Sloane is, too. Do you think I'm not aware that when he looks at me what he's seeing is the Culhaine Collection?"

"Oh, Damaris." I lifted my hand, then let it fall.

"And pray don't cry over me. I cannot bear it."

"*I* cannot bear to hear you put such a low value on yourself."

"Stop being sentimental," Damaris snapped. "I assure you I'm being neither maudlin nor self-effacing. I'm not afraid to see things as they are. That's my saving grace. What I see is that Warren Sloane, whatever his weaknesses, is a person I can understand, and thus forgive. And that he is the one person in my life who had ever given me the things I really want."

"It appears," I said daringly, "that you have a great deal more to give to him, than he to you."

"That," Damaris said carefully, "is the trouble with judging by appearances, don't you think? One sees only the outside. It seems to me value is also determined by the need. When I am with Warren, I feel for the first time in my life that I am not defective merchandise."

"Oh, Damaris!"

"And I think, I hope, that I am able to do as much for him. And if that's too blunt, well, you must forgive me, but it's shanty Irish I am, and below the finer points of proprieties."

"Damaris, don't."

"Why not?" Damaris said harshly. "Why not call a spade a spade? I'm more my father's daughter than he knows; I don't like sham. If it's the truth you'd have me be knowing, let's say it plain. Warren Sloane is in love with the Culhaine

Collection. It's like a sickness in him, a hungering after the kind of beauty he's been starving for. He'd give his life to that beauty, to taking care of it, to never letting it be damaged or come to harm. Well, maybe I can understand that hunger, for there's an emptiness in my own soul, too. And I understand something else too, so put your mind to rest if you're worrying about how he'd treat me. It's what *I* am, too, you know, a piece of the Culhaine Collection. Just ask my father. And now, if you don't mind, Lavinia, I think I'd like to be alone."

IX

As a result of that conversation, the relationship between Damaris and myself was altered, and oddly enough, for the better. It established Damaris as a woman grown, it broke the old boarding-school pattern of adoring, dependent child and protective mentor.

I noticed a change, also, in Marina's attitude towards me. Heretofore, with the casual arrogance of the very rich, she had scarcely acknowledged me at all, save as some object present for the family's convenience. The incident at the coffee shop, apparently, had forced her recognition of me as a person. Suffice to say that at times I now was conscious of her watching me with veiled, measuring eyes, she no longer looked directly through me on occasion, and there was, at our shared luncheons, a tangible current in the air through which Warren Sloane moved with sublime masculine indifference. And when Warren casually asked me later if Marina had remarked upon our coffeehouse tête-à-tête, I answered him not a word.

Another, and more surprising, incident which grew out of the whole affair was that the next afternoon, while Warren and I were working in the conservatory, a servant appeared with a message bidding me to tea in the library with Ross Culhaine.

Warren whistled. "A royal command. Will you be a royal subject or a rebel?"

I ignored him. "Tell your master I will join him as soon as I have tidied up," I told the servant crisply, pulling off my apron, and went upstairs to wash my hands in the bedroom bowl and smooth my hair.

My first reaction to the message had been an ignominious nervousness and a chill stab of fear, which no one who has not been in my recent state of homeless penury can understand. And if, when I sailed downstairs and rapped upon the closed library door, my manner was too brusque and stiff, it was only to keep my courage high.

Ross Culhaine himself opened the door at once. His first words took the wind from my carefully and precariously hoisted sails.

"I owe you an apology," he said without preamble. "It occurs to me that you must have thought me yesterday not only an insufferable boor but an egocentric Philistine as well."

I gaped at him.

"If I gave the impression that I—ah, doubted your probity or judgment, let me assure you that was not what I intended." He smiled, an oddly attractive smile that softened the death's-head contours and made him much more human. "Please, Miss Stanton, come take tea to show you accept my apology, which I assure you is a devilish hard thing for a Black Irishman to make. And do let's sit down, for I feel a fool standing here, and I'm sure you do as well."

He led the way to the Florentine chairs beside the fireplace, where a great blaze roared, throwing dancing lights on the lovely lines of the tea service on its silver tray. "Will you do the honors, or shall I pour as a sign of my abject humility?" He could, it seemed, employ upon occasion Damaris' trick of rattling on with charm when someone else was ill-at-ease. I busied myself with the tea things while he continued.

"In point of fact, your blunt announcement yesterday precipitated a dilemma. That is the only excuse which I can offer. You were right, of course, you know. The box is counterfeit."

I did not speak, and after a moment he went on. "I have suspected for some time that there are irregularities in the Collection. However, although it is possible to document that certain objects are indeed forgeries, it is most difficult, as you must know, to substantiate any charges against the perpetrators without hard proof. Since I have none as yet, it seemed the wisest course for me to remain ignorant of the whole affair, in the hopes the thief or thieves would grow overconfident."

I nodded.

"Then you will understand the difficulty in which you placed me. My first thought was to try to convince you that I did not know." Ross smiled ruefully. "My second was to realize that you would consider me a hopeless fool. I might have gotten by with anyone else, but not with Eustace Robinson's niece."

"Then you did buy the box from him?"

"Oh, yes, and was told of both the scratch and its history, and the peculiarity of hallmark. I was not aware that this particular piece had since been forged, but as soon as you left I took a good look at it myself, and I was sure."

"And you have no idea of how the substitutions have taken place?"

"I have several ideas. The matter which perplexes me is not so much *how* as *when*. The Collection was shut up here for years; the house itself closed and guarded. Did the substitutions take place since our return, or in the months directly preceding our departure? There was considerable—confusion —in the house then, for some period of time, and I was giving scant attention to works of art." Ross looked somber. It was the period of his wife's death to which he referred, and remembering my dear mother's last illness, I could understand.

"Would it not help," I said at last, "if some piece acquired on your recent travels can be identified as forged? It would at least prove the pilfering is being managed by someone with current access."

Ross looked at me with respect. "An excellent thought. Miss Stanton, would your proprieties be offended if I suggested some midnight intrigue?"

"What do you mean?"

"Tonight, after the household is asleep, slip down and meet me in the conservatory. There should just be time before morning for us to make a cursory inspection of the contents. Then if, later, any further substitutions are made, we will know the thief is still active, and will also be able to witness for each other. To be blunt, I would prefer to have someone else's testimony to corroborate my own, and I do not wish anyone else to know about the thefts."

I felt a wave of guilt. "You had better know that I have already told someone of our interview of yesterday."

"And who was that?"

"Warren Sloane."

Ross grimaced. "But he does not know that I do concur with your findings, and I can rely on your not telling him, can I not?" He correctly interpreted the expression on my face. "I am not implying any doubt of his honesty. Nor of his integrity, although I'm well aware he's probably passing a detailed inventory of the Collection on to his home museum. Every major collector and dealer in the Western world wants to know what I own, and I've no objection. It's only the social Philistines who have no right to knowledge. But I do think that if the antiques grapevine doesn't know I know I'm being robbed, I have a better chance of reclamation. If it places you in an awkward position with Sloane, can you not excuse it as professional loyalty to your employer? Speaking of which, we have never discussed the matter of remuneration, since you now have taken on a professional assignment." He named a sum which left me breathless. "Will that be satisfactory?"

"It is far too much," I said faintly, "since you are already supplying me with room and lodging."

"That has nothing whatever to do with it," Ross said sharply. The death's-head look had returned. "I respect both work and money, and since I expect full value for every cent I spend, I prefer to pay for the best possible professionals in all fields. You are hardly a live-in servant, Miss Stanton, nor for that matter a genteel female for whom charity need be diplomatically disguised. As for your staying under my roof, that is a purely social matter. You are a friend of my daughter, and her guest."

"Under the circumstances, I should prefer to look for private lodgings for the balance of my employment in this city."

"That is as you wish, of course. But I hope you will reconsider. Damaris would be very disappointed. You've been good for her; she has been much more normal since your visit here."

I did not much care for his choice of words but we parted, amicably enough, to dress for dinner. My mind was whirling with unanswered questions. And late that night, after all the household was asleep, when lying wakeful on my bed I heard a tap upon my door, I did not turn over and close my eyes again as discretion bade me. I rose and, not putting on the lamp, dressed in the dark in a serviceable work gown and soft slippers, and presently crept through the hall and down the servants' stairs. A single lamp burned in the conservatory and Ross was waiting for me inside the door. "Good girl," he said approvingly, noting my preparations and the fact that I had brought pen and notebook with me. He shut and locked the baize door after us and lit another hanging lamp. I saw that he had closed all the heavy canvas shades that protected the plants from too much sun in summer. "A melodramatic touch, but no point in exciting notice," he said briefly. Holding the lamp high, he led the way directly to where the Culhaine Collection gleamed in the flickering light.

It was a night of magic, a night outside of time. The quietness, the lush perfumed air and the white tropical flowers glowing through the darkling green, the gleam of precious jewels set in gold and silver, and above all, that sense of stillness, of something shimmering and splendid hanging suspended, waiting. We spoke but seldom, our voices hushed, intent upon our search. Ross Culhaine's hands were long and slender, like a surgeon's or an artist's. I close my eyes and can see them again, so curiously gentle and experienced, turning over the treasured objects as if they were living things.

We finished shortly before dawn, having discovered some dozen objects of dubious worth. Ross removed all traces of our labors and pocketed my notes, and we crept off to our delayed slumbers before the servants stirred.

I was half afraid Damaris might have come in search of me and found me missing, but her manner the next day was just as always, and she asked no questions. I concluded with relief that she had had an uneventful night.

Damaris was, as her father had said, much better lately. The fits of vagueness or depression, alternating with hectic brightness, were evening out, and she was both more animated and more serene. This continued as November and preparations for her debut progressed. She even expressed some interest in the plans. She did not, however, as she had suggested, invite me to go to the attic with her to look for lace. Some time or other she went on a secret pilgrimage of her own among her mother's things, reappearing with a drawn face and the return of that haunted expression in her eyes, but she quite calmly showed me the lace which she had brought, and begged my assistance in repairing it. The lace was a heavy band, about five inches wide, alternating thread-work with a heavy padded satin stitch of scrolls. It looked quite like the embroidery in the portrait, and I was happy to repair it for her. The portrait itself was cleaned and framed and hung, and that night at dinner Ross Culhaine took our collective breath away by suggesting that a few pieces of the Collection be set out on display. I wondered immediately what he was up to, but Damaris and her aunt were over-joyed.

Damaris' gown for the affair was well in hand, and a few days later Mrs. O'Shaugnessy brought it for a fitting. The style capitalized on Damaris' period air rather than warred against it as most of her wardrobe did; she looked pale and weary when the fitting was over, but I could tell she had been pleased. Marina also had a gown in work, which we were not shown. As for myself, Damaris had delicately inquired into my resources and offered to assist me, but I shook my head. The salary I was receiving made it possible for me to have my own conference with Mrs. O'Shaugnessy.

She was a birdlike little woman with a decided manner and a sensible head, and grasped at once that I was not one of those idle women who, as she put it, "spend fortunes on fripperies because they've nothing else to occupy their foolish minds." Fortunately, it was quite the custom for ladies to have a second, décolleté bodice made to match with the skirts of their finest gowns, and I had a few lengths still on hand of the aubergine silk. I also found enough pieces of old lace to weave together for a low deep bertha. Mrs. O'Shaugnessy produced for me a bodice so low and scant of sleeve that when I beheld myself in the mirror I felt like the old woman in the nursery rhyme, "This never can be I." But I was not displeased.

I modeled the completed turnout for Damaris the night before the ball, and Damaris clapped her hands. "Vinnie, how splendid! You will put me to shame."

"Hardly," I laughed. "It is your party."

"Aunt Marina's, you mean."

". . . And the meek companion will fade unnoticed into the shadows."

"You have never, in all the years I've known you," Damaris retorted, "been meek. And I intend that you shall be a belle." She overrode my practical observation that since I knew no one I should scarcely be asked to dance at all. "Mr. Sloane is going to engage you for the cotillion. It is all arranged."

I did not much care to be the object of arrangements, but Damaris did not notice. "I do hope," she said slowly, "that Mr. Sloane enjoys the ball. He has worked so hard." She picked up the sketches of the floral decorations, which were lying near. "Society will be shocked. Ivy and lilacs and violets and wildflowers, instead of palms and roses. 'Friendship, sincerity, purity and innocence.' He either has a very romantic outlook, or a strange sense of humor."

"At the risk of sounding impossibly sentimental, they seem to me to be appropriate symbols."

Damaris smiled somberly. "Ah, Vinnie, you still see a little girl in boarding school, long ago. There is no innocence here. We are all as wicked as can be, and that's the truth."

I had thought the European *jeune fille* was kept more sheltered than we Americans, but if that was a sample of the sophistication Damaris had acquired abroad, then I was wrong. I looked at her and was astonished to find that her eyes were full of tears. That sort of invisible translucent shell she used to have was gone, with the illusions lost God knows where, and I could have wept. We always ache for the loss of someone else's innocence, if not our own.

Damaris swung round suddenly, and grasped my hands. "Oh, my dear, is it dangerous of me to tempt fate thus? I'm afraid because I'm *not* afraid now, and it's all your doing."

"Mine?"

"It was you who dreamed that dress for me, my lovely, lovely dress. When I put it on I believe in life again. It becomes an armour for me." Damaris added with uncanny prescience, "Like your ring."

Instinctively I glanced down at my finger, at the great stone. I was still shaken by Warren Sloane's discovery and had found myself, oddly, unable to examine the ring closely since.

"When I look at it," Damaris said, echoing my thoughts, "I feel as if I am looking at pools within pools, drawing me down and down. You must guard it carefully, Vinnie. It's a wonder Papa hasn't tried already to add it to the Culhaine Collection."

"It's not for sale."

"You did not have it, did you, when we were in school? I would have remembered, surely."

"I—received it recently. It was my mother's."

"Her betrothal ring. Was it an heirloom in your father's family? Why, Vinnie, there are tears in your eyes. Have I said something wrong?"

I shook my head, but could not answer. The tears, which had been so absent at Eustace Robinson's funeral, which had been stirred to life in the coffee shop, brimmed at the floodgates of my will and would not be checked.

"I am a foolish, meddling, curious girl," Damaris said gently, "and if I have hurt you, I am very sorry."

It was the moment which I had known inevitably would come, when I had to knock down the last wall of pride between us and tell her the aftermath of Eustace Robinson's death. I did so, all of it, even the humiliation and shame and emptiness which the Hon. Mr. Blyden, Esq.'s revelations had brought to me.

"So you see," I finished, "I came here, if not under false

pretenses, with mixed motives. I needed a corner to crawl in, and I hoped to find in Boston some clue to who I am. Your letter was the answer to a prayer."

"At least," Damaris said with devastating frankness, "that relieves me of the burden of being the recipient of your sense of charity. Also vice versa; you must believe that, Vinnie." She was right. My head cleared suddenly. We were friends who owed each other nothing, and therefore were free to give.

"And you *shall* find something out about your father. It's the most romantic thing I've ever heard. I'll help you. Perhaps Warren, or my father—"

"You are not to tell them! Do you understand? I know quite well what most persons' interpretation of my story would be."

"I'm sure your father was a fine man," Damaris said firmly. "I *know* you are a gentlewoman. And a gentle woman. You have given me faith in myself, Vinnie, now you must allow me to give it back to you."

Naturally, we ended up crying on each other's shoulders, which was undoubtedly maudlin, but made us feel much better.

The day of Damaris' debut dawned chaotic. I use the term "dawned" loosely, for only the dullest grey light showed and snow was falling. It continued all the day as florists' attendants and caterers' men streamed through. Quantities of floral tributes arrived for Marina and Damaris. The long ballroom, across the hall from the dining room, was unlocked, and the house servants, orchestrated by Hopkins, flew about continually, looking harried. There was no work on the Collection for me that day, for all traces of our labors had been swept clean from the conservatory, but I kept busy trying to distract Damaris, whose tremulous nervousness had returned.

Warren was in and out of the house, but I did not see him.

He had been authorized by Ross Culhaine to arrange the display of a few carefully chosen Collection pieces on a library table I heard being carried out to the conservatory for the purpose. Damaris and I lunched on trays in her room, and took tea in mine, and afterwards I succeeded in persuading her to retire for a few hours' nap. I lay down, also, but I could not sleep. Sooner than it seemed possible, old Maggie was coming in to help me dress.

Maggie was most approving of my remodeled gown, and laced me into it to the accompaniment of a stream of family confidences. She took a proprietary excitement in Damaris' debut. "Lord love ye, child, seems like it's only a day since we beheld her after her christening, like a little princess in lace in her mother's arms."

"It's sad her mother cannot be with her now."

"That's as may be," said Maggie darkly. "If you're ready now, will ye not go in to Miss Damaris? She's already dressed, and it's such a time I've had making her sit quiet."

Damaris was sitting dutifully, but she jumped up eagerly on my entrance, her soft silks rustling. "Vinnie, how fine you are! Vinnie will you do my hair up for me like in the portrait? You're so good at it, I wouldn't allow Maggie to attempt it."

So I looped Damaris' hair up in the pale arrangement of coils and braids, as in the little portrait which had been cleaned and framed and hung at Ross's instructions on the wall near where Marina and Damaris were to stand to receive their guests. Last of all I brought out something Damaris had not seen. "I made this for you, for luck." It was a spray of lilies, white for debut, which I had fashioned of beads and wire after the manner of the garland in the portrait. Damaris was enchanted when I set it round her hair.

"Now we must go downstairs and show ourselves to Papa." She picked up her fan with its delicate ivory spokes. "Have you yours, Vinnie? We must let the gentlemen write their names on the sticks for the dances they request. It's the way, Aunt says, when there are no programmes." Damaris slipped the silken cord around her wrist. "Stay with me, Vinnie. I begin to feel quite giddy."

We rustled out into the hall. From somewhere below us in the ballroom came the faint strains of a fiddle as the musicians tuned their strings. Candles burned in all the crystal-hung bronze brackets high on the wall and the scent of tuberoses assailed me. Warren Sloane had made alterations in his floral decorations, after all. Damaris frowned faintly, as though puzzled, and ran the back of her hand across her brow.

"You *are* giddy."

"I shall not be, I shall remain quite well no matter what this night may bring." Damaris' words were curiously stilted, almost like a novice taking vows. Her bosom, beneath the low-cut lace, rose and fell. "Stay beside me." She grasped the banister with one hand and my wrist with the other, and descended out of the shadows into the well of light.

The scent of the flowers swelled. They were everywhere, everywhere in the lower hall. The flames of the candles in the chandelier danced and sparkled, sending forth shimmering rainbow fragments refracted and magnified in a hundred prisms. Beneath them, aureoled in light, stood two figures, motionless. I felt Damaris' fingers tighten painfully around my wrist.

Ross and Marina. The mask of the Prince of Darkness was upon him, from faultless dead-white ruffles to the dark gleaming black of his evening tails, and diamonds twinkled coldly in his cuffs. The only color was the Titian glow of Marina's hair, for she had chosen, how cleverly, to dress as well in black, alluring knowledge contrasted to Damaris' virginal white. Her gown was velvet, cut daringly plain and bare with *diamanté* straps, her only ornaments the canary diamond flashing on her finger and the diamond dog-collar

Ross was fastening around her neck. The familial task invested the moment with a curious intimacy. Her head was tilted forward and when he had closed the clasp he reached up one finger to smooth into place a tendril of golden hair which had escaped. Then, in a careless, almost automatic gesture, he pressed his lips for a moment against her nape. Only an offhand instant, yet as if a match had been struck, illumination flared on all the crosscurrents I had heretofore but dimly understood. Behind me Damaris breathed a faint negating sound.

"There you are. Do come, guests will be arriving soon," Marina had caught sight of us and spoke in her natural imperious manner as though nothing had occurred. Really, nothing had. Yet I was breathing hard and there was a ringing in my ears. Now it was I who lagged, while Damaris hurried down ahead, pirouetting in a sort of nervous excitement before her aunt and father. Marina nodded with critical approval, but Ross stood motionless, looking past her, a strange expression on his face.

"I will try to do you credit, Papa," Damaris said quietly. There was a hard desperate resolution in her voice that must have reached him, for his eyes focused on her and his face relaxed.

"I am sure you will, my dear. I have something here which I would like you to wear."

I divined his meaning even before I recognized the velvet case which he drew from a nearby niche. He pressed the catch. Damaris gasped audibly and shrank back, her eyes fixed with a kind of terrified fascination on the legendary Collar of Culhaine.

X

I had thought myself inured to dazzle, but I had been wrong. The portrait, all the word-descriptions, had done scant justice to the sheer *presence* of the great collar of reticulated gold. Some unknown artisan had shaped it carefully, shaped the heavy squares of beaten yellow with their great cabochon rubies, the flexible connecting scale-like leaves of paler, greenish hue, frosted with a tracery of pearls, so that it would fit close to the nape of a slender neck and lie flat upon proud shoulders. It lay coiled upon the velvet of the case like a living thing.

"No," Damaris whispered. "I don't want to wear it, Papa, please!" For a moment I thought that she would faint.

"Damaris is right. It is too heavy for her," I struck in boldly. "But this is a special night. Could it not, this once, be put upon display? Might she not select a suitable location among the other pieces in the conservatory?"

Damaris flung a look of sheer panic at her father.

"It will remain in the library, beneath the portrait. I will see to it." Ross bowed briefly and was gone.

"I must say," Marina began with some asperity.

"I couldn't! Aunt, *you* must understand!" The back of Damaris' hand went to her brow again, and her nostrils flared, then she straightened and her eyes darted feverishly about the room. "The flowers—the flowers have changed . . ."

I followed her gaze. And she was right. The bouquets, the garlands, sheaves and sprays that were everywhere were as Warren had meticulously sketched them, as I had seen him supervising their arrangement that very morning. But in the hours since, they had been embellished. Among the violets and lilacs were other flowers: silver-leaved geraniums; white hollyhocks and peonies and cherry blossoms, seemingly incongruous in a drawing room but strikingly effective. And everywhere among the white, glowing notes of gold. Gold lilies, yellow tulips; gold roses, each above two buds; lady's slipper and marigold and acacia, half-hidden among the ivy tendrils and the luminous white. It made a marvelous Renaissance effect. And tuberoses, hundreds of tuberoses, blanketing the air with their singular heady scent.

Damaris' frantic gaze turned to her aunt, and a tangible current passed between them.

"Who has done this?" Marina said harshly. "If the servants dared—"

"Do you like it? I planned it as a surprise," Warren Sloane said pleasantly behind us. He had come in without our notice. "Intended as a courtesy to you, madame, but you have undone me. I had anticipated you would be wearing your favorite golden shades."

"A courtesy." Marina had become at once taller and paler, like royalty encroached upon. Then she snapped her fan open with a short laugh. "You are not undone. You ought to have come to me first for my response, but since there is no harm done—"

"And none intended, I assure you."

"—it shall be as you have planned. You ought however to have remembered that tuberoses affect my niece most strangely."

"I forget nothing," Warren said calmly. "I used the tuberoses with great care, as an—undercurrent, shall we say?—to counteract the prevailing innocence, which could grow cloying."

"You need not fear." Damaris' chin was up and her voice was very quiet. "I will be quite all right."

"You are quite pale." Warren scanned her face intently. "Believe me, madame, I would not have Miss Damaris frightened for the world. Perhaps I ought remove the objects of our controversy at once."

"They will stay. Everything will stay as it is. Our guests are arriving. If necessary, we will make adjustments later."

Warren bowed. "As you will. In which case, may I beg the honor of a dance with the debutante before the festivities begin?"

"Certainly not." Marina's voice was sharp. "She must stay with the family to receive our guests."

"Then I shall claim her later." Warren bowed again, offered me his arm, and bore me off in style to the front parlor. His eyes were very bright, and he had the look of an eager squirrel.

"That sounded," I said when we were out of earshot, "suspiciously like a threat."

Warren laughed. "Incorrigible, aren't I?" he said, unabashed. "When the marchesa puts on her Lucrezia Borgia air, I cannot resist taking her down a peg. Don't look so disapproving, Lavinia. After all, I know her fairly well, for all her title and aristocratic airs. And know even more about her, which the lovely lady does not like at all." He correctly interpreted the expression on my face. "Do not ask what. May I tell you something? This is an Italian family—"

"Only half Italian."

"—be that as it may, it has an Italian character and it reeks of intrigue. Take advantage of your status of outsider and don't allow yourself to be drawn in."

"Is that a warning?"

"Call it an expression of concern. You are a charming woman, Lavinia, and an intelligent one. There are things in this house you are better off not knowing. I should hate to see you hurt, just through the chance of having learned too much."

"It is hardly likely. I am, after all, as you remarked, an outsider and an employee. As you are, yourself." That was malicious of me, but I was nettled. He was referring to Marina and Ross, of course. I was annoyed at having it recalled to mind, and even more by the implication that I could be hurt by knowing.

Warren left me, at my request, in a quiet corner where I could see the guests arriving, and scurried off after cocking a sardonic eyebrow. I took refuge behind my fan and a cold manner and disciplined myself into composure by watching the spectacle of Boston society crossing the threshold of the House of Culhaine. There was a good deal of ironic amusement to be derived in the role of detached observer. The flirtations and maneuvers, the differing characteristics of Boston bluestockings, the old merchant prince families of clipper ship days from whom the stigma of trade had long since vanished, the cultured internationals, the Revolutionary War families and the *nouveaux riches*—Boston balls embrace no one exclusive age group, and there were doddering, aristocratic old gentlemen here, as well as blooming belles. But soon, by virtue of my observer's role, I began to perceive the worm in the bud, the blight beneath the rose.

This was, as Marina had intended, a glittering affair. The Cabots had appeared, like a fleet of proud ships sailing into foreign port. But I suspected they had come—would it be indelicate to say—for business reasons? It was one thing for them to attend a soirée in the Culhaine mansion; I wondered whether the Culhaines would be invited to their own. This house and all that's in it, I thought, is tonight like a new exhibit in a Barnum circus. I overheard more than one Boston dowager and dashing dandy evaluating with patronizing carelessness the debutante, the entertainment and the Culhaine Collection. It made my blood boil.

Warren, joining me in my corner presently, confirmed my thoughts. "The Cabots showed up, but not some of the others Marina hoped. She's going to be angry. Marina's done Damaris proud, hasn't she? And vice versa. This is quite a dasher." He ran his finger around the edge of his collar and grinned at me.

Despite myself, I felt my earlier displeasure with him melting. He seemed a breath of fresh air in this artificial atmosphere. "Did I think to tell you how grand you look?" he said, surveying me approvingly. "How is our Cinderella bearing up?"

"Well, I hope. I've not seen her since the receiving line broke up."

"Culhaine has performed his paternal duty and the sticks of her fan are filled up with the names of the scions of his business friends. That's a delicious redowa they're playing at the moment. Will you venture?"

"By royal command?"

"We will dance the cotillion, as I presume you've heard, to please Damaris," Warren said calmly. "I was suggesting that we dance this one to please ourselves."

Dancing was one of the graces stressed as part of a young lady's education at Miss Milbrook's Academy, and as it happens I am an accomplished dancer. Undoubtedly more accomplished than the Misses Cabot, a small voice whispered impudently in my head, and added the postscript that Warren Sloane undoubtedly would be surprised. "My pleasure,"

I heard myself respond with spirit. And shortly we were bounding breathlessly with the society folk.

How out of place these modern dances looked, I thought, in the ordered serenity of that great hall-like ballroom with its tapestried walls and its grey stone chimney breast from some European castle, flanked by the high-backed, carved, needlework-covered settees. A hundred candles gleamed above our heads in the branched iron chandeliers. Damaris alone looked properly in place, with her Renaissance gown and air. I caught a glimpse of her whirling past in the arms of some young Boston blueblood, and was glad I had asserted myself in the matter of her gown.

The music changed from the redowa to a waltz, but as the set was not yet completed, Warren and I continued circling slowly. His steps fitted excellently with mine; I was, perhaps snobbishly, surprised at how well he danced. We did not talk, we drifted into the same easy companionable silence we had found in working together in the conservatory.

When the set was over Warren suggested a visit "to observe the observers inspecting the Collection. Or such small parts of it that have been allowed on view. I have contrived some lighting effects of which I confess I am inordinately proud."

He well had right to be, I thought, when I came to see them. He had covered our work table with black velvet and on this spare simplicity some representative pieces were set forth, few but choice. I noticed that the counterfeit silver box was not among them. The objects were spread out at some distance, so that no one competed with another. They were labeled with brief handwritten titles on chaste white cards, and among the flowering baskets overhead—here was the touch of genius—Warren had concealed small lamps. Their beams shone down through the foliage precisely on the raised bas-relief of silver, the rim of a golden cup. The result was masterly, and I told him so.

"Damaris must see this. Has she been here yet?"

"She won't come. She never enters the conservatory, haven't you noticed? Her mother died here."

I stared at him.

"It's never spoken of," Warren said. Some others had entered the conservatory to inspect the exhibit, and he guided me down a side aisle between the plant beds and dropped his voice. "Apparently there was some dreadful accident out here, and she knows of it, and it is supposed to have affected her markedly. You knew her before that, did you not? You have remarked the change? You must never mention it to her, you know. Isabella's death is a forbidden subject in this house."

"Warren," I said, "how did she die?"

"I've learned," Warren said ambiguously, "never to learn too much about any household into which I come on business. Or socially, either, for that matter. It's the better part of valor." He drew out a handsome gold watch and looked at it. "It's time for supper. Will you honor me with your companionship? Then let's within."

Which left unanswered both of the questions in my brain: how Isabella's death had come about, and whether—or how— he knew.

I can best describe the supper by saying it was up to all the standards of the house. Afterwards came my first experience of a cotillion, or German, as it is called here, that lengthy programme of mixed round dances interspersed with varied figures, so beloved of society of late. The figures are so arranged as to determine the choice of partners, by chance meeting in some evolution or by mock trial of skill. Needless to say, the figures the marchesa had devised were most elaborate, as were the small favors provided for the gentlemen to bestow upon each successive female partner. My hands were full of dainty tissue paper trifles, gay *bon bons*, flowers and ribbons. I danced in turn with various Boston nabobs, and whether it was deviltry or champagne possessed me I could not say, but presently I began to flirt with the best—or worst —of them and enjoyed myself most reprehensibly.

Warren, claiming me again in one of the turnings, twinkled at me. "Enjoying the metamorphoses? So is our Cinderella." We caught a glimpse of Damaris, whirling by. Her eyes had a fevered brightness but she seemed exhilarated, and I was glad for her.

"Interesting things, cotillions," Warren was saying in my ear. "Almost more interesting to observe than join, though Damaris wished us so. One can relish the patterns better from afar."

"Who do you mean?"

"Surely you've noticed." He cocked an impertinent knowing eye. "The patterns in the tapestry, my dear. Wheels within wheels." And all at once I did see.

There is a kind of tapestry from late medieval times made up of many tiny figures, each in his own sphere going about his business against a flowery ground. They seem of separate unrelated pictures—until one stands back, and the groupings fall into place, and one perceives a dominant and overpowering theme. The figures become not people then but puppets, performing a set round, controlled by that invisible spiderweb of force. As earlier, in the hall, I had that peculiar moment of absolute clarity and I saw us all. Ross. Marina. Warren. Myself. Damaris. Even that unidentified young Boston blueblood with whom she danced. Figures in a tapestry, figures in a dance, and the invisible force that motivated and controlled us all was the Culhaine Collection.

Figures moved, rather than moving, through the formalized patterns of intrigue to a dance motif. The pavane of the two sisters?

I had had too much champagne. "I wish to sit down," I said abruptly, and Warren looked at me first with astonishment and then concern.

"Lavinia, are you ill? Can I get you anything? A glass of wine?"

"No! Not that. Just let me sit for a few moments by the window, please. Alone."

He took me to a palm-shielded alcove and, with unexpected delicacy, left me as I had wished. I leaned my head against the cool pane of glass and closed my eyes. I was startled at myself, at the force of my fancies and at my giddiness. I would have only a few moments to myself, I knew, for the nature of a cotillion obliges one to complete the pattern once it is under way. Already I heard male footsteps approaching and a voice behind me saying, "I believe the pleasure of the next turn is mine."

I looked round into the Lucifer face of Ross Culhaine.

I did not trust myself to speak, and was too proud to plead an attack of momentary illness, so with head high I moved in silence into his outstretched arms.

I could say my response was due to the effect of the champagne, but that is the coward's way. I am not sure whether it would be more or less embarrassing than the truth. Nor am I speaking only of his request to dance. The truth, which I knew then as I know it now, was that I was stepping quite deliberately into the very maelstrom Warren Sloane had warned me of. And doing so, which was the more frightening, in the full knowledge that I was impelled not from without but by some force within myself.

I could not allow myself to think about it then. The dance engulfed me. I yielded to it, blotting out thought and sight, conscious only of the music and the motion, and the scent of tuberoses, and Ross Culhaine's arms encircling me so that we moved as one. Then the music ended and I was breathless, the blood pounding in my ears, and I had learned more truth about myself than I was ready yet to know.

This dance concluded the cotillion. I stood dazedly, scarcely joining in the others' clapping. "Come. There is

: 123 :

something you must see," Ross said, and I found myself following him through the hall quite as a matter of course. The front of the house was quiet now, and cooler, for almost everyone had gone to the ballroom to watch or participate in the cotillion. We stood together, Ross and I, in the doorway of the library gazing towards the fire.

"I wanted you to see it," Ross said, "since it was really your idea. And a good one, too. It has been wrong to keep it shut away from sight."

On a plain pedestal, some three feet before the fire, stood a classic, quite simple marble bust. It showed the head and shoulders of a young woman, and round the slender column of neck the golden collar gleamed quietly in the firelight, making the artful arrangement of hidden lamps in the conservatory seem suddenly contrived.

I could not speak, and knew I did not need to. We stood together, united by the beauty. And by something more. The blood drummed in my ears again, and I was afraid to turn my head, afraid to look on the tall man beside me lest I betray too much of the new self-knowledge I did not wish to have. I stared at the glowing jewels in the golden collar, and the echoing ruby on my finger seemed to burn like fire. There is an old saying that rubies draw their flame from their wearer's heartblood, and it seemed so now.

Only a moment, yet it seemed like hours. Then we were no more alone. Guests were making ready to depart, there were voices in the hall behind us, and the spell was broken. Here was Mrs. Cabot, sailing up with her fleet of lesser attendants in her wake. Come for a last covetous look—there was a wry taste in my mouth, which was otherwise quite dry.

"It is indeed magnificent." Why was it the Culhaine Collection always evoked that word and made it commonplace? I was reminded, out of nowhere, of the old, old concept of the touchstone, which revealed all that came in contact with it in its true nature, pure or dross. Perhaps the collar was such a touchstone, I thought hazily. But Mrs. Cabot, unaware of her part in any revelation, was being gracious. "Now that I see it, I can understand why you guard it closely. But my dear man, such treasures should be shared. It must be shown at the fête, and not on marble but on flesh and blood."

Automatically, almost involuntarily, her wrinkled ringed hands reached out.

How shall I write about what happened next? It has been recounted in every gossip paper, and even to tell it in the simplest words is to reduce it to melodrama. Or to farce. One minute the plump, aging hands were lifting the golden collar from the statue, lifting it to rest against the upholstered satin of her own effulgent bosom. The next, a long slender hand shot out, forcing hers sharply down, tearing the golden circlet from her grasp. Ross Culhaine's voice, dangerously controlled, said quietly, "That collar belongs to the women of the Clan Culhaine. It was fashioned for a queen. It will never be worn by any Brahmin cows."

Thank God, there were few persons in the room. Only the lord of Culhaine, and myself and Mrs. Cabot. And two of her colorless hangers-on, like scandalized shadows. Damaris and Warren and Marina, silhouetted like shadows in the doorway's light. I caught a glimpse of Marina's face, indelibly, like the face of one who had looked upon an ancient Fury.

Someone, I thought wildly, must do something. But I knew not what. I was paralyzed by my own inadequacy. Then I heard Damaris moan.

Damaris moaned, then cried out and fell forward, grasping Warren's arm, and at once the focus in the library changed its center. The necklace, and the words it provoked, were quite forgotten. One thing society accepted with understanding, it seemed, was a fragile female. Mrs. Cabot and company crowded around Damaris, offering assistance, smelling salts and brandy.

Damaris pressed her hand against her heart and shook her head. "I'm so sorry," she murmured faintly. "These silly spells . . . dancing too much . . . I'll be quite all right. But I'm afraid . . . Dear Mrs. Cabot, Aunt, I am so sorry. Will you forgive me if I retire?"

Mrs. Cabot, mother and grandmother, nodded with understanding. "Bed's the best place for the girl," she declared robustly. "Getting late anyway. Time we all went home. You see to the child, my dear marchesa. Everyone will understand."

"No! Take care of—your guests. Lavinia will come with me," Damaris said forcibly. Her eyes locked with her aunt's, and Marina, with that cool discipline I so admired, simply nodded.

"As you wish, my dear. Mrs. Cabot, will you do us the honor of assisting me in the farewells?"

I do not know what had become of Ross Culhaine, but it was Mrs. Cabot and Marina who made up the guard of honor at the door. And it was Warren who carried Damaris upstairs, and laid her on the bed, looked at me, and left.

Concerned as I was, the remarkable convenience of Damaris' attack at that precise moment had not escaped me, and I was not altogether surprised when, as soon as the door had shut after Warren Sloane, she pulled herself to a sitting position, with a bit of color returning to her face.

"Those bitches!" she said distinctly. I was not sure exactly to whom it was that she referred. After a moment she leaned her head forward again and her face went pale. I was afraid that this time she would make herself genuinely ill.

"I don't care if I do," Damaris retorted grimly when I remonstrated. "Somebody had to do something, and everyone else just stood round like gaping fools. It was the only thing I could think of on short notice. Everyone's used to my sick spells by now, thank God."

"I thought you were going to be really ill. You went into such spasms and were so pale."

"I held my breath," Damaris said ruthlessly. "I've learnt all sorts of tricks. Spare me the sermon, Lavinia. One does what one has to do." Her breathing still was labored, genuinely so, and I rubbed her wrists to try to still her pulse.

"How dare she!" Damaris whispered. Her eyes were black with anger. "That was my mother's necklace. How did she dare . . ."

"Hush," I said. "Don't think of it. It's over now."

"It is not over, and you know it." But she allowed me to lean her back against the pillows. After several moments she opened her eyes. "Do something for me."

"You know I will."

"Go to my father."

I was rendered speechless. After a silence she went on quietly. "I will not have him hurt. I told you, Vinnie. And he'll be hurting now with a deep hurt, thinking he's shamed my party, shamed Marina." It was not an image I would have had of Ross Culhaine.

Nor was it I, I felt quite sure, whom he would wish to see. My mouth felt dry. "Surely your aunt—"

Damaris' eyes, curiously adult, met mine. "Marina is different. She can eat humble pie to gain her ends, and not lose pride. She does not understand. Tell him I do . . . and tell him I was proud!"

But I could not tell Damaris what it was that held me back. "He'll think me—presumptuous," I said at last. "He scarcely knows me."

"He respects you. And you understand." Damaris looked at me squarely. "You are the only person whom he does respect who knows what it's like to stand outside and hurt because you don't know who you are."

She was the devil's own daughter. I would not do it, I could not. It would be misunderstood. Yet all the same, an hour or more later, when Damaris was at last asleep, there I was going downstairs through the dark and silent house. My mind told me I was a fool, but my feet still moved me on.

The lower rooms were black, for even the servants had retired, but a faint light rimmed the library's heavy door. It was not tight shut, then. I touched it lightly, steeling myself to knock, and it swung open slightly.

The room within was dark, save for the fire which had burned down low, and at first I could not discern whether the master of the house was there. Then I saw him, bent forward in a chair beside the fire, his head bowed, his hands dangling still and empty between his knees. And I knew, irrevocably, there was no turning back.

A finger of flame flickered on the diamond in one cuff, and it shot forth black fire. He was so motionless he seemed a figure carved in stone and anguish. "What do you want?" His voice was low, and hard, and he did not look up. I could not answer and also, stupidly, I could not move. Then he did look up, and his tone altered. "Oh, it's you. I thought it was another. So you've come down to sit up with the corpse, have you? It's a good old Irish custom. They used to keep it with thieves and highwaymen, the night before they hanged, you know. So it's in the grand tradition. Well, everyone's had a look at the highwayman, so you might as well sit down."

I came in, shutting the door behind me. Better my reputation should be compromised than the servants find further food for gossip, should any of them be stirring. I sat down opposite him, silently, in the Florentine chair, and Ross pulled himself to his feet and went round behind the desk to pour brandy into two slender Venetian glasses.

"Here. This house is cold as Acheron tonight. Drinking with the corpse is another old Irish custom." He had been drinking already; his voice was faintly slurred, but his appearance was still as coldly immaculate as the Lucifer image. Brandy was nothing for a gentleman to offer to a lady, but then by Boston standards, neither of us qualified for those titles. I sipped from the glass he handed me, finding it liquid fire.

Ross sat down again, watching me sardonically across his glass. Behind him on the desk the golden collar lay coiled and brooding. Its rubies glowed darkly in the light of the dying flames.

What power it exercised, I thought. For it did have power. Marina sought it, Damaris shrank from it, Ross was possessed by it. As for myself, I was strangely fascinated. It stirred some atavistic recognition deep within me which I could not fathom and which made no sense.

"Well, Portia, pronounce sentence. I am armed and well prepared." I stared at him, and he laughed shortly. "My dear young lady, you did not come down here from the innocent goodness of your heart. Go ahead and say it. I have made my daughter ill, I have disgraced my noble sister-in-law, I have brought shame on the Clan O'Houlihan and proved myself exactly what was expected, an uncouth boor. You think I have not already realized it all?"

"I cannot conceive of you," I said steadily, "being uncouth in anything."

"Not even when I have had the bad taste to speak the truth plain to the reigning bossy of the herd?"

"Nor can I conceive of your taste ever being bad." I smiled faintly; the brandy was proving warming. "Your manners, possibly. I have noticed that speaking truth is generally bad manners."

"Your eye, as always, is unerring. I salute you." Ross lifted his glass. "How is my daughter?"

" 'No sick, my lord, unless it be in mind.' " I stopped, annoyed to find myself also speaking in quotation, and put the glass from me firmly. "You need not worry about Damaris."

"Meaning she employed falsehood in the name of manners. Lord, what a shameful thing is man when a woman has to cover up his weakness! How she must despise me."

"You do not know your daughter at all, do you?" I said bluntly. "She has an Irish temper too. It was fortunate she had no knife at hand or she might have used it. Not on you; on Mrs. Cabot. You see, she shares your sentiments exactly."

"She would not even wear the collar."

"Its weight is too great for her. And not alone in gold." If this was the brandy speaking, then so be it. There was a time for keeping silent, and a time for speaking truth. "She is much afraid, you know, of failing you."

"I know nothing," Ross said shortly. "As you have just with brutal delicacy pointed out. We Irish bogfolk are supposed to have the gift of second sight, but never you believe it. I never know a thing until it is too late. That is the curse upon the Clan Culhaine."

He drained the brandy glass and poured another.

I ought not be here. It was the one thing that I knew, and knew with the clarity of insight that had come to me on the dance floor: if I stayed longer in this room I was stepping into a morass from which there was no drawing back. I rose.

"Sit down." He swung around. "Sit down, my dear Miss Stanton, and I will tell you the story of the Clan Culhaine. It's tragicomic, as all we bogfolk are, and sure it should interest you strangely, for you're an antiquarian lady. Unless you're too afraid."

With each sip he was becoming more markedly "Irish," and more bitter. "The Clan Culhaine. Hereditary rulers of one of the Old Kingdoms, my father always said. Those days were long gone by his time, though. And so he came to Boston in the Famine Years, came with his bride and his babe and naught but the shirt upon his back. Came to where the streets were said to be paved with gold, and opportunity beckoned for any lad embued with the strength of his youth and energy and dreams! Boston told the truth of that to him soon enough, after those singing falsehoods. But he never forgot he was the son of a hundred kings. When he was in his cups he'd sit at that harp and sing of it for hours. He died when I was but a lad. My mother was a little slip of a thing, hardly more than a girl, but with a cast-iron backbone. We were all of the Clan Culhaine now, she told me, and she set herself to keeping us head high. We were lace-curtain Irish, and never would she let you forget it. My shoes were spit-and-polish shined each morn before I went out selling papers in the streets, and herself laid the tea table ready, with a scrap of lace cloth, before she left to scrub the steps of those holy-high Boston ladies who couldn't soil their hands with honest toil. My mother had had lovely hands. By the time I was twelve the lye and the rheumatism had eaten at the knuckles and she played the harp no more."

In the fireplace a log broke, sending forth showers of sparks. The room was dim with shadows, and the gold necklace gleamed dully in the flickering light. I didn't speak. He seemed to have forgotten I was there.

"It eats a man's soul to see his mother work like that and he too young to change it. I said nothing, but my heart was on fire with determination. Then one dark wet morning a notice in the papers I was peddling blazed out at me. One of the clipper ships in Boston harbor was looking for a cabin boy. When my mother came home for tea that night, she found me gone." His smile was ironic. "Not for nothing had I inherited the hot head and fey mind of the Clan Culhaine. I waited till I was far enough away to be beyond her reach, then I wrote her I'd be back when I could bring with me her weight in gold."

This time he was silent so long I feared he was slipping

into some black interior abyss. "And did you?" I ventured at last.

"I did. And that collar also, fit for a queen of the Clan Culhaine. I found our flat let to strangers with six squalling brats, and my mother's things sold at public auction to pay back rent. She'd died a year earlier of penumonia and neglect. And I with the gold I'd been hoarding to bring home for a fair fine showing! I went on a monumental bender to wrestle with my guilt, and sobered with a hard determination to make those Boston bezoms pay for how they'd broken her. There was nothing to hold me here. After I'd had the satisfaction of beating the agent who'd seized her things to a bloody pulp, I put half my gold out for investments, and taking the other half sailed back across the seas. I had some fierce conviction that the native Culhaine turf could fill the emptiness within my soul."

He poured another shot of brandy from the crystal decanter and drank it off straight. I half feared he would lapse again into black silence, but I was wrong. He stood by the fire, turning the delicate Venetian glass between his long fingers, and laughed without humor.

"I went to Europe to find my roots, and isn't it passing strange? I fell in love with a century in which being sent to Ireland was the equivalent of being sent to hell. The cold damp of Ireland chilled my bones like Boston, but Renaissance Italy warmed my heart. I fell into it head over heels like a boy with his first love. But with the love of the man I was, I loved a woman."

His eyes traveled to the portrait above the chimney breast, and his voice went so low that I could scarcely hear. "The curse of the Culhaines. To blight each fair thing that we touch, each thing we love. I wed, and brought her here, and saw it all repeat. Scorn, rejection, disillusion, failure, disintegration. If I had not brought her here she might have lived. And now it starts again." With a swift savage gesture he flung the fragile glass into the fire and it shattered on the hearth.

With the sound, something seemed to snap within me, and I could move again. I did not look at him. My pulses pounding, I stumbled blindly toward the door, impelled by some sense of having blundered into secret rites I ought not know.

"I said don't go!" His hands grasped my arms brutally and swung me round. He was not Ross Culhaine, but the brandied shade of those tribal chieftains who once strode like giants over the proud green land. My arms hurt from his grip but I scarcely noticed. "My mother went. My mother . . . You have the look of her."

His voice dropped, and his hands relaxed. His eyes traveled from me to the golden collar and it drew him from me like a magnet. He picked it up, and turned it over and over in his fingers. I was free now, and I could have left; I remembered that afterwards. But I did not go.

"A dark woman, like banked fires." His words came so softly I had to strain to hear. "Moved like a queen, and could have borne a queen's collar and not been broken as the others were. I used to dream as a lad, lying on deck staring up at the night sky, of her in a purple gown like a queen, with her shoulders bare. My wife was fair."

Before I knew what he was about he was beside me again, the collar in his hands. "Never seen it worn as it was meant to be." With an abrupt gesture, he dropped the golden weight around my throat. Involuntarily, the necklace still upon me, I made a sound and drew away. The movement seemed to recall him to a momentary reality. He stared at me with the look his eyes had had earlier that evening.

The look, my brandy-hazed senses told me fuzzily, of a soul in hell. I could not help myself. Involuntarily I moved again, but not away. God alone knows what he read upon my face. The next moment he was in my arms, his face buried against my neck, crushing me tight the way Damaris sometimes clung to me in nightmare panic.

It was not I he clung to. I knew that even as my arms instinctively held him close, held him for what seemed like hours, on his knees before the dying coals, myself in the Florentine chair with his head against my breast.

When, later, I went at last upstairs, I found the marks of his fingers on my arm, and the indentations of the weighty collar still on my shoulders.

XI

Everyone was enervated the next day. I myself slept till nearly noon, and awoke feeling curiously drugged. That was due no doubt as much to the brandy as the late hour. Recalling, foggily, the events of the evening, particularly the latter half, I felt deeply embarrassed. Actually the encounter in the library, as it came back to me in scattered pictures, seemed so improbable as to have been a dream. But I had no wish to come face to face too soon with Ross Culhaine.

"He was in his cups," I told myself. "Probably he won't even remember."

The matter of the Brahmin cows was something else. Mrs. Cabot had certainly not been tipsy. My face burned, though I had done nothing, after all, other than being an unwitting bystander, twice over, to things which I ought not have heard.

Or a catalyst. The word came to me out of nowhere and I had that odd feeling, as one sometimes does, of being on the brink of some profound discovery which as yet made no sense.

Which would in time make all things clear. Touchstone. Catalyst. If the collar were some kind of touchstone in this house, it was I who had caused it to be put upon display.

Catalyst indeed. Catalyst. Questioner. I had come to Boston, had I not, to question? The Questioner was the devil's advocate. Also called the Old Guiser, for he walks in many masked disguises. Damaris had been in a sort of disguise last night, and the mask which she customarily wore was dropped.

Definitely I had been reading too many books of late. I wondered if this was a hangover I had, but decided not. I had not drunk that much brandy. Hangover from too much fantasy, perhaps.

I rose and dressed, avoiding my reflection in the mirror, looked in on Damaris, who was still sleeping soundly, and went downstairs. Already the house was fresh and shining, as though a magic wand had been swept over. No trace of the festivities remained except for the cut flowers drooping in their vases. A neat pile of engraved cards lay on a silver salver, left by ladies during their morning drives as expression of thanks for invitations to the ball. Two sets of cards; now that Damaris was officially "out" she received calls too. Boxes of hothouse flowers were arriving also, punctiliously sent Damaris and Marina by bachelors who had attended. How artificial are the rituals of society, I thought, feeling suddenly oppressed.

Laid out on the long oak table was the morning mail. More out of habit than any expectation I glanced over it and was pleasantly pleased to find two envelopes which bore my name.

The first was a brief note from Warren Sloane inviting me to tea and ice-skating in the afternoon. My spirits rose. Outdoor exercise was exactly what I needed. I thrust the envelope into my pocket and opened the other, which carried no address.

It contained, without salutation, a terse one-sentence apology from Ross Culhaine for insupportable conduct and any liberties he might have taken. I thrust both note and envelope into the fire and saw to it they were well destroyed, wondering why the only emotion they aroused was a faint and inexplicable regret.

The house was still, and the library door shut tight. I rang for Sarah, told her to bring me coffee in the conservatory, and went there myself directly, prepared to restore myself with the discipline of work. Here, to my astonishment, however, I found that things had neither been left as they were nor been restored. All trace of the Culhaine Collection had vanished.

Sarah, bringing my coffee, leapt at the excuse for volubility. "I don't know, miss, I'm sure. When we got up this morning it was locked tight, as always, only there's a light shining round the door, and through the glass, we can see it from the kitchen window. 'I don't like this,' Mr. Hopkins says, and he goes and knocks upon the door. And the master himself answers, 'Go away,' he says. 'I'm tending to this myself, and you're to let no one in until I say.' At five o'clock in the morning, miss, it was."

So Ross Culhaine had not gone to sleep all night.

Sarah went on, evidently taking my silence as further prompting. "Then an hour ago he rings for Hopkins and he tells him, 'You can clean in the conservatory now,' he says, which we did, and found it exactly as you see it, miss, all the gewgaws put away. 'Only you're not to tidy the library,' the master says, 'I'm locking the door and no one's to come in.' And what's a body to make of it, miss, lessen there's something strange going on, that's what I'd like to know. Are you all right, miss? You look kind of wan. Her ladyship's not feeling too pert neither, seems as if. She's sent down word if anyone calls this afternoon she's not at home."

"That will do, Sarah," I said repressively, and she left, not bothering to conceal a sullen look.

Eustace Robinson had told me once that the first sign of disintegration in a great house often showed in its servants. "If I'm called to make an appraisal, or even socially, and the servants seem careless, or overproud, or as if they're covering secrets—sometimes it's just the faintest hint, but my nose knows—and sure enough, sooner or later things go up for sale, or into storage, and there's news of business losses, or a hidden scandal, or a loss of tone. Whether the servants are loyal or opportunist, they're the first to know, and if you've eyes to see, it shows."

I wondered what was the change the state of this staff portended, or whether it was a filtering down of the shock waves Ross Culhaine had dealt society last night. The staff knew of that, naturally; they always did.

Since there was no work to occupy me here, I wandered back upstairs to find Damaris awake, tired and determined. "Tell," she said without preamble.

"Tell what?"

"What happened last night." I had not reckoned on the fact that naturally Damaris was going to want a full account. She punched the pillows behind her back and pulled herself up, wincing as she did so.

"What's the matter?"

"My legs hurt. It's stupid, I don't know why. It's happened before but never so bad as this. Vinnie, how is my father?"

"All right, I think." And I did think so. As I had held him in my arms I had felt the tension drain from him as if in some crazy way I had given him absolution. But I was not going to speak of that to Damaris. "He was worried about you. I reassured him. I also told him he ought to know you better, that you shared his sentiments and were proud of what he'd done. Damaris, I think you ought to tell him that yourself."

Damaris flushed. "I cannot. You have seen it, Vinnie. When I'm with him I'm—I think he's disappointed, I know he's thinking of my mother. Like last night. He was angry I would not wear her necklace but I could not do it."

But I knew, as apparently she did not, that it was not Isabella whom Ross associated with the necklace. I wondered how much she did know of that story.

"Damaris," I said, "where did the collar come from?"

Damaris' brow puckered. "I don't really know. It's a Borgia piece, according to stories, but who can say? Papa won't speak of it. I do know it was the start of the Collection. My mother told me the story once. I gathered that she'd thought it rather thrilling, but Aunt Marina cut her off. She's always hated to be reminded of Papa's rude beginnings."

She chuckled, her face softening. "My father shipped as a common seaman when he was just a boy. It must have been terrible, from the way Mama spoke. But he had one friend, an Englishman, who was first mate on the ship and took my father underneath his wing. They were in Italy, in some waterfront place where sailors congregate, and the mate won the collar from an Italian seaman playing cards. Neither one of them had any idea of what it was."

"How did your father get it?"

"There was a fire," Damaris said vaguely. "The other man was killed. Papa saved the collar, because it was beautiful. Later, when he needed cash, he pawned it, and that's when he discovered what it was. He took the money and bought other merchandise along the waterfront, and sold it and bought more." She smiled. "Probably all illegal, but who'd dare ask? Always, he kept the best pieces for himself. That was the beginning of the Culhaine Collection and the Culhaine fortune. Personally, I've always thought my father belonged back in the Renaissance, with cloak and dagger. Or in the seventeenth century, with a patch across one eye!"

It was an image which I myself could not completely disassociate from Ross Culhaine.

Damaris was growing tired. I saw her wince once or twice

when she thought I wasn't looking. So I rubbed her legs for her, and rang for tea, and left her to Maggie and a nap.

Warren's note had suggested our meeting in the park, which I approved as a prudent thought. There was no point in adding to servants' gossip—or, for that matter, adding fuel to other fires. He was already at the skaters' benches when I arrived.

"I was not sure if you would come," he greeted me.

"On the contrary. This is exactly what I need."

"Skating? Or a different face?" Warren looked at me shrewdly. "How are things at Casa Culhaine?"

"Ambivalent. I've not seen the marchesa. She's given orders not to be disturbed. And Mr. Culhaine himself has removed the Collection from the conservatory."

Warren whistled. "That bodes ill, I fear. Personally, after last night's fiasco, if I were Culhaine I'd pack bag and baggage and go back to Italy at once."

I doubted this would happen. He was not reckoning on the stubbornness of the Culhaines. Nor on the fact that Ross Culhaine's main aim was to humble Boston, not to win it over.

"At any rate, all the wounded are bearing well. There were cards and bouquets galore this morning."

"Naturally," Warren said drily. "Boston is showing its civility. We must have manners at all costs, especially for the sake of the Arts Museum."

"Oh, do let's forget all that," I exclaimed pettishly. "I am sick to death of Boston and its precious culture!"

"All right, all right," Warren said soothingly. "What you need is a good run against the wind." He laced my skates and we took off down the long length of the ice. I was not at all sure this excursion was particularly proper, but at the moment I simply didn't care. It was an invigorating and thoroughly refreshing afternoon, which we concluded with coffee in a little Italian place on a side street. I did not realize how tired I was until, at my request, Warren had left me with a bow at the corner of Marlborough Street.

My weariness met me as I went up the path. The hothouse heat inside for once felt comforting and I paused in the lower hall a moment, after Hopkins had relieved me of my wraps, letting it warm my bones.

"May I speak with you a moment, please."

The door of the library had opened and Ross Culhaine stood there behind me. His voice, cool and stiff, threw me into a state of most confused disorder. I did not look at him as I passed, head high, into the library before him as he held the door, and I disciplined my tumultuous thoughts severely. It was not I who had cause to feel embarrassed. Then my eyes fell on the great library desk, and all thoughts of personal discomforts fled.

"I retrieved them between dark and daylight," Ross said, watching me take in the objects from yesternight's display, laid out with the notes he and I had compiled together. "Would you examine them, please? I'll explain later; if my conclusions are correct, I will not have to."

He was right. This time it was a Cellini medallion which had been counterfeited.

"I examined the display personally immediately before the first guests arrived. I am convinced the medallion then on view was genuine." We looked at each other. "This confirms one thing," Ross said. "We are not dealing with a pilferage in the past."

"But the box could still have been taken in the past."

"Of course. There may also be two separate thieves, six years apart." He brushed this aside impatiently. "The point is, substitution is going on right now, in which case steps can be taken."

"But how? The Collection has never been displayed," I said stupidly. "Whoever switched the medallions came prepared. No one knew you had it." *Except those in the house-hold* . . . I felt the thought unspoken.

Ross shook his head. "Cellini pieces are not unknown. The antiques world is small. When articles change hands, the word leaks out. Pictures have even appeared in the gossip press from time to time." As you would know, were you not being sentimental, his tone implied.

"What happens now?"

"Nothing, for the time. The entire Collection will be on display for the Renaissance Fête. The date for that, by the way, has now been settled. Three days before Christmas, to take advantage of the prevailing charitable mood." He gave a brief mirthless smile.

So there had been a diplomatic conference in my absence, and evidently this was the price Marina had exacted. I had to admire her singleness of purpose.

"It is the best thing possible," Damaris said firmly when we discussed it later. "It will serve notice to all of Boston that we are not ashamed. The Cabots will be forced to come; they have proclaimed too loudly their espousal of the Arts Museum. And they will suffer." She ran her fingers through the blond hair hanging lank around her shoulders.

"Suppose they make another attempt upon the collar?"

"They will not." Damaris' eyes went dark. "I will even wear it myself, if necessary. We must begin to plan at once. You shall help us, Vinnie. There is only a month's time, but they shall see how quickly my father can summon splendors."

I voiced a thought which had been growing in my mind. "It is time I should be thinking of when I have to leave."

"Vinnie, no."

"I must, Damaris," I said gently. "I cannot remain all winter. You know I must find work. The catalogue of the collection is almost complete."

"You must not think of it," Damaris said stubbornly. "I will not let you. We will speak of it no more."

I let it pass, for she did look fair to working herself into a state.

Neither Damaris nor Marina came down that evening, so Ross Culhaine and I dined tête-à-tête, if such term could be applied in that vast dining room with servants standing by. By unspoken consent we talked of art and music, rather than matters that were more personal, and such were our mutual interests that the stiffness of us each dissolved, and we continued our discussion for some time over the coffee cups in the library. When I rose at last to retire he took my hand and bowed.

"Permit me to thank you for one of the pleasantest evenings I have spent here in some time."

It was not until I was halfway up the stairs that I realized I had never broached the subject of my visit's ending, as I had fully meant to do.

Though the hour was late, I sat for some time brushing my hair before the fire. I had, I found, a great deal on my mind. It was time I came to some definite decision as to whether to leave or stay. Common sense and independence said go, before the luxury of this life became addictive. Staying implied accepting a measure of dependency I was not prepared to face. And other ties as well.

Damaris said she needed me. And there had been other requests as well for help.

Catalyst. Odd how that word kept coming back to mind. Did I serve that function? It was better at times to allow sleeping dogs to lie.

One thing was certain, if I stayed I had better work out some decision I could adhere to in the matter of Warren Sloane. Considering how Damaris felt, it was, to say the least, unfeeling of her companion friend to slip out on such excursions as I had today. I had known that, even as I had selfishly rejoiced in the opportunity it provided me for escape. I had no illusions about how Warren felt about us both; I also had no illusions about Damaris' will power—or mine.

My departure could alleviate that pressure. On the other hand, in view of what I considered highly unsuitable emotions on her part, would not my leaving her unattended be the coward's way out? Especially in view of—

Say it, Vinnie. Especially in view of what you have been trying not to face all evening. Although many persons could have known what objects were contained in the Culhaine Collection, the switch of the medallions could only have been made by one of the persons who knew for certain that the Cellini would be on display: Ross Culhaine himself, or Warren Sloane.

I refused to think about it any further, and such was the state of my tangled thoughts that I trusted neither, nor even my own logic.

I read for a while, in an effort to compose my mind, but found myself staring into space more often than at the page. At last I gave up and prepared for bed, and it was not until that moment that I realized something was wrong. Leonardo was not in the room.

At first I was not disturbed, not until I had checked all his accustomed hiding places in the drawers and the armoire and beneath the bed. Neither was he in the neighboring boudoir nor where I half expected, curled with Damaris among the quilts and comforts of her bed. It was difficult to search in the blackness, for I did not wish to disturb her with a light, but at last I sat back, forced to recognize that he was not there.

Someone—Damaris, or a servant—had left a door open and Leonardo had slipped out on a journey of exploration. I was not really worried about him if he had gone outside, for he was a city cat, but I could well imagine what Marina would say if he were elsewhere in the house.

"At least I needn't worry whether he's in her room," I thought grimly. Marina would have promptly tossed him out with a few choice words. I was going to favor him with a few myself, when I once got my hands on his orange excellency. There was no help for it; I would have to search. I put on robe and slippers, lit a candle, and descended into lower blackness.

Hall, public rooms, even with some trepidation the library, but no Leonardo. Thank fortune that Culhaine's taste in decoration was fifteenth-century spare and provided few hiding places for rotund orange fur. The baize door to below stairs was shut and locked, and in any event if Leo had ventured there the servants would have restored him to his proper place. This left only the upper floors—I retraced my steps, my candle flickering eerily in the darkness.

From somewhere in the upper regions came a faint sound, as of a door opening, and a draft ran chill fingers over me, causing the flame to stream and waver, sending forth a long streamer of smoke. I shrank against the wall, feeling like a fool about to be discovered, pulling my wrapper tighter round my throat. But no footsteps came, and I relaxed. I was imagining things, no doubt, impelled by the loneliness and the late hour. I continued, more quickly, up the stairs, resuming my exploration of the second floor, past the tight-shut doors of the apartments of the sleepers, where I knew my missing feline could not be.

Two other bedrooms were there on this floor, as well as several lesser ones, with the sewing room and school room on the floor above. I did not relish the prospect of ascending there; I was growing more and more uncomfortable and with no reason.

"What if he has gotten into the attics, to the rest of the Collection?" I was being ridiculous, I told myself sternly. The storerooms were kept always locked, and probably the unused bedrooms were as well. I tried the door knob of the nearer one, and it turned easily in my hand. The room was empty, handsome and austere, and contained no missing cat. I shut the door carefully behind me and went on to the next. Here, as I reached out my fingers to the knob, I heard the sound again, a so-faint creaking, and the door itself moved slightly, as if recoiling from my touch. As if it already were ajar.

It was then I felt it, that strong intangible sense of presence, of another person breathing near in supposedly empty blackness.

"Is someone there?" My voice, striving to sound normal, came out as a cracked whisper. There was no answer. After a moment, I pushed the door open further and stepped inside. For the instant before I raised my candle, I seemed to see a vague whiteness, like a woman's figure, across the room.

"She comes to me in the night." Damaris' words, in palpable terror, came back to me from that first night. *Isabella.*

I found that I was holding my breath, and my lungs hurt me. Firmly I raised my hand, and the candle flame pierced the darkness like a small act of faith. The whiteness dissolved. There was nothing there.

Nothing but a magnificent, opulent room, perhaps overcrowded with furniture that was worthy of a palace. On a dais stood a gilded bed fit for a Doge. And on the bed—

"Leonardo!" I gasped. And then began to laugh. If anything could have brought me back from the edge of nightmare to the ridiculous, normal everyday it was the expression on Leo's face, like an angry baby, as he stretched and yawned, annoyed at having his comfortable nap disturbed.

"At least you had the sense not to shed on the velvet spread," I scolded, picking him up as he gave voice to indignation. One of his clever tricks is to drag onto a bed something to make a cozy nest, and he had done so now. He will use anything at hand—a velvet skirt, a paisley shawl. Fortunately this time he had chosen only a dull old rag. Or so it seemed at first, until I shook it out—awkwardly, with one hand, for I still held the candle in the other, with Leonardo pinned beneath my arm.

It took only a moment for me to recognize what it was. The missing tapestry Damaris had spoken of, the tapestry round which she had written the "Pavane for Two Sisters." It was at that moment of recognition that I heard Damaris scream.

XII

I got out of that room so fast that, afterwards, I had no recollection of so doing. One moment I was standing there, Leo clutched beneath my arm, staring down at the tapestry in my hands, dully glowing. The next I was in the hall, the door of that other bedroom shut behind me. The screams had started in Damaris' room, but by now they had traveled into mine. I ran towards it just as Damaris catapulted out my door. Behind me, other doors opened, feet came running. Ross and Marina, flinging on dressing gowns, pushed past me towards her.

"*No!*" Damaris recoiled backwards, her eyes wild with horror. One arm came up to shield her head; the other, rigidly extended, thrust two trembling fingers towards Marina's face.

Marina gasped. "*Malocchio.* Ross, she doesn't know us!"

"She's still in nightmare," Ross said tersely. He grasped

Damaris by her upper arms and shook her roughly, although his voice was not ungentle. "It is all right. You are here, safe, at home."

"No! Not safe, not home . . . Not ever . . . She's here, she's come for me. I tried to tell you . . ." Ross's treatment, however cruel it may have seemed, had been effective. Damaris was coming up out of the depths of nightmare and her voice grew more rational, childlike and tired. She pulled herself free and bent over the banister, her breath coming in shuddering sobs. "I cannot do it," she whispered. "I *have* tried. I'm sorry, Papa."

"I told you it was wrong to bring her back." Marina swept down on Damaris, turning on Ross a face magnificent in its wrath. "Poor *bambina*, the weight of her memories, they derange the mind. You hear her, Ross. She thinks again that Isabella has returned. I said that it would happen. She should be back in Italy where she can forget." Her speech was becoming more markedly Italian than I had ever heard it. She reached out to enfold Damaris, but Damaris flung herself away.

"No! Don't touch me. You don't believe me, either of you!" It was in my arms that she sought refuge.

She was now trembling violently, and I asserted myself, though it was not my place. "She should be in bed. I will see to it. Can this not be talked about tomorrow?"

"You are right. Come, Marina." It was impossible to tell what Ross Culhaine was thinking. I did not wait for more response but hurried after Damaris as she stumbled to my room.

Once inside, I shut and locked the door, lit the lamp quickly, and built up the fire. I wrapped Damaris in blankets and Leo settled in her lap like a comforting hot water bottle. I commenced to heat the spirit lamp, but she gasped and jerked her head to tell me no, so I sat beside her rubbing her wrists and murmuring commonplaces until I felt her pulse grow slower. Then, "What frightened you, Damaris?" I asked quietly.

Damaris did not speak at once, and when she did, her voice was not hysterical but low and still, as though despairing comfort. "She was here again. My mother. As God's my witness, Lavinia, I did see her. And I am not insane."

So that was what she feared. "For sure you're not," I said briskly. "We'll speak of it later when you're calmer, if you like. For now, you must sleep."

"Not in my room! I won't go back in there."

The edge of hysteria was back in Damaris' voice. "Then you shall stay here," I answered soothingly.

"Leave the light on. And lock the doors!" She would not close her eyes until I had demonstrated to her satisfaction that they both were bolted. I sat beside her, and Leo purred, but it was some time before we got her off to sleep.

It was not till then, when I rose and rubbed my aching back, that I noticed what seemed like a pile of torn fabric on the bed. The tapestry. I had had it in my hands when Damaris' screams had sounded, and in the ensuing tumult it had passed unnoticed. It ought to be returned at once, but I feared to leave Damaris. Oh, I'll be honest: my curiosity was great! And most unseemly, though that stopped me not; my antiquarian instincts triumphed over virtue. Cautiously, being careful not to wake Damaris, I threw it out across the bed in shimmering folds.

It was a tapestry such as I had felt myself drawn into, that evening of the ball. A dark ground like a midnight sky, thick-starred with flowers. Against that darkness, figures glowed—small figures in many separate groupings, dancing, making music, courting; central figures, large. Progressively, the tableaux portrayed the legend of the Two Sisters. My throat tightened. Here they were, in that central grouping, exactly as Damaris had written of them in the song, two men, two ladies, golden-haired, the one with her hands clasped demurely at her bosom, covering the place where the great golden collar met her breast. Even through the dust and wear of four hundred years, the spun gold threads shone fire.

The one dim lamp still burned, as Damaris had begged me, on the table by the chaise. I lifted it and brought it closer, that I might feast upon the richness with covetous eyes. Then I saw what I had not before, and the lamp tilted perilously in my hands. The tapestry was not perfect, across central figures ran three great tears, elsewhere the threads of gold and wool and linen were frayed and pulled.

At first I thought the damage had been caused by Leo's claws. But when I bent to examine it more closely, I knew I had been wrong. The threads had not been pulled. They had been cut, as with a knife.

Would things have worked out differently, I sometimes wonder, had I done as I ought and returned the ruined tapestry to the closed bedroom the next morning, and said no word? That was what any sensible woman would have done, but I was no such person, I was an antiquarian and a restorer. My first impulse, thinking Leo had caused the damage, had been to use my special skills to repair the rents. My second, after I had realized he was not to blame, was to do it all the same. I could do it well; I could surprise Ross Culhaine with it on Christmas morning. That was not the antiquarian thinking, but the woman who had fallen under the Lucifer spell.

I awoke the next morning to find Damaris huddled on the chaise, regarding me with grave and troubled eyes. "It happened again, didn't it?" she asked me somberly. "I tried to convince myself it was a nightmare but now I look at your face, I know that that was wrong."

"What do you mean?" I responded guardedly.

"No games," Damaris said. "Not any more. My father knows now." She stopped. "I have tried to believe it was sick fancies, as Aunt says. I have tried to face up to it, as Papa wished. But oh, Lavinia, I am so tired of pretending. I saw my mother, I am sure of it, she—touched me. I was awake, it was no nightmare. It is impossible. Either I am wrong, or I am going out of my mind."

"There are alternatives," I said firmly. "One is that your mother could be still alive—"

Damaris shook her head. "I saw her die." A shudder ran through her, but her eyes were stern.

"—or you saw something, and believed it was your mother." I did not voice the other two thoughts which came to me: one, that the fact her mother was still living could have been kept from her for some strange reason, or—more incomprehensible, and more alarming—that someone was deliberately trying to make Damaris believe that she had seen her. Out of my unconscious the memory came back to me, the sensation of someone standing watching me last night in the empty room, and for a moment my own pulse raced.

"Or else I *am* insane," Damaris finished starkly. "And so we come full circle." She sighed. "I almost wish I knew I were, it would be—easier. That's what's so frightening, the not knowing."

"One thing is certain. For the rest of my stay here, you had better sleep in here with me, or I with you. Then if anything does happen, I will be there to see."

Damaris' eyes widened. "Surely you are not still thinking of leaving now!"

"Perhaps it would be best. Your father might relent and take you back to Italy, as you wished."

"He will not. Never. I do not think I can bear it here alone." Damaris pushed herself upright and her voice took on that false gaiety which meant she was plotting something. "We will not speak of it. Ring for breakfast, Vinnie, do. We will tell Sarah that I have come in to have it here with you. Maggie will guess, but she won't speak, I can trust her always. And this afternoon, Vinnie, we will go for a walk and you will show me why you find that museum so fascinating, as you say!"

For whatever reasons, I was glad to see Damaris perking up. And if she wanted to get herself worked up over my relationship with Warren Sloane, well, perhaps that was better than having her preoccupied with midnight visions of the dead.

I hoped to get an opportunity for a closer examination of the tapestry that morning, and perhaps a start on the repairing, but this was not to be. My conscience over retaining it was eased a little by my discovery that the room across the hall was now tightly locked. I tried the door, surreptitiously, on my way downstairs. When I reached the lower level, I was greeted by the message that the marchesa wished to see me in her rooms.

Marina looked dreadful. I had not seen her since the ball, save for those tumultuous moments last night in the upper hall, and I was shocked by the change in her appearance. Her hair was down, there were dark circles beneath her eyes, and faint lines showed around them. She seemed, though I do not wish to be melodramatic, haunted. But she greeted me with a travesty of her gracious charm which struck me, since she did not usually exert it on my behalf, as twice pathetic.

"Do sit down, Miss Stanton! Forgive me for receiving you in my bed, but I find the strain we have been living under has taken more toll than I thought."

"The strain, madame?"

"Damaris' condition." Marina looked at me directly. "Surely you realize now. And you will understand as well, I hope, the reasons for my—inhospitability—heretofore. One does not wish strangers to see those one loves in this deranged condition. I have tried to protect Damaris from public knowledge of her aberration. Perhaps that was wrong of me; I do not know." She shrugged sadly. "Then, too, I hoped that if you were not here her father might comprehend at last how unbearable life was for her in this house, and allow me to take her back to Italy where she belongs. But my sister's husband, Miss Stanton, is a very stubborn man. He refuses to give way, even now that he has seen the effects upon our poor *bambina*. Therefore, my dear Lavinia—may I call you that?—now that you know the truth about Damaris, will you not join with me to keep her safe? I understand you have been thinking of terminating your visit in the near future. I beg of you, for Damaris' sake, to change your mind."

So Marina had been discussing me with Ross Culhaine. I wondered suddenly whether he had made my staying the price of his capitulation in the matter of the Renaissance Fête.

"Perhaps," I said deliberately, "you had better explain precisely what you mean by 'the truth about Damaris.' "

Marina's eyes opened wide. "The painful memories this house holds for her have deranged the poor child's mind. It happened before, when Isabella died. Her condition improved when she was away from here, safe, in a different world. Now that he has dragged her back, the old delusions have returned. She believes her mother has come back from the dead to punish her."

Her choice of words struck me at once. "To punish?"

"Please, Lavinia, do not harrow my memory by asking for details. As a child I adored my sister. Her death was a terrible, shocking accident, which I still find most difficult to accept. If it is so for me, how much worse then for Damaris, who saw it happen? There is an agreement in this house that for her sake the circumstances of it will never be discussed. Believe me, *cara*, they were more than sufficient to drive the poor child mad."

She lay back against the pillows, exhausted by the earnestness of her words. The resemblance between her and Damaris had never been more marked. Nor had I ever liked her better . . . or agreed with her less.

"I do not know what to say," I said at last. "As for my staying, I am not sure at present what would be best. I can tell you that if I decide that I must leave, I will discuss it with you first."

I left the marchesa's apartment with much to think of. Not the least was the situation I could not put into words to anyone—the developing attachment between myself and Ross Culhaine.

Duty and selfishness warred within me that afternoon. I knew Damaris needed outside diversion, and that I ought to have rejoiced in her suggestion of a promenade to the museum. All the same, I hoped fervently that she would forget it, and when she did not, I am afraid I gave her during the excursion few of the attentions due from a friend and a companion. I needed time alone; I needed time to think.

I should not have been surprised at the direction my heart and other emotions had been leading me, step by inevitable step, since that first night when I had read *Paradise Lost* and dreamed of a fallen angel. How often had I not sensed it, even though I had shrunk from facing it in conscious thought? I would have been all right, if Ross Culhaine had not been in his cups and poured out his story to me the night of the fiasco at the ball. The night Damaris—knowingly, I wondered?—had sent me to him. The Last Culhaine, Damaris' father, Marina's lover (as I believed ever since that same night). I could resist all that, but not the lonely little Irish paperboy setting out to amass a fortune that came too late. It was that boy, that man, to whom I had reached out that night. He had known it, he could not ignore it, however much he tried now. And I had known, even as my arms had gone round him before the fire, that in so doing I was making a kind of covenant.

I walked unseeing through the serene classicism of the museum, and responded absently to Damaris' soft comments, and thought upon these things.

"Lavinia." Damaris' voice cut through my troubled reverie with a new note that made me look at her and then look again more sharply. Her face had gone very pale and drops of moisture had come out upon it. She clutched my arm and doubled over slightly.

"Are you ill?" She nodded. "What is it?"

"Don't know . . . My legs . . . Pains in my legs, and here . . ." She pressed one hand against her stomach and bent again, convulsively. "Help me, Vinnie."

"Come sit down." I steered her towards a bench, but she shook her head.

"No. Home. Quickly." She was right. By the time I got her to the door she could scarcely walk. I summoned a cab and managed somehow to bundle her inside, where she sank back against the cushions, moaning slightly. I untied her bonnet and undid the top buttons of her basque. She scarcely noticed; she seemed to drift in and out of consciousness. The short ride home seemed an eternity, and when we reached the house I sent the cabman to the door to summon Hopkins. He came quickly, sized up the situation with experienced eyes, and carried Damaris up to her room himself.

"With your approval, miss, I'll pay the cabman and send him for the doctor."

"No!" Damaris, bent double though she was, struggled up. "It's the old trouble, Hopkins. No doctor . . . Send Maggie . . . Maggie and Vinnie will take care of me. Don't tell family . . ."

He hesitated, but he was accustomed to taking orders from Damaris, and she was so wrought up that I did not in her presence wish to overrule her. "Fetch Maggie," I said sharply, and he left.

As soon as he was gone Damaris' fingers closed like a vise around my wrist. "I lied—in museum. *Do* know—what it is. Isabella—trying to poison me. *They* don't believe, won't listen . . . You must help me, Vinnie. Mustard, salt, warm water . . . oil and butter . . . Maggie knows. Only hurry, do!"

"It's here, dearie." Maggie loomed behind me. Together

we got the nauseous mixture down Damaris' throat. Then vomiting, violent and persistent. Then she lay back, exhausted, and we undressed her and got her into bed. Her temperature was rising and her pulse was rapid. She was moaning, doubling over with pains in her lower body. I feared it might be appendicitis, but Maggie, probing with expert fingers, shook her head.

"Pain the wrong places. It's just what that poor angel thinks it is. Stranger things have happened, miss, and it's my advice not to inquire why or whither but just try to control it best you can." She went downstairs and fetched more warm mustard water.

"Told 'em you and Miss Damaris were dining in your rooms," she reported, giving me an even look. "They wouldn't understand. Fancy doctor tries to stop them convulsions, worst thing possible. Up to you and me, dearie, if we're not too late."

Reviving Damaris long enough to swallow more cathartic; more sickness, bathing her convulsed limbs and trying to reduce the fever. Damaris moaning; struggling up to consciousness; the pattern all repeating. The night wore by. Outside the walls, rain began to beat against the windows, slowly at first and then accelerating into sleet. Damaris grew quieter and her pulse diminished. Across the bed I heard Maggie muttering her rosary to herself. When at last a pale dawn began to glimmer fitfully outside the windows, we agreed that the poison, if such it was, must by now have been ejected from Damaris' system.

"Can't be nothing at all left in her, poor lamb," Maggie said in her earthy fashion. "I'll fetch some bicarbonate of potash and chloroform to ease her retching. And some strong tea for you, dearie, you look fair done in."

I rubbed my arm across my brow. "Just so Miss Damaris will recover. Are you sure she's all right, Maggie? Perhaps now that she's calmer we ought to fetch a doctor."

"*Them!*" Maggie's voice was large with scorn. "I've seen

them with her, paying no attention, saying she brings it on herself with nerves! I've brought her through it before, and I may again, God save her from it, before things get better. She'll sleep now, and be as right as ever she can be, all things considered, in a few days more."

"But all the same . . ."

Maggie turned on me that blank closed face of servant-dom. "But for what, miss? Call the doctors for them to ignore her and do nothing? Or to tell lies about my lamb and cause a scandal which *she* don't want herself? We'll take care of her, dearie, you and I, and do more good for her than a peck of doctors." She lumbered out and returned with tea and toast for me, and a dose that smelled fragrant of oranges for Damaris.

I sipped my tea, staring somberly at the dying fire. Now that the immediate emergency was over, I must decide whether to accede to Damaris' wishes and keep the silence. It did not seem right. Whatever Ross might believe was the cause, Damaris had been seriously ill and her father ought to know it. Before I came to a decision, I became aware that Damaris had awakened and was watching me with fevered eyes. As usual, she read my mind.

"Promise," she whispered sternly, and against my better judgment I agreed. How easily I acceded to her wishes, aligned myself with the conspiracy of silence, I did not realize till afterwards. It was a measure of how completely I had fallen under Damaris' spell.

Concealment came naturally, I found, in such a household. No one expected to see us, no one inquired. Damaris' illnesses were accepted as emotional disturbances and ignored. Marina herself, apparently, was keeping to her room; remembering the ravages that had shown on her lovely face the last time I had seen her, I was not surprised. I saw Warren Sloane coming in and out of the house during the next two days, but he apparently had been told that Damaris was having one of her spells and that I was with her, and he sent no word. Ross Culhaine was round and about, but he too sent no message. I wondered what he was thinking . . . About the theft of the Cellini medallion . . . ? About the night in the library when he had dropped his guard?

How carefully he had avoided references to that during our next interview; how impossible that, drunk as he was, he had not been aware of my response. I wondered, and I waited, and the more time that passed without my seeing him, the more uneasy of our eventual encounter I became.

When, on the evening of the second day, I received a summons to the library, my heart was palpitating. Whatever I expected, or feared, I am not sure. Certainly I was not prepared for what I found: Ross Culhaine standing behind his enormous desk, scowling darkly and as frigid in manner as on the first day I had come.

"I have taken you into my confidence on several matters, as you well know. Although I made no such demands upon you, I would have expected you, Miss Stanton, to do the same—at least where my own family is concerned!"

"What do you mean?"

"My daughter has been seriously ill the past two days. I have learned of it at last, belatedly, through the servants' grapevine. Hopkins, at least, it seems, has come to a realization of a father's rights, if you have not. Kindly forget any misguided notions you may have about protecting persons from the facts, whatever they may be, Lavinia. I want an explanation."

There are times when the needs of another take precedence over one's own integrity.

"Damaris was poisoned," I said baldly.

I was prepared for many reactions—shock, fear, even anger at concealment. What I had not anticipated was a coolly lifted brow and a sardonic "Do you know this of your own knowledge, or is it a deduction?"

"Observation," I snapped. "While we were at the museum Damaris exhibited signs of illness. She became pale, plucked at her garments, doubled up, complained of nausea, dizziness and stomach pains. I brought her home in a cab, during which time she lost consciousness at times, went into cold sweat and began experiencing convulsions. I spirited her into my room and locked her there because she said it was the only way she could feel safe."

"It did not occur to you to send for a physician?"

"Damaris made me promise to tell no one." No need to drag poor Margaret into this. "She stated her belief she had been poisoned. I undressed her, administered heat and certain other treatments she directed, and she was ultimately able to—to rid her system of anything that could have contained harmful substances. I sat up with her all night; she suffered severe convulsions and attacks of pain, but by morning appeared much better, though very weak. She repeated her demand for my vow of silence."

"And you gave it?"

"It seemed necessary to her physical and mental state that I should do so!" I straightened and got my voice back to Boston level. "Afterwards, I did research and discovered the symptoms and treatment coincided with those for arsenic poisoning."

"And how," Ross inquired, "do you suggest the poison was administered?"

"That is scarcely for me to say."

"Damaris made no suggestions? She accused no one in this household, or outside powers? Did not that strike you, now or then, as odd?"

I did not answer. Damaris' panic-stricken eyes, the rigid wall that shut me out, that despairing "No one would believe" were things that for mixed reasons I could not share. Since my silence, in itself, was an admission, I said at last, "My immediate concern was with Damaris' health. Questioning would—upset her."

To my relief Ross did not pursue the subject. "You did

research, you said. Did it never occur to you Damaris might have done so, too?"

"She must have, since she knew the proper treatment."

"There is another explanation, which surely you would have seen did not blind loyalty cloud your judgment. Did it never occur to you that Damaris deliberately might have ingested the arsenic herself?"

I stared at him.

"Many Boston belles take arsenic on lumps of sugar for their complexion. I believe it's supposed to induce an interesting pallor."

"Damaris is no such fool."

"Damaris is no fool at all," Ross said evenly. "Lonely, hysterical, dream-haunted, yes; and extremely intelligent."

"A short while ago you were saying you could not remain within our home, despite Damaris' pleading. Now she has your undivided attention, unquestioning faith, your love and mothering. She needs those desperately. Perhaps desperately enough to risk her own death?"

One thing was clear. Whatever Damaris was, whatever the explanation behind these seemingly senseless things, I was needed here.

XIII

I was much troubled in my mind that night, and though I tried to dispose myself for slumber, I could not sleep. Too many unanswerable questions stirred within me, and my thoughts rambled as in a maze, now here, now there, down twisting alleys which were not blind but seemed to run to endless caverns, opening beneath my feet like the Abyss of Acheron and quite as fearsome. When at last I did lose consciousness, it was to dream of a vast shifting wasteland lit by sporadic fires and peopled by haunted shades. I found no rest.

The next day was Sunday, when it was quite my custom to walk alone the few blocks to hear the noted Dr. Brooks preach in the stylish new redstone Trinity Chapel in Copley Square. The Culhaines and the Orsinis, of course, were Catholics, another fact which alienated them from social Boston. I recollected Damaris, in boarding school, going through the period of intense mystical devoutness peculiar to young people.

How sad that she seemed to have lost it with her other losses; it might have been a comfort to her now. I knew that I myself found solace and renewal in the ordered beauty of the Episcopal service, and I needed that, especially today.

I had awakened early and unrefreshed, and on an impulse determined to rise and attend the Early Eucharist. When I slipped outside, snow was falling, blotting out sound in a hushed pale Gothic world. The skirts of my dark gown, trailing the drifted banks, became spangled with frosted crystals. The sanctuary was only a quarter full, and I knelt in a quiet pew to the side to order my troubled heart.

Candlelight, and faint sweet smoke, the whisper of the choir boys' vestments, and the gleam of altar gold. The timeless measured liturgy of the Eucharist unfolded, but my mind could not discipline itself, my thoughts continued to scamper endlessly down new aisles opened by Dr. Brooks's voice intoning the gracious words.

. . . Forgive us our trespasses . . . I had done those things which I ought not to have done, and left undone those things which I ought to have done, and there was no health . . . *Lead us not into temptation . . .* I would not think on that . . . *Deliver us from evil . . .* there was evil around, intangible and waiting, like the omnipresent scent of tuberoses in the air . . . *Almighty God, unto whom all hearts are open, all desires known, and from whom no secrets are hid; Cleanse the thoughts of our hearts . . .* I needed that. Or was it escape, a shrugging off of responsibilities from which I shrank? *Lord, have mercy upon us . . .*

Almighty God, give us grace that we may cast away the works of darkness, and put upon us the armour of light . . . The church had cast aside her drab serviceable green and put on the purple splendour of Advent Sunday. I had been in Boston a long time. And what had I accomplished? Nothing of my original intention of learning my identity by tracing down the Medici ring. Nothing, apparently, except to serve in the House of Culhaine . . . As a catalyst? For good or evil? *Thou shalt not commit adultery.* Ross, Marina? *Thou shalt not kill.* I wonder how Damaris' mother died. *Thou shalt not steal, Thou shalt not bear false witness. Thou shalt not covet* . . . Forgive me, Lord. . . . *all things visible and invisible* . . . My thoughts were like the tangled threads in a tapestry in which the pattern was sensed but was not yet distinct. *Come unto me, all ye that travail, and are heavy laden* . . . How I longed for rest.

People always talk, I thought with irony, of the struggle between duty and temptation. The real difficulty was in knowing which was which.

Mr. Brooks was speaking of the Annunciation, talking of angelic messengers, recalling the old cryptic words to Sarah that in strangers we have all of us entertained angels unaware. *Lucifer was a fallen angel . . .*

I received Communion and walked out of the church, straight into the impish angelic face of Warren Sloane.

"I saw you go in and didn't want to intrude, so I loitered outside the gate," he said, grinning cheerfully. The man was everywhere. "Come and let me buy you breakfast."

"Certainly not."

"Then shall we step inside the church a moment after everyone has gone? I need to speak with you, Lavinia."

I allowed him to escort me into the by now almost empty chapel. In the nave a stocky acolyte was extinguishing candles, and the sweet smoke drifted down. We sat in a back pew and Warren turned to me. His voice was hushed, whether through reverence or an instinctive adaptation to the setting, I did not know.

"I have tried to see Damaris, but hatchet-faced old Hopkins in the hall won't let me. I did pry out of him the information she was ill. How is she now?"

"Better. She is—what is that phrase?—resting comfortably."

"What happened? Genuine illness, or the sort she brings upon herself? Don't look at me in that governessy fashion, Lavinia. I also know Damaris well, you know."

"Quite genuine, I assure you."

"What sort of illness? Something new, or female troubles? I'm not being offensive, there's a reason for my asking."

"We believe it was something that she ate," I responded primly.

"Convulsions? Pains in the abdomen and lower limbs, same as before? The same complaint she suffered from before? Oh, yes, I know of that, you see."

I did not answer. The church was filling again, for the second service, and Warren stood abruptly, his hand beneath my arm. "We had better go for coffee, where it's private. Hang your reputation, if that's what you're being so nice about. This is important."

He hustled me off down Boylston Street without so much as a by-your-leave. "Coffee and sweet buns," he instructed the waiter briefly. "Be quick about it, and then let us be."

"You have the audacity . . ."

"I do indeed," Warren retorted grimly, "and it's time that someone did. What are Damaris' symptoms, Lavinia? You won't tell me? Very well, then, I shall tell you. Convulsions, pains, pallor and perspiration, fluctuating pulse, painful and recurrent regurgitation. Am I correct? And she herself knew exactly what to do? Has it occurred to you that she could be systematically being poisoned?"

I stared at him, considerably startled.

"Damaris was extremely upset," Warren said, "the evening of the ball."

"About what?"

"I do not know. She would not tell me then. She wanted to talk to me, she said, in private. Then that—episode with the necklace occurred, and I had no chance to speak to her again. I have tried to see her twice but she sends back word she does not wish to be disturbed. I was not sure whether the message came from her or from the powers that be."

I wet my lips. "Why—what made you suggest poison?"

"Because something is considerably wrong in that mausoleum," he said bluntly. "Don't tell me you haven't felt it. You're a sensible woman, and not likely to blame it on some Machiavellian aura lingering on."

This hit so close to the mark that I blushed faintly. "Like a curse upon despoilers of old graves?"

"If there is one, it's quite real, and not based on any spiritual emanations from artifacts. And the grave may not be quite so old."

"What do you mean?"

He responded with a question of his own. "How much do you know of Damaris' mother's death?"

"How much do *you?*"

"Nothing. I wasn't here then, after all. And the subject is *tabù*. But I do know this: Damaris' illnesses started with Isabella's death. I cannot help feeling that is the key behind it all." We looked at each other. "That child is in some way involved. And Culhaine adored his wife."

"Are you suggesting—"

"I suggest nothing," Warren said. "Other than that you try to protect Damaris. Something is very rotten in the state of Denmark, as we both know."

Somewhere in the stillness of the breakfast room a clock ticked loudly. "I must go. I should not be here. I did not mean to leave Damaris so long alone." I rose, gathering up gloves and prayer book.

"I'll see you home."

"*No*. I mean it, Warren." I rushed out blindly, and with, I fear, some loss of dignity. I needed to be alone. Too many thoughts rolled round my head like tangled bobbins of a tapestry.

By the time I reached Marlborough Street, I had resolved

upon two things. I could not leave. And I must find out what lay beneath the concealment of the death of Isabella Culhaine. If the inhabitants of the household would not tell me, I would begin at the other end. With the "Pavane for Two Sisters," and the tapestry. I would commence to repair the tapestry that night.

I hurried up the icy steps, my mind eased somewhat. Ross Culhaine met me in the hall. "Come in here at once." He grasped my arm and steered me into the library and shut the door.

I had had enough for one day of such peremptory treatment. "How dare you?"

"How dare *you* make a common fool of yourself by sneaking out for secret assignations?"

For a moment that took my breath away, for many reasons. Then my blood surged. "You have no right—"

"I have the right as head of this household," Ross interrupted coldly, "to keep any of its members from jeopardizing it. Warren Sloane is not a fit companion for you, and you are not to see him."

"Considering that I was introduced to him beneath your roof—"

"To work with, yes. I scarcely thought you would sink to choose him as a personal companion."

"I scarcely think you are in a position to dictate to me whom I may choose! As for his suitability"—I took a deep breath—"I did not think you such a snob as to consider an educated antiquarian inferior to a newsboy bootblack!"

The words flashed in the air, and our eyes met like crashing swords. Then the red mist rose, and my blood drummed in my ears. I turned away. For a moment I thought that I would faint. I could not look at him, but when I lifted my head at last, he spoke, and I knew the Rubicon we had both been avoiding had been irrevocably crossed.

"Well, Lavinia," Ross said. He was smiling crookedly, but

looked as though he had been running hard. "So here we are, it seems, at Thermopylae Pass." He was turning the little dagger he used as a letter opener over and over beneath his fingers. There were no lamps lit, and the wan light filtering through the lavender panes rimmed his profile.

"You are correct. I *have* no right. I cannot; it is—dangerous to have an intimacy with me. I have learned that to my sorrow."

"Perhaps," I said shakily, "we should confine our discussion to the matter of Warren Sloane."

"He also is dangerous. And unsuitable, though not for the reasons you so graciously ascribed."

"Because of the medallion and the silver box?"

"Perhaps. I do not yet know. There are other reasons. I cannot tell them, nor, as you have devastatingly pointed out, have I the right to make demands. I can only ask you. Please, Lavinia, do not become involved with him. For Damaris' sake, if not for ours."

So he knew about that too, it seemed.

"I don't know what to say," I said at last.

"Nor I, either. Perhaps it would be best to just say nothing." He came toward me, and stood for a moment, then took my hand, and raised it to his lips, and bowed, and showed me in silence to the door.

I spent, all in all, a most disturbing day.

The snow continued well into twilight. It was Sunday, and no callers came. Marina did not appear, but by late afternoon Damaris felt well enough to venture down for tea. That was good; it ameliorated the tension between Ross and myself and softened our constraint of silence. Damaris was pale, and alarmingly thin, but her conversation fountained in sporadic spurts of gaiety, between which she kept glancing slant-wise at her father and myself. I wondered how much she guessed. Far more than was good for any of us, I suspected.

She stayed down for dinner, too, and afterwards insisted

on Ross's favoring us with some of his Irish songs. At last—to Ross's relief as well as mine, I'm sure—I persuaded her it was time for us to go upstairs. She made me sit with her until she fell asleep, and lock our doors onto the hall, and leave the ones between our rooms wide open. I would infinitely have preferred to have them shut. Finally, when I was assured that she was deep in slumber, I was able to return to my own room. I lit the lamp on my work table, brought out my work basket and the magnifying glass I had procured from the library downstairs.

Then—the tapestry. Strange how my hands shook and my heart beat faster. Strange how I suddenly felt a *voyeur*, a player of dangerous games. I was quite irrationally glad that Damaris had insisted that our doors be locked. I spread the somber folds out across the table, and the convoluted flowers glowed at me like malignant things.

I had intended to approach the mending of the tapestry in the disciplined manner in which I had been schooled. Instead, spurred by the memory of the magnifying glass's harsh enlarging truth. The tiny, elegant figures sprang to life and seemed to move.

To move; to dance a slow pavane . . . What was I thinking? Imagination and scholarly precision warred within me. My mind moved swiftly, seeking clues, even while my artisan's eye would be caught and held by tiny, infinitely skilled details. A lily in a lady's hair; an elegant gentleman with a dagger in his belt—a dagger much like that I had seen that morning in the hands of Ross Culhaine. Better not to think upon that morning. Better move on, noting the hand harp slung over another masculine shoulder . . . the man of craft? The words of Damaris' song echoed in my brain.

> "He saw a woman seemed so fair,
> A-wearing lilies in her hair,
> And oh, she caught the craftsman's eye."

Was the man of craft Ross Culhaine? He was crafty; he had begun his climb to wealth in craftsman's fashion. Think not on that; move on. Here in this tiny grouping was the lady wearing the famous collar once again.

The magnifying glass slid from my fingers with a crash that could have, but did not, wake Damaris, but I paid no heed. The room went dark; went light; my breathing hurt me. Here was the collar, but not the same, no, not the same as in the portrait and the jewel case in Lucifer's library below the stairs. With the glass I could see that something was added. A pendant; Damaris had told me of it months ago, and I had nodded, imagining the usual cross or heavy irregular pearl. But this was different, this was a blood-red ruby, se´ in a curious serpent head of reticulated gold. Only for a moment had the glass of magnifying truth illumined it, but I had no need again to see. I knew the pattern as I knew my name. The twin, the double of that golden snake was even now coiled on my finger, coiled round the enigmatic pigeonblood ruby of the Medici ring.

XIV

Like a drowning thing struggling through depths after depths of murky waters, I came to consciousness again, and my lungs hurt with the pain of my own breath. Though only one lamp burned, the room seemed overbright. Mechanically I folded the tapestry and placed it in hiding, mechanically I disrobed, prepared for bed, blew out the light. In the darkness I sank into the engulfing featherbed, and pulled the covers tight, and my thoughts like rats chased their tails around my mind.

Twin rubies, tapestry and real; twin serpent heads. Twin, or double? "Spit and image," my mother would have said. *Mother. "I have had Marianne's ruby made into a ring."* "Where did it come from?" Damaris had asked me. "Was it her betrothal ring?" I never knew my father.

"Lavinia has the right to know the truth. Marianne wished to live without restitution." For what? my brain shrieked within me. Eustace Robinson had determined to

write to Boston. Damaris had written me. Here, now, was Boston, here the Culhaine Collar. Ross Culhaine's collar and my mother's ring.

No, no; my thoughts were running wild. This was not Greek tragedy. This was some deadly game. Ross Culhaine had looked at me as if he were seeing ghosts. His mother's ghost, he said.

Ross Culhaine had known Eustace Robinson, who was not my uncle. Eustace Robinson and a ruby, links between myself and Boston. Damaris, another link. Ross, now another. Links of emotion drawing me, holding me here, stronger than ties of duty or of blood. Links that once fastened a ruby to a golden collar.

Begin again, begin at the other end.

"Damaris, where did the collar come from?" "Papa won't speak of it. He had a friend, an Englishman, in Italy, won the collar from an Italian seaman playing cards. There was a fire. The other man was killed."

Was that man my father?

Some time, long ago, the ruby once pendant to that collar had reached my mother. I had never known the story. A story Eustace Robinson had been at some pains to conceal. A story I had come here to uncover. Instead I had plunged into the Culhaine Collection, and the tale of the two sisters, and had found—what?

"A Medici poison ring. Truly, Lavinia, did you never guess?" Damaris had been poisoned; Ross said, by her own hand.

Warren's voice saying, "I have the oddest feeling I've seen this serpent's head before." Damaris, speaking of a tapestry, speaking of another portrait in which the collar was somehow different, saying she hadn't seen the portrait since they returned from Italy.

Damaris saying her dead mother was trying to poison her, to punish her. Warren hinting there was something strange about Isabella's death, about Damaris' illness. *"Something is very rotten in the state of Denmark . . . Culhaine adored his wife."*

Ross, his eyes a living pain: *"It is dangerous to have an intimacy with me . . . To blight each fair thing that we touch . . . the curse of the Culhaines."*

" 'I die of love that is not true . . .' "

How had the ruby left the collar and reached my mother? Why?

Restitution. Damaris, vague: *"He saved the collar from a fire . . . The other man was killed."*

God, let me sleep.

At last, mercifully, from the dead of night, sleep came. And with it, dreams.

"Damaris," I said to her casually, next morning, "I've become interested in that song of yours. Where did you find the story? Is it from history, or a book, or did you make it up?" Seeing her face take on that shuttered look, I improvised quickly. "I've been thinking of doing a bit of writing on my own. I used to do so at school, you may recall. It occurred to me, if I could support myself by writing poems, I might not have to leave to seek employment."

Damaris was immediately eager to be of help. "Of course you can!" Fortunately she was ignorant of my professional arrangement with her father, and of the world of publishing as well. "There's scores of things to write of! The two sisters were real, I found part of the story in a book downstairs, and because I was interested I looked for more."

"Why were you interested?" I pinned her down ruthlessly. "Because of the tapestry?"

"Tapestry?"

"The one you told me of, that showed the sisters' story." Instinct held me back from revealing I had found it. "That showed the collar, and proved the Bianca in the portrait was one of the two sisters."

: 173 :

"I don't know what you mean." Wide-eyed, astonished innocence.

"Yes, you do," I said grimly. "Don't play games with me, Damaris. I know you well."

"Do not you play games. I've tried to warn you." Damaris stopped pretending. We were having breakfast together in her room and she pushed herself upright, staring at me with dark agitated eyes. "Do not pry into our family legends. It is dangerous."

"How so?"

"You know, you've seen it! I became involved in the tale of the two sisters, and now something is trying to stop me—to punish me. Laugh if you like, but such things happen. There *is* a curse on the Culhaines and it will not end till it has killed me too . . ."

Then gasping breath. Hysteria. Pains. Damaris clinging to my hand. At last falling into an exhausted sleep. Myself feeling guilty . . . doubly so, because I wondered if it all were feigned.

There was something diabolic here, but whether it emanated from some source of ultimate evil, or from persons, or from memories imprisoned in the walls—who was to say? I felt as if it came from within myself, distorting my vision, making me doubt the things of which I once was sure.

I rooted quite shamelessly among Damaris' papers that afternoon and finally found a copy of the "Pavane for Two Sisters."

There were two sisters, dark and fair,
The one was skilled in subtle art,
The other pure in garb and heart,
And she wore lilies in her hair.

Still through the dark pavane they move,
A dark pavane of death and love.

One sister loved with virgin truth
A stranger gallant, strong and sure.
The other, with her wiles impure,
Stole off the heart of that same youth.

One sister wore with brazen pride
The favor once to t'other shown;
And she, forsaken, mourned alone,
Till in her bosom love had died.

A man of craft came passing by,
He saw a woman seemed so fair,
A-wearing lilies in her hair,
And oh, she caught the craftsman's eye.

Alas for faithful love once scorned,
And for false love that seemeth true;
For failing old and choosing new,
Death came upon a grey-eyed morn.

"Oh sister, you have loved well,
I die of love that is not true,
But who chose better, I or you,
Is secret time alone will tell."

Time would tell many things.

My head ached; though I had a cowardly and quite childish impulse to run away, too much trapped me, too many
unspoken covenants into which I voluntarily had joined. I
dreaded going down to dinner that evening, but I did.
Marina had emerged from her seclusion also, and Damaris—
they both looked ill, and preoccupied. Our circle round the
dinner table was reunited, like some dreadful parody of a
family grouping. The scene reminded me somehow of a
Dürer etching, the real distorted just enough so as to seem
faintly ominous. I did not look in Ross Culhaine's direction,
nor did he in mine.

"I have had the Collection returned to the conservatory," he remarked to the room at large. "Sloane is coming round first thing tomorrow to resume the work. He suggested Miss Stanton might do some work repairing tapestries if she is willing."

I quaffed wine quickly, hoping no one saw how my hand was trembling.

Marina looked startled. "*Caro, why?* I thought you would not wish—"

"My dear, your fête, had you forgotten?" Ross said sardonically. "Sloane had the audacity to remind me also that he has obligations to the New York museum and cannot 'linger here forever,' as he puts it. He bade me pass the message on to you, as well. You have encouraged him overmuch, Marina; he's grown too familiar."

"I hardly have encouraged him of late," she retorted tartly. "Indeed I had assumed the fête out of the question, with Damaris ill. You surely must see by now she should be taken away from these surroundings."

"We are remaining here." Ross' voice was still, and very quiet. Yet, even without looking at him, I felt its force. In that overheated room, I felt a chill.

"If you are sure," Marina said uncertainly. "We have received invitations, to balls and holiday parties—Damaris' name has been put on all the hostess lists since she's 'out'— I've held off responding . . ."

"Of course you must accept, Aunt." Damaris' voice came in high and clear. "It is what you have been wanting, certainly we shall go."

"*Cara,* that was before. You've been so ill, you said yourself that you could not keep on."

"It does not matter. I did not understand. It would make no difference, Aunt." Damaris sounded like a young Cassandra, walking clear-eyed into an inexorable fate. I remembered her, on one of those first nights in Boston, with her father's own hardness: "*One does what one has to do.*"

The table was cleared, and we withdrew to the library for coffee. Damaris sang. Patterns repeating. Damaris looked ghastly, but she kept on determinedly, eyes overbright. She came at last to that song which I knew had been on her mind all evening long, behind the madrigals and Early English airs.

"There were two sisters, dark and fair . . . "

A faint susurrus of breath ran through the room, as if others beside myself had been also waiting, were waiting still for some move to be made to release us from a spell. At last Ross rose. "It is quite late."

"So it is. I have engagements in the morning." Marina was the first to get away, with Damaris close behind her. I made to follow, but Ross stopped me, his hand upon my arm.

"Lavinia, are you ill?"

"My head aches. If you will excuse me—"

"Are you sure that's all?" His voice was kind, concerned. "You scarcely ate. Nor hardly spoke, at dinner. Is something wrong? If you don't wish to work on the tapestries—"

I had all I could do to discipline myself not to break and run. I murmured something, I knew not what, and made my escape.

Warren Sloane, the next morning, took one look at me also and demanded to know if anything was wrong. It was easier to lie to him than to Ross Culhaine. And yet, to my discomfiture, I found myself torn between the instinctive shuttering of my inner walls and the compulsion to pour the whole nest of serpents out to Warren's sympathetic shoulder and so-willing ears. Ross Culhaine was right, it was dangerous for me to be around Warren Sloane, although for reasons he did not suspect.

What a blessing it is to have a professional vocation. It imposes a discipline at once rigorous and soothing; so must the inhabitants of cloisters find their rituals, I thought. By dint of intense concentration on the Culhaine Collection I was able to steel my mind from the Culhaines themselves, as well as from the comfortable attractiveness of the sympathetic presence by my side.

I even welcomed the arrival of Ross Culhaine and a servant with a trunk of tapestries. Such needlework demanded concentrated solitude, demanded all one's mind as well as hands. I realized I had been half braced against some remark of Ross's about a missing tapestry, but none came. This lot of hangings was of a different sort, smaller, and on religious themes. I seized one which seemed to require the least amount of work, and fled.

A footman came and lit a fire for me in the third-floor sewing room and lit the lamps, so the place was cheerful despite the snow falling outside the lavender-tinted panes. Coward that I was, I rang for lunch to be brought up, and worked in a blessed half-consciousness until the tapestry was all repaired. I emerged from my fog to find my eyes aching and the hands of the mantel clock standing at half-past four. Warren would be long gone by now. I would go down to the conservatory and refresh my troubled spirits with the scent of flowers.

The conservatory was deserted, as I had hoped. No lamps were lit, but a luminous purple winter twilight filtered through the vines to bathe the objects on the work table, where it touched them, with a limpid sheen. I did not go to them, but walked instead down a side aisle where I was lost in a world of green and growing things. I had some peculiar distaste, at this present moment, for the Culhaine Collection.

What was I to do? I came upon a small bench hidden by ferns and sat down in the fragrant silence. I could not continue in this fashion, ever more sensitive to the pervading aura of evil, yet buffeted to and fro by winds of chance and uncontrolled emotion; determined at one moment to trace the emanation to its source; at the next, shrinking from what I had uncovered. I had come here, had I not, to discover who I was? I was discovering *what* I was, instead, and I was not at all easy in my mind with what I'd learned. But I did not know which was the greater cowardice—to leave, or stay.

I know not how much time passed, with myself lost in my own thoughts, when I heard footsteps hurrying down the aisles between the planting beds. I drew back into the fernery, for I had no wish to meet with anyone I was likely to encounter here. But the footsteps, muffled by the tanbark, so I could not recognize them, passed by my alley and went instead down the long corridor on the further side. There was a faint creaking, then a cool draught of air eddied all the overhanging leaves. I looked up, startled. Was there some door to the conservatory from outside which I had not known of? There must be, for I had heard but one pair of footsteps yet now there came that muted indistinguishable murmur of voices locked in rapid conversation. Conversation? Quarrel. A voice I recognized as Marina's flared out suddenly, low-pitched but clear. "It must stop, I tell you. Do you understand? I have been weak, I have wanted to protect. No more. It will go no further—" Once more the indistinguishable murmur, then her voice again. "I will not allow it! No more thefts, substitutions, this pretending of not coming here. You understand me? It is dangerous.
Non permetto—"

Abrupt cutoff; a swift faint ejaculation; a crash, as of some heavy crockery flowerpot. Then silence. Then footsteps, rapidly retreating to the house. My heart was pounding. It was several moments before I ventured out.

Whatever lurid picture my imagination painted, it was not what I found. Only the stillness greeted me, and the fragrant, the overpowering scent of flowers. No figure, alive

XV

I was astonished to find Warren Sloane in the front hall when I went down in response to the dinner gong that evening. He looked up, smiling pleasantly, as I stopped short on the stairs.

"Surprised to find me here? I, also. But the snow has stopped, the night is glorious; a sleighing party's being gotten up to benefit the museum. When I called to tell the marchesa, she insisted that I stay to dine. We will all of us travel out to Milton afterwards. Madame has graciously consented to chaperone. You will come, won't you?"

Clever, clever man. He was determined to see Damaris, and by making his bid in the guise of a museum benefit, he made it impossible that he should be refused. I hadn't a doubt in the world that the sleighing party had been all his idea, although Marina was murmuring something about Madame Cabot's generous patronage.

"Ought Damaris go?" I temporized. "She's not been well—"

"Oh, yes!" Damaris said rapidly, from behind me on the stairs. "It's warm as toast. The sleigh's lined with furs, I've heard. I'm perishing for adventure, and I'll not be kept away, so you mustn't try it! Perhaps Papa will come also, we'll be a Happy Family like in the children's game! Will you come, Papa?"

Ross's smile twisted, and he bowed faintly. "If it would not be an intrusion in the young people's gaiety." He spoke his words to the room at large, but it was at me he looked, and my eyes were the first to look away.

What a strange dinner that was, the five of us together round the table, candlelight falling on bare polished wood, the omnipresent servants hovering by. "Happy Family," Damaris had said—ironically?—referring to the card game of our youth. Not quite happy, not quite a family, yet bound together by some bond as spiderweb strong and as invisible. Who, I wondered, had been Marina's *vis-à-vis* in the conservatory conversation? I scanned her face closely, but could find no clue. Marina wore a gown of albatross, with long tight sleeves which encased her to the wrists, so if there was a bruise upon her arm it did not show. No disturbance showed in her gracious manner, either, although the fine lines of which I only recently was conscious were noticeable round her eyes. Of us all, Warren Sloane appeared the most relaxed, but his glance was watchful. He was up to something. All of us were up to something. My head began to ache.

The sleigh called for us promptly at the appointed hour and we hurried out, bundled in furs or, in my case, in my warmest dolman and a down-edged hood. Marina's Titian hair glowed against sealskin and sable, while Damaris was muffled in chinchilla. The sleigh also was lined with furs, with more in robes to pull up to our chins. Its prow curved up like a swan's breast to form a sort of cave or grotto in which the more fortunate, or least winter-hardy, could recline. Several gay souls already were ensconced, but they made room with good-natured banter for our party. My head commenced throbbing. There were foreboding starbursts at the corner of my vision, and I paid scant attention to where I was being placed, save to note Warren's contriving to have Damaris by his side some distance from us. Her face was apprehensive and her eyes were overbright. Then a familiar voice, very near, said, "Are you comfortable, Lavinia?" and I realized I was bundled, Colonial courting fashion, tight by Ross Culhaine. By Ross Culhaine, with Marina on his other side. Packed in like three peas in a pod. Like the three monkeys, I thought with a trace of hysteria. See no evil, speak no evil, hear no evil. I would be See No Evil, I would not even think it. I closed my eyes, not answering, and tried to blot out sight and sound and mind.

I more than half succeeded, but was it due to self-discipline or to my senses all responding? As we sped through the still night the air was fresh and cold and clear, and the ache in my head receded. Ross put his arm about my shoulders to steady me as we careened around a curve, and when the sleigh righted itself he did not withdraw it. The jingle of sleigh bells, the scent of pine boughs with which the sleigh was decked, the hothouse violets pinned to ladies' furs, the cold ice crystals that stung my cheeks, the warm bodily presence of Ross Culhaine so close beside me, the smooth wool of his dark greatcoat and the silkiness of its sealskin collar . . . I sank into a timeless sensory world.

We reached at length a gracious old house where candles burned in windows, and great logs blazed in tall open fireplaces. There were oyster stew, and soda biscuits, and Flaming Bishop Punch. There were apple-peel tossing, and snapdragon. I heard Damaris' laughter peal out, over-high, but I paid no heed. There were old-fashioned contra dances. There were waltzes. There was Ross Culhaine, not asking me to dance but swinging me peremptorily out onto the floor.

"Please—I do not wish to dance—my headache—"

"Not until you tell me what is wrong," Ross said firmly.

"What makes you think anything is wrong?"

"Because you have not exchanged two words with me in as many days. Not since both of us said a great deal more, without words at all. Both of us knew it. I thought that it did not displease you." I could not speak, and he looked at me sharply and swung me round in a secluded alcove without missing a step. "Since then something has happened. You have changed. I know you well enough to know you are not clever at dissembling."

"Really, you do not know me well at all! Now, do you?" My voice had taken on Damaris' quality, and I tossed back my head. "As for dissembling—really, have not all of us been merely playing games?"

Ross's face changed. "I have no wish to force myself upon you if it is distasteful," he said coldly, made a faint bow, and strode away.

Considerably disconcerted, I emerged from the alcove alone into the conscious gaze of Marina Orsini's level eyes.

Would this evening never end? I made my way over to the fireplace and sat down in a concealing settee, taking refuge in the so-convenient headache which was beginning to revive. At last the festivities came to a close, but this was no relief, for it was back to our pre-established positions in the sleigh. I withdrew into myself as much as I was able, and retreated into the lapping quicksand of my thoughts. Some of the young beaux of the party were in high spirits, stimulated no doubt by the Flaming Bishop, and began to sing. At first most everyone joined in, but as the miles passed some musically-trained commenced to offer solos. Miss Cabot did so; she was, surprisingly to me, quite good. She seemed both younger and more alive tonight, perhaps because her overpowering mamma was not present. Damaris sang, at Warren Sloane's persuasion, but she did not sing the "Pavane for Two Sisters."

We reached home. Ross helped me out and turned back to Marina's waiting hand. I escaped into the house as rapidly as I was able, for my head was raging now. Let Damaris keep her quicksilver rhapsodies to herself until the morrow, when she would undoubtedly need my attention more. I pulled my clothes off and fell into bed. Leonardo, annoyed at being left so long alone, jumped up beside me, but he soon sensed my mood and stalked off to join Damaris.

It was some hours later when a faint piteous cry penetrated through my slumbers. I stirred and sat up, wide awake, my headache gone. The cry repeated. Leo was beside me, pulling at the covers, his body jerking. He was going to be sick, on the brocade covers. I reached for him quickly, then my arms froze. His back legs dragged stiffly, an odd gurgling sound and a rime of yellowish foam came from his mouth, and his body jerked and contorted as Damaris' had. As Damaris . . .

"*Damaris!*" I did not know I was shouting until I heard the words.

She must have been awake; she was there in an instant, her face alarmed, a candle flickering eerily in her hand. "Vinnie, what—" Her eyes fell upon Leo, and the change which came over her was awful. "Oh, dear God . . . I didn't do it, I swear I didn't . . ." Her face had gone corpse-pallid and she had commenced to shake, but she fairly pushed at me. "Get Maggie, quick!"

I looked around helplessly until my eyes fell on the bell-pull, which I grabbed.

"I'll go. I know her room, it will be faster. Stick your finger down his throat, it may help some—" Damaris flashed out and I heard her bare feet running up the stairs. I seized Leo and tried to follow her command, to which, sick as he was, he offered violent protest. Then Maggie was there, red-faced and puffing, salt and mustard in her hands. Good heaven, I wondered, does she keep it in her room? My thoughts did not stop then to analyze, they were only grateful. Maggie took over, with Damaris' and my assistance, and presently Leo—as annoyed as he was weak—was pronounced well on the mend.

"How did it happen?"

"Something he ate," Maggie said firmly, gathering up the debris of our operations. "He'll be fine by morning. All he needs now's sleep. Same's you two young misses." She lumbered out.

"It's not safe here for cats. I ought to have remembered that. I lost my kitty," Damaris said rapidly. Her voice was skyrocketing in that fashion I had come to know and fear, and she sounded suddenly like a very little girl. "Not safe for any of us. But we're trapped. Can't leave. *You* can, though! Vinnie, don't listen to me, I oughtn't to have begged you, take Leo and run. Before it's too late, before you're caught too, like me—"

Maggie, reappearing, looked at Damaris sharply. "No more of that," she said firmly. "You're getting wrought up, dearie. What you need's your nice bed, and Maggie to sit by you to keep the evil things away." Her eyes met mine over Damaris' head. "It's all right, miss. I'll see to her. She gets like this at times, I expect you know." She steered Damaris out, and I heard the locks turned on the doors.

The poor child's mind is deranged, Marina had said. I flinched from the disloyal worm of doubt twisting in my mind, only to ricochet from its even more terrible alternative. For Leo had almost died.

Christmas was coming. The Boston shops wore evergreen and holly, and sleighbells jingled everywhere. Leo recovered, none the worse for wear. Damaris grew thinner and brighter. Marina was haggard; Ross, remote. And I? I retreated into the preoccupation of my work, and tried to close my mind. I did nothing.

As Marina had said, invitations now were coming in for the winter season. Not the important ones. There were no bids to the Assemblies, nor was Damaris asked to join a Sewing Circle. I had learned—again by way of Warren's know-all gossip—that each season a charity Sewing Circle was organized among that year's impeccable-family debs, and that Boston women remained members of their particular Circle their whole life long. It was hard to envisage either Damaris or Marina in such a provincial setting, but their exclusion was nonetheless significant.

They were invited to lesser social functions, though. An afternoon tea, a musicale, a pre-Christmas Ball. I was bid to this also, as an afterthought. Marina, naturally, chaperoned, a role to which her lustre seemed oddly suited. Damaris went willingly; she was no longer running from her secret fears, whatever they might be, but had adopted the fatalistic attitude that whatever was meant to happen, would. She permitted Marina to dress her up splendidly in silks, but she did not have the fragile new-discovered loveliness that had blossomed forth the night of her own debut. Nor was this ball nearly so magic-making, although we both danced and had a pleasant time. Warren was not there, of course. Neither was Ross Culhaine.

"I have put in my time for this season," he told Marina briefly. "Chaperoning is your department." So I was spared the problem of avoiding circling the dance floor in his arms, and I was irritated at myself for feeling, in spite of everything, let down.

Damaris and Marina went Christmas shopping, and I with them. I prepared remembrances for them both. But I did not continue repairs on the tapestry of the two sisters.

Then came Christmas Eve. No one thought to prepare me for Boston Christmas, and I was surprised and, to my astonishment, enchanted. Boston—social Boston, that is—goes caroling and calling on Christmas Eve. All that grey afternoon

Hopkins was busy supervising Maggie and Sarah and the others in setting forth an exquisite collation in the parlors. Etched crystal cordial glasses, thin as breath, came out, and cut-glass port jugs, and brandied cakes. Della Robbia wreaths were hung in the lavender windows. Beneath them, commencing at twilight, candles burned. Hopkins looked pleased and proud.

Ross Culhaine and the coachman and gardener were shut up in the conservatory all the day, and at intervals there issued forth splendid period arrangements of fruits and flowers, of evergreen and bay and holly and out-of-season roses like crimson blood. The skies were lowering and hinted sleet, and for a time there were anxious predictions that the customary festivities would have to be curtailed. But by dinner time, as a grace-note to the season, the skies had cleared. We were scarce risen from the table when the first sounds of caroling and laughter were heard in the street outside.

I had not looked forward to Christmas—not here, not now, not after all that had happened to me of late. The approach of the holiday had brought periods of an empty loneliness and an occasional undisciplined tear, but my sensibilities had hardened, I believed, into an independent, spinsterish mold. I would find time on the morrow to steal away to a church alone, for brief solitary observation of the holiday's true significance, and that would be all.

But I was wrong. Christmas Eve, in that insidious fashion which is perhaps its true and genuine magic, contrived once more to knit separate and alien souls into a common bond. Boston itself was asserting its spell. Not Irish, or Brahmin, or Italian Renaissance now, but that rooted city of the Adamses and Quinceys and Old South Church and Faneuil Hall. In the old stately fashion, the ladies of the households stayed at home receiving, while the gentlemen and the youthful of both sexes paid their calls. Some calls were brief, some long; there was much opening of doors and whiffs of pine, coldly fragrant on winter furs. The house rang, as I had never heard it, with gaiety and laughter and a kind of warmth that tugged my heartstrings.

I caught glimpses of Marina in the front parlour dispensing aromatic punch and heard flashes of her silvery laughter. From the library came the sounds of men's voices and, for a while, the sound of Damaris' harp. But I stayed well away from the library myself. I was introduced to a distinguished greying man who proved to be a member of the famed Saturday Club, and found myself plunged deep into an engrossing intellectual discussion which was as wine to my soul. I was, in short, having a very happy and heartwarming time which banished far away the dark tides which had of late so lapped at the edges of my thought.

When, presently, my new-found acquaintance bowed and left, having made hints of future invitations to all sorts of intellectual delights, I saw him and his friends off smilingly and turned, almost without thinking, towards the conservatory. The doors had been tight shut all day, but they were open now, and a tall spruce towered to the ceiling. On the tips of all its branches candles burned, and on its depths hung jeweled and filigreed ornaments of odd and curious work. Russian, Bavarian, Florentine . . . I stepped closer, staring. Here and there among the gilt and tinsel swung baubles of genuine value and real art. Ross had interspersed the Christmas ornaments with lockets and Medallions; with *enseigne*—hat ornaments—similar to the forged Ghiberti; and with those curious pendants, shaped like ships or mythic creatures, once worn by elegant courtiers as sleeve jewels. *Ross* . . . my mind was back again in the dark tides.

I left the conservatory and turned on impulse into the quiet and deserted ballroom to cool my face. The long room was very still and it was several moments before I realized that it was not empty, after all. Half lost in shadows of a high-backed settle by the open hearth, a couple was locked in a motionless and passionate embrace. The blush silk of Damaris' gown billowed softly against familiar tweed, and her thin hands tightened round his shoulders. I averted my eyes and turned away, feeling a *voyeur*, feeling too a sad and unwelcome emptiness inside.

The front rooms were still thronged with people. Crystal and laughter tinkled. I drifted through them, unnoticed as candle smoke, and found a refuge in a bay half-hidden by palms. It was the same bay to which Ross Culhaine had come to claim me the night of the cotillion. I looked back on that as in another world. Presently, from outside the tinted windows, a new sound came, distant and growing nearer, odd and enchanting. A sound of bells like a miniature carillon, ringing golden music. The people round me began moving towards the street, and the front door was opened, sending in a gust of cold pine-scented air. Carolers on the sidewalk, bell ringers in the street. Carolers in velvet and broadcloth and furs, coming in for Flaming Bishop. Music in the air. There had been carolers in Minetta Street also, when I was small, and for a moment my eyes stung with tears.

"Lavinia?" Damaris was standing beside me, her face soft and flushed and her eyes like dew-starred flowers. "We are going to Midnight Mass. Will you come with us?"

More candles, hundreds of them, and the sweet medieval scent of incense, drowning the senses. Choirboys' frail poignant sopranos soaring in *Alleluia!* Priests in lace vestments over purple and crimson. Flashes of gold in chains and crosses. Kneeling and rising, kneeling to rise again. Ross Culhaine beside me—by plan? by chance? The scent of sandalwood clinging to the fur collar of his dark broadcloth coat. An old voice chanting Latin in an unfamiliar liturgy, though I had studied Latin well in school.

Into my heart, for the first time in months, there stole a kind of peace.

The final benediction was pronounced, and the congregation flowed like a shining river out of the close sanctuary into the cold reviving air. Our party became separated in the crowd, and I found myself jostled in the vestibule against Damaris. Her fingers were trembling as she sought to hook her chinchilla hood, and she stopped to press one hand against her heart.

I fastened her furs for her. "Are you all right?"

"Yes, oh, yes!" Damaris said breathlessly. Her face was radiant. She reached up for my shoulder and pulled me close to hear her whisper. "I am so happy! Vinnie, I must tell you. I have a secret—"

"Damaris!" came Marina's voice from the church steps.

"Later—when we are alone!" Damaris breathed hastily. "Yes, Aunt, we're coming!"

We were being offered a ride home in the carriage of a business associate of Ross Culhaine's, and when we reached the house our hosts accepted his offer of a last refreshment. The house was quiet now, and although stubs of candles still burned beneath the della Robbia wreaths, the front rooms were dim with shadows.

"Let us go into the conservatory. I left word for the tree to be re-lit." Ross turned to Damaris, who had gone motionless at his words like a bird poised in midflight. "My dear, I have a Christmas present there for you. If you would give *me* a gift that I would truly value, you will join us there."

For an instant Damaris' eyes flared. Then her head went up. "Certainly, Papa, if it will please you," she said quietly. Had her happy secret, whatever it was, banished the old shadows, or was this Cassandra-fatalism? I did not know. She moved as calmly as the rest of us into the conservatory. Only once did she falter, and went all pale as she crossed the threshold, but her father did not see. As for the others, their gaze was caught and held by the splendor of the tree. Ross rang for Hopkins, and had a small collation served us where we sat in the wicker chairs, and Damaris to my admiration maintained her quiet poise. She sat in silence in a high-backed peacock chair, holding an eggshell cup in an equally translucent hand, her eyes opaque. I wondered what was going on in that convoluted mind. Was she reliving those terrible moments in this room which had so haunted her, or was her memory mercifully dulled by the narcotic euphoria of that embrace to which I had been an involuntary witness? Well, Damaris had wanted Warren to make her feel a woman, however high the cost. And who was I to blame her?

Beyond us, on the far side of the conservatory, branches rustled. Ever so faintly, muffled by the tanbark, came footsteps not so much heard as sensed. All at once, as such things happen, the memory of that other encounter to which I had been silent witness swept back on me. I looked up sharply, just in time to meet Damaris' startled eyes. She was looking not at me but past me, her lips half-parted. "Why, that was it! That was exactly how it was. I had forgotten. Someone stood there—"

The branches rustled, the curtain of cascading ivy hanging overhead was parted, and into the aisle toward us stepped the solid everyday presence of Warren Sloane, smiling pleasantly. I almost laughed at my relief, so caught up had I been in my own imaginings, when I chanced to catch a glimpse once more of Damaris' face. Something had struck it, freezing it into a kind of terror. She went white, then flushed, and wet her lips, but no sound came. Involuntarily I reached out to her.

"Damaris, I was speaking to you." Marina's voice interrupted, gently chiding.

"Yes, Aunt. I'm sorry." Damaris wrenched her gaze away with almost physical force; her face turned from us, and when she looked up again her eyes were shuttered.

The small word of Christmas eddied and swirled around us, and the moment was gone. Ross's friend and his family were rising, murmuring farewells. Ross bade a pointed adieu to Warren also, and that same gentleman caught my eye and made an ironic face. We saw them all to the door, which was then shut and locked. Already, in the front rooms, the candles had gone out.

"Christmas morning," Ross said, looking at his watch.

"It shall not yet be." Marina slipped an arm around Damaris' waist, scanning her face intently. Her own eyes looked troubled, but her voice was rich and warm. "To bed, *carissima*, while you can yet walk. I shall send you up some of the *panettone* you love, and some warm milk."

"There is no need. Lavinia will prepare some for me," Damaris said dully.

Her tone must have struck her aunt also, for the marchesa looked at her closely. Then she stepped into the library and came back with a small package in her hands. "You must sleep late. We will have our gifts in the afternoon, as usual. But you, *cara*, I would like for you to have this now." She pressed the tissue-wrapped package into Damaris' hand.

Damaris nodded absently, running the back of her other hand across her eyes. "You are right, I am—tired. Lavinia, would you fetch the milk for me, yourself . . ." She began pulling herself up the stairs while Marina watched her with a grave regard.

Ever since the poisoning attack Damaris had refused to take any nourishment prepared only for her by any but myself. I could not blame her, but it was not pleasant descending by candlelight into the cellar reaches where the dairy foods were stored on ice. I fetched a jug of milk as quickly as possible and returned to find Damaris, half undressed, sitting by her back window gazing out at the conservatory roof. A plate of *panettone* stood on the little table, and she gestured to it. "It should be safe, it was made for all to eat. Will you have some with me?"

It did not seem wise for Damaris to retire to sleep with

that sort of thought at the forefront of her mind. I sought to divert her. "Have you opened your aunt's gift yet?"

"It's on the table. You may look at it." I picked it up, a lovely little painting on ivory of a young woman in the style of a hundred years ago, mounted as a pendant and framed by pearls. "My great-grandmother Orsini," Damaris said. "Aunt knows I've always loved it."

So Orsini was Marina's family name. How odd; somehow I had taken her for a widow. The title, of course, was effective marital disguise. Damaris still sounded lifeless, so I pressed her further. "You wanted to tell me your happy secret when we were alone."

Damaris shook her head. "Not now. I am too tired. Perhaps tomorrow. Vinnie, please, would you just heat up the milk."

I did so, adding the sugar and vanilla she liked from the private stock kept in the armoire of my room, and saw her into bed, and then turned towards my own, wondering what it was that had troubled her. I advanced to turn down my brocade spread, and then all thoughts of Damaris fled.

A small package I had not noticed heretofore lay on my pillow, and I could guess at once from whence it came. Alas for my Puritan conscience which whispered sternly that I should set the gift aside unopened. I had Pandora's curse of curiosity.

Inside, on cotton wool, lay a Ghiberti *enseigne*, enamel glowing richly on the beaten gold. A small raised figure of Athena, goddess of wisdom . . . the card was unsigned, but I knew Ross's writing well. "I take this method of presentation to avert the strength of your displeasure. Pray accept this small token in gratitude for much."

Would I have heard Damaris sooner if I had not been so engrossed in my own thoughts? Over and over, in the days that followed, I asked myself how many times she had to call me before my ears caught the frantic terror of that faint sound. I found her on the floor beside her bed, grasping her stomach, her face convulsed. The overturned cup of hot milk lay beside her.

There was no time now to run in search of Maggie. I thrust my fingers down Damaris' throat, as she had bid me do with Leo, and screamed for help with all the strength at my command.

XVI

They were all there in moments—Ross, Marina, the frightened servants, Maggie clutching her little collection of cures.
Their images registered before me in distorted vision. Ross,
bending over Damaris, swinging round to grab the bewildered footman. "Run, you fool! Fetch Dr. Martinson! Don't
stop to dress, take my coat from the hall. But hurry!"

Marina, crying out, "*Caro*, no! It will all come out. Maggie will see to her. No one must know!"

Ross thrust her aside. "It doesn't matter now!" He knelt
beside Damaris, seizing her from my arms, holding her tight.
Maggie was there, trying to force the familiar mixture down
her throat, but it was no use. Damaris was too far gone in
convulsions to even swallow. It was not nice; it was nasty and
disgusting, and I had to steel myself to try to help. Marina
could not even look but turned away, holding tight to the
bedpost, ill and shuddering.

It seemed an eternity before the doctor finally arrived. He
came in bustling and precise, and the tight circle round us

opened to give him way. Damaris still lay on the floor, for we had feared to move her. She looked so pitifully helpless, lying there, and the way we were watching her seemed suddenly obscene. I shut my eyes, hearing the matter-of-fact elderly voice murmuring professionally, asking "Was this a sudden attack? Something she ate earlier, perhaps?"

"She was well all evening," Marina's voice said clearly, and Ross's even tones added, "There was nothing wrong at the time we went to bed."

The doctor murmured again, pontifically, and said something about acute gastritis. All at once what was happening began to register, and I opened shocked eyes onto the ring of faces. Closed faces, determinedly silent, shutting back some nameless horror. Maggie's eyes, troubled and defensive, met my accusing ones. Dear, well-meaning, stubbornly loyal Maggie! Ross was cold and still, hiding a well of anguish; if ever Damaris had doubted her father's love she should have seen him now, but he still did not intend to speak. Even now!

"You had better," my own voice said clearly in the stillness, "treat her for arsenic poisoning, not gastritis."

The stillness, silence, broke like shattering glass. The doctor, shocked: "Vast difference in treatment . . . Serious accusation . . ." Ross, emotionless, even: "We have reason to suspect she has been taking arsenic, yes." The doctor, taking charge with sudden authority, ordering us all out of the room, snapping requisitions to servants, telling Maggie alone to stay. Then we were out in the hallway, Damaris' door shut behind us. I grasped the banister, feeling sick inside.

"You should feel sick!" Marina's voice battered at me, harsh with venom. "If she has taken poison, I hold you responsible! You were here to take care of her, you should have done it better. I thought that you could help, but I was wrong. There has been trouble, trouble ever since you came!"

"Be still!" Ross snapped sharply. She must have gone. I

didn't know; I bent over the rail and prayed I would not faint. Then Ross's hand touched me. "Lavinia—"

I did not answer. I jerked myself up, and went into my room, and shut the door.

I did not undress or even try to sleep. I sat rigidly on the chaise beside the fire, seeing nothing, thinking nothing, hearing the sounds of sickness from the room next door. Those sounds grew weaker, and a grey glimmer of light began to filter through the lavender panes. Christmas morning. I rose stiffly and crossed to the window, resting my face against the glass, not knowing whether the silence portended good or ill. How long I stood there motionless I do not know; it seemed like hours.

There was a knock on the door and Maggie entered, carrying a tray. "Thought you'd best eat some breakfast, miss. There's no one feels like sitting downstairs proper, the good Lord knows."

"Miss Damaris?"

"Resting comfortably's what the doctor calls it." Maggie's face twisted. "She's stopped being sick, poor lamb, like there's none of that vile pizen left to get out of her no matter what we give her. She just lies there quiet, and the doctor says we must leave her be till she wakens, and time will tell. And he makes me leave her alone, poor frightened love, and says I'm to go and rest myself, but I'm that wrought up, miss, I cannot do it. There was naught for me to be doing, so I made some breakfast, and I've brought it up."

"She's not alone?"

"The doctor's with her, and one o' them nursing females." It was clear Maggie had no high opinion of the medical profession. She heaved a sigh, and I looked at her and saw, as the doctor must have done, that she had about reached the end of her tether. I forced her down into a chair, overriding her protestations, and poured her a hot, strong cup of tea.

"I just can't eat alone, I'm too upset," I told her artfully, and thus cajoled, the poor old soul gave way. The meal did her good, I was relieved to see, but she still was troubled, and after a few preliminary twists of her apron it began to emerge. She needed a confessor; she was uneasy over the vow of silence Damaris had exacted.

"Seeing her lying there, miss, so pitiful, and him with medical learning doing all the wrong things! But what could I do, miss? She'd made me swear before the Holy Mother not to tell."

Evidently Maggie assumed I was privy to all Damaris' secrets, and I did not undeceive her.

"What did you swear? Not to tell that she was being poisoned?" Maggie nodded. "They knew it, Maggie," I said gently. "You heard me tell the doctor the last time it happened. Her father knew." No need to pass on Ross's suspicions to Maggie.

"But not who's responsible," Maggie said uncompromisingly. "He'd never believe, she said, and just as well, the hurt of it being more than he could bear." But beyond that she would not go, and I could not budge her.

"It has to do with her mother's death, doesn't it?" I asked, carefully casual, and saw an answering flicker in Maggie's eyes. "I know about that, but I've never quite understood . . . Damaris saw it, didn't she? It's what's made her—queer?" *Forgive me, Damaris,* I murmured silently.

"Is it any wonder?" Maggie flew to her lamb's defense. "The acid eating away at the lovely face, and herself screaming like the souls in torment and falling to the floor, and the poor child standing by her, seeing—It was an accident! The two vessels on the work table side by side, in the one the acid with which the marchesa'd been cleaning off the master's precious metals. She used to love to work with the Collection in the old days, but she's never touched it since, no more'n my lamb would go out to that place of haunting till last night. What happened was an accident. In the heat of quarrel, who was to tell one of them vessels from the other? But *she* don't see that."

I understood now. No wonder, I thought, sickened, that Damaris flinched from such a memory. A terrible death; the smell of burning flesh; a young girl, impressionable and sensitive as Damaris, standing by, paralyzed by inadequacy, even as I had felt last night. Yes, Damaris would hold herself responsible.

"She thinks her mother's trying to punish her, doesn't she?" I asked boldly, and had my answer in Maggie's eyes.

I went over and put my arms around her. "You know what I think?" I said bracingly. "I think you must go upstairs, and try to sleep; you can, now that we've talked. Then you must get up and go to church and say a prayer for Damaris' safe recovery. And for her and her mother's souls. You *can* go, can't you?"

Maggie sniffed. "They won't care, they'll not even notice. *He's* downstairs in the library with the marchesa, and her holding him against her breast like he was her child." Something inside me twisted. "Repenting his cruel harshness to the poor lamb all these years, he is, and let us pray by all the saints it's not too late. There's been evil done in this house, miss, and good souls led astray by the wiles of the Evil One and the Scarlet Woman."

She was referring to Marina and Ross, of course; apparently their intimacy was public knowledge.

What a strange, quiet Christmas that was, as still as death. I was able at last to get Maggie off to her room comparatively calm. I promised to send for her if any change occurred, but no news came. The morning passed, the doctor came and went, murmuring professional generalities, promising nothing. He was anxious to get home to his own feast and family, no doubt. As for us, the holiday was forgotten. We were not allowed into the sickroom, and I comforted myself with the thought that were Damaris failing we should certainly have been sent for. I speak of "we," but I did not see the others. I sat alone, thinking disjointed thoughts, and I went down to a solitary lunch only because it seemed to help the servants to have something practical to do. In the afternoon, having been assured that no crisis was expected, I bathed and dressed and slipped out to the church in Copley Square to say my private prayers. When I emerged it was into twilight and snow softly falling. A wave of loneliness washed over me, and my mind flitted back to that other church visit when Warren Sloane had accosted me while leaving. Warren had warned me Damaris was in danger. I wondered suddenly whether he knew yet of Damaris' illness. I had half expected him, with his audacious brashness, to come Christmas calling, especially after the intimacy I had observed last night. Last night; how long ago it seemed.

When I reached the house, Hopkins informed me that the doctor had been and gone, and that Damaris seemed improved, although still lapsing in and out of consciousness. Yes, Mr. Sloane had called. Hopkins had informed him briefly of the accident, and he had gone off much disturbed. So that was the line the servants were taking, I noted. Accident; the family was to be protected from scandal at all costs. "And tea is ready for you in the front drawing room, miss, if you'd care for it."

I didn't, but I partook anyway, to oblige. Rituals must be observed, and they were helpful. For the same reason, I dressed for dinner and came down, and so did Ross and Marina, impelled no doubt by the same atavistic need. Murders and suicides might come and go, but one must keep up the form and one must not fail the servants. I thanked God for those omnipresent servants who impelled control and inhibited the free expression of our thoughts.

So Christmas passed, observance of a holy birth amid unholy death . . . I would not think that way; Damaris must not die.

Snow continued falling through the night, but it stopped by noon. The doctor came again, there was some bustling round in the room next door. In midafternoon a knock on my own door came, and I opened it onto the dark enigmatic figure of Ross Culhaine.

"The doctor wishes us all to come into Damaris' room at once."

My heart lurched. "She's not—"

"No. She's regained consciousness, in fact. The doctor is trying to determine exactly what she took, and how, and he seems to feel it would be better if we were present." His mouth was wry. "He has a report to fill out. It seems one cannot very well refuse."

Damaris looked so small in that cocoon of bed, like the child that I remembered. She was all frailty and pallor, but under the pallor, steel. I knew the signs by the way she would not meet our eyes but gazed over our shoulders at the window. Marina was even more shaken than I at Damaris' appearance; she turned away, weeping softly. Ross stood silently; it was impossible to tell what he was thinking.

The doctor was determined to brook no nonsense, that was clear. He spoke to Damaris in a grave, fatherly tone, telling her precisely what had happened, that she was now on the mend, but that "the call was very close, very close indeed, my dear. The question now is how you came to—ah, ingest this harmful dose. We must make very clear whether it was an accident or not. For instance, my dear young lady, did you partake last evening of anything out of the ordinary, anything the others did not?"

"But I told you—" Marina broke in. The doctor held her off brusquely.

"I asked the child, madame."

"Answer him, Damaris," Ross said evenly.

What would happen if Damaris blurted out her tale of visitations from a long-dead mother?

"But this is silly," Damaris said in her clear high voice. "It was an accident!"

"We can't be sure—"

"*I* can," Damaris said rapidly. "It was an accident—an overdose. I took the arsenic myself, you see. For my complexion!"

We stared at her.

"Lots of ladies do!" Her voice rattled on, determinedly vivacious. "It gives one an interesting pallor. I do have that, you know. Arsenic's quite the fashion nowadays in Boston. It used to be done all the time back in the old days. I read about it in a book."

"What book?"

"I don't know," Damaris said vaguely. "An old one somewhere. So write up your reports, doctor, and I'll sign them. But mayn't I rest now? I'm really very tired."

We turned to leave, much shaken, yet I was aware of a tangible current of relief among the others. Damaris' voice reached after us. "Lavinia can stay, mayn't she, for a few minutes? I want to talk to her. Just Lavinia."

Marina offered protest; it was her place to stay, Damaris was her niece and needed her. But Ross overruled her firmly and thrust them all out, shutting the door and leaving me with a Damaris summoning up reservoirs of strength and hard as stone.

"Why did you do it, Vinnie?" she demanded.

I was so thrown off guard I could only stare at her. "What do you mean?"

"No different food. No milk left by my bed at night. You fetched that milk from the dairy case yourself, and fixed it in your room, because I trusted you. Only you; no one else could have touched it. Vinnie, *why?*"

"But you said—"

"I said *I* took it," Damaris said harshly. "Did you think I'd let them hurt you? But I must know *why.*"

This was becoming a crazy nightmare I could not believe. "You thought your mother . . ."

"My mother was not here last night," Damaris said inexorably. *"You* were. Was that why you wouldn't share the milk with me last night? I wondered at it. I should have guessed, right then." So this was what people meant by the strange logic of the insane. "Why, Lavinia? Because of Warren? Because of Father? I'd not have stopped you there. Are you an agent of my mother's come to punish me?" Her voice was becoming shrill and her breathing labored, but when I moved toward her impulsively, she thrust me off.

I must go; I could not help her now. But before I went. . . . "Last night," I said rapidly. "Last night at church. You said you had a secret."

"You are imagining it." Damaris said forcibly. "I said no such thing." But there was a strange look in her eyes. She knows, I thought, that I know she lies. But why?

I left, because there was nothing else to do. The nurse bustled in to take charge, casting me a baleful look. My legs felt like they were about to buckle under me, and my brain was whirling.

One thing I felt sure of; Damaris genuinely believed what she had said. Whatever she had thought or done, earlier, she believed this now. She was right, too. The milk was the only draught that could have held the poison; I alone had touched it, pouring it from the common pitcher, carrying it up the stairs—

The sugar. The sugar and vanilla. I kept them openly accessible in my armoire, and most of the household knew it. I ran into my room and threw the carved doors open, staring with growing alarm and panic into its cavernous depths.

The sugar tin and the small brown glass bottle both were gone.

XVII

I sat rigidly on the end of the chaise, pressing my hands together tightly on my knees, and though the central heat was suffocating, I felt icy cold.

Murder. Attempted murder, anyway. There was no reason for my private stores to vanish unless they had contained the arsenic. If they had, then—my stomach contracted. Whoever had placed it there had not cared if I died as well, for I often shared Damaris' late-night brews. Had *wanted* me to die? But why? Because I knew too much?

What did I know? Doggedly I laid out the facts, arranging them this way and that, like pieces of the Collection, as if by ordering them I could order as well my trembling body and my skittering thoughts.

Damaris was afraid. That was the beginning. Damaris' mother had died, and Damaris had gone away, and she had come home again from Italy and she had been much afraid.

Home. Boston. Where the proud and ancient Orsinis and

Culhaines were new-rich immigrants and as such despised. Where Ross's mother had died a pauper, for which he blamed the city. Where Damaris' mother had died by accident of acid, and Damaris blamed herself. Whom did Ross blame?

The Culhaine Collection. The Collection, Damaris' debut, the projected fête, all designed to shame and humble Boston. For injuries done to Ross's mother, and Damaris'.

The Collection. Warren Sloane, brought from New York to catalogue the Collection, disliked by Ross Culhaine but not his daughter. I, Lavinia Stanton, antiques expert. Child of I knew not whom. Ward of Eustace Robinson, antiquarian extraordinaire connected in some way with Ross Culhaine. Confidante of Damaris' troubled dreams.

Dreams. Fears. Visions. Damaris, believing her mother came to her in the night. Belief fostered by Maggie, simple, superstitious, loyal? Damaris, insisting all along she was being poisoned. But Ross said she was doing it herself. Myself, susceptible to the atmosphere of this strange mansion—was that only my imagination, or was it more? Myself sensing another presence watching, that night with the missing tapestry in the shut-up room.

Things missing. A ruined tapestry. A portrait. A counterfeit *enseigne*, a counterfeit silver box.

Intrigue. Patterns of intrigue, past and present. Skeins carefully, ambiguously interwoven by Damaris in the "Pavane for Two Sisters." Two sisters, good and evil—Isabella and Marina?—and a stranger and a man of craft. And death. "There's been evil done in this house, miss," Maggie'd said. And gone on to speak of the Evil One and the Scarlet Woman. Marina was Ross's mistress. "I'd not have stopped you there," Damaris had said. She had been speaking of myself and Ross Culhaine. I had been too bewildered at the time to notice, but now my face flushed. Damaris had guessed. Damaris knew so much. Was that why she was being poisoned?

Intrigue. Warren secretly courting Damaris, out of compassion, some genuine caring, and self-interest. Damaris encouraging it, although she understood it all. Warren half-courting me as well, adopting the offhand, half-mocking friendliness he must have known was the only approach I would accept. Warren discovering so casually the secret of the Medici ring. Warren wrinkling his brow, saying in the chocolate shop, "I have the oddest feeling I've seen this serpent's head before." A slashed tapestry, long missing, the only link between the Culhaine Collar and my mother's ring.

Intrigue. Conversation overheard in the conservatory. Marina's voice. Threatening? Warning? Marina knowing of the theft, saying there was danger.

It was no use; it made no sense to me. I had the oddest feeling that I stood on the edge of something, some piece of fact or logic which would make all things plain. But I could not see it. And suddenly I simply didn't care. Ross and Marina were so sure, so positive that the source of all Damaris' illnesses was herself—her unbalanced mind, her need to punish herself, her need to bind us near. Why could not I accept that and leave the problem in their hands, where it belonged? Marina had flung the truth at me that night: there had been trouble ever since I came.

I should not have come. I had known that for some time—for many reasons. I stared down into the depths of my mother's ring and the great ruby gleamed at me quietly like molten blood.

What impulse or what thought impelled me, I cannot say, but the fingers of my other hand moved steadily, inexorably, to the serpent head and pressed down the tiny darting tongue. Pressed it as Warren had, that day in the chocolate shop, and as then, the stone sprang up, revealing the shallow well beneath.

As then—no, *not* as then. Lightning-sharp, an acute clarity of thought descended. Then there had been a faint sediment as of jeweler's paste in the well's corners. Now the hollow was half-filled with a whitish powder.

I slammed it shut, breathing as though I had been running hard. I was jumping to conclusions. All the same, no power on earth could have persuaded me to follow one's usual impulse and taste that powder. And it was at that moment that my nebulous feelings crystallized into rock-hard conviction.

Damaris might be poisoning herself, but she would never have put that powder in the ring to incriminate me. Had she wanted me accused, she had only to have voiced publicly her belief about the poisoned milk. Stay; had the sugar and vanilla vanished because they were *not* poisoned? No, it would have been easier to have adulterated those than to have put this suggestive powder in my ring . . . which, for all my facile words to Warren Sloane, stood easily accessible on my bureau every night.

Damaris would never have wanted me accused.

Unless, as Marina said, she really was insane?

Start over; start from logic, not belief, on solid, provable ground. Start with this latest poisoning attempt. Damaris had either taken arsenic herself, or it had been in the milk I served her. If the arsenic had been self-administered, Damaris knew enough, had been scared enough the day of her earlier attack, not to take a lethal dose. The alternative could only be that she had meant to kill herself. But why? Damaris had been happy on Christmas Eve, genuinely happy. I would stake my life on it. It was not only the passionate embrace onto which I'd stumbled, but the look in her eyes at Midnight Mass, her breathless voice saying, "I am so happy! I have a secret—" She had been radiant at that moment. What could have happened afterwards to make her want to take her life?

I had seen it, hadn't I? Her startled look, as memory rushed back, then terror, cold and still. Afterwards, the light had vanished from her eyes, and she had never told' her happy news.

I willed my mind back, thinking hard. What had happened in the conservatory at that moment? Nothing much. Only a hint of footsteps, a sense of hidden presence bringing back another memory to my own mind. Only the ivy parting as Warren Sloane appeared.

From where? The house? Or that hidden, as-yet-undiscovered outside door? Was it Warren Sloane whom Marina had met in secret and had threatened?

It added up, to a sum which made me ill, not only for Damaris but for myself.

Warren Sloane poisoning Damaris? I could not believe it. *If they were wed,* an evil serpent whispered in my mind, *if he stood to inherit, then perhaps . . .* Damaris' voice came back to me: *"Warren Sloane is in love with the Culhaine Collection. It's like a sickness . . . He'd give his life for it."* Damaris had also said, *"I am a piece of the Culhaine Collection."* Damaris had trusted him, without illusions. She needed him. Enough to kill herself if something happened to destroy that trust?

Yes.

What was not in character was her accusing me. If Damaris really meant to die, she would do so openly, and damn the world. I dropped my head on my hands. I was exhausted, and no closer to a solution than I had been before.

The days of the week dragged on as we went through the motions of our daily lives. The Christmas tree in the conservatory was taken down. I kept my hands busy mending tapestries and laces, wishing I could keep my mind profitably occupied as well. I went for walks, through other parts of town, keeping clear of my accustomed routes and any chance encounters. I dined formally with Ross and with Marina, making inane small talk for benefit of the servants. Marina looked terrible. As for Ross, who could tell what he was thinking? Special nurses, spelled occasionally by Maggie, stayed with Damaris night and day. She did not wish to see any of us, the doctor reported, looking sober.

"Undoubtedly a feature of her illness. You must not alarm yourselves. She is at present suffering from many strange delusions, but it will pass."

Ross nodded coldly, but the muscle in his temple worked. "We will take her back to Italy when she is able. My sister-in-law was right. I hoped by bringing her here to force her to accept reality, but instead I've fair destroyed her."

So it was from Maggie that I received most of my bulletins about Damaris. Dear loyal, loving, garrulous Maggie—what would I have done without her? Maggie would hear gossip in the servants' hall, would overhear bits of technical shop talk when she served the nurses' meals, would observe with her own folk wisdom when in Damaris' room, and then, lacking anyone else she felt free to speak with, she would come to me.

"They do be sayin' she took the dreadful stuff herself. She'd never! That's a mortal sin, that is, and the sweet lamb knows it!"

"Would it still be a mortal sin if she were not in her right senses?"

"And that's another wickedness they're sayin'!" Maggie retorted darkly. "I tell you, miss, if my sweet child be out of her right mind, it's because evil souls are seeking to drive her from it!"

Another time, "The poor lass is fair delirious, and that fine doctor doing nothing for it! That Mr. Sloane, no better than he ought to be as I've often said, but meaning well, sent a beautiful boo-kay. And her that loved flowers won't have it in the room! Got it into her head the flowers are messengers whispering evil things!"

Damaris was not rallying as she should. Whether it was the result of a brain fever, or the arsenic, or her general poor health we were not sure. Shut up together by our mutual apprehension, we waited, and snow fell inexorably outside the lavender window-panes.

One day—the afternoon of New Year's Eve, it was— Hopkins came to me. "There's a person on the doorstep, miss, with a message for you. Refuses to give it to anyone but you."

I went down to find an urchin of indeterminate age and sex awaiting me. "Be you Miss 'Vinia Stanton?"

"Yes, I am. You have a message for me?" I held out my hand, and the mite nodded in approbation.

"You're the right one, miss. 'E said I was to know you by the ring." A smeared and wrinkled envelope was pressed into my hand and the child was off, lost in the steadily falling snow.

Some instinct bade me go at once upstairs. In my room, door shut, I turned immediately to the envelope. It was sealed, and its address blurred by wet, but the writing inside was immediately recognizable, though with no salutation and no signature.

I am half out of my head with worry, and that Cerberus at your door will tell me nothing. Will you please come? I must know what is going on. You can come safely—not proper, perhaps, but here at least there's no chance of your being seen.

It concluded with an address; a mews lane I recognized which ran off Beacon Hill.

I dressed and went. I told myself it was to find out what Damaris was keeping from me, that elusive "secret"; I went armoured with heavy winter wraps and with suspicion.

I did not walk toward the Public Garden in my usual manner but cut through Exeter to Beacon Street and beyond, to the lane along the river. The water itself was grey and turgid and I followed it, behind the backs of houses, until the river curved and I went inland up a steeply cobbled hill. Narrow brick houses, one room wide, with black shutters and shiny knockers, marching one higher than the other in tight-packed rows . . . This was old Boston, the Boston of colonists and patriots, and despite my mind's preoccupation, it soothed my soul. My footprints were lost at once in the soft whiteness of the all-concealing snow. No one was about; here and there in windows, lamps burned softly. I turned into the lane I had come to find and began watching for the number. The dwellings here were poorer, mostly flats over stables or rooms rented out by impecunious genteel widows. The one I sought had paint that was slightly peeling, but the brass dolphin doorknocker shone smartly.

Warren opened the door at once and pulled me in and up the stairs. "Lavinia, thank God. You're a saint of mercy. Take off your wraps, and your boots too, if the suggestion won't offend you. You must be soaked." He marshaled me into a Boston rocker by a small coal fire. "What in the name of all that's holy is happening in that Marlborough mausoleum?"

"Damaris almost died," I said baldly. "An overdose of arsenic. As I believe you know."

"I got that much out of your guardian dragon, but no more. He said it was an accident."

"Damaris says she took the stuff herself. Did he tell you that?"

"I don't believe it!" His astonishment seemed genuine. "It makes no sense!"

"You have been saying all along she was being poisoned. Doesn't it seem a bit odd you had so much foreknowledge?"

Warren stared at me. "What in God's name are you saying?"

"Only what you have said, that something's going on. I have an odd feeling that I'm being used as some kind of connecting link, and I don't like it." I felt myself commencing to shake, but I kept my voice in control.

"And you're saying I'm part of this—deception?"

"I think you are. Damaris was happy on Christmas Eve, that's why I don't believe she'd kill herself. Or take an overdose, either, after the last experience. She had a secret. She wouldn't tell me what it was. I think I know, although I have no proof. That's why I've come to you."

Our eyes met in silence. "Perhaps I should tell you," I added, "that I came into the ballroom the night of the twenty-fourth."

"Oh," Warren said. He ran his fingers through his hair. After a few moments he murmured, "What am I thinking of? You must be perishing for some hot tea," and went over and busied himself with the little brass kettle that was steaming on the hob. He had, it seemed, a remarkable tea prepared—lemon slices spiked with cloves, cakes from a pastry shop, apples roasting on the hearth. His room was small but charming; a few good pieces of furniture, a few good prints. "My home away from home," he said, handing me a teacup. "I'll not be here much longer now, though. My permanent position, of course, is with the museum in New York."

Warren sat down on the sofa opposite, gazing at me with an equivocal expression. "You are right, of course," he said at last. "I did—how shall I put it?—lay at Damaris' feet my hand and heart, and she paid me the honor of accepting." He raised his own hand. "You needn't speak. I know quite well what the reaction of her fond pater would be. Hence the deep dark secret." His face belied the sardonic humor of his tone. "A deception, granted, and highly improbable, but if it makes her feel good, what's the harm?"

"Does that mean you were not serious about it?"

"You think I would do that to her?" Warren asked sharply. "I am very much in earnest. I am also cynical enough to

know that such a marriage will not be allowed to happen—
one way or another."

"What does *that* mean?"

"Damaris was poisoned," Warren said bluntly. "Since then
I've not been allowed to see her. She refuses my messages and
flowers. They've gotten to her somehow, and Lord only
knows what she's being told."

He did not know that nothing we could say against him
would be any news to her. Besides—

"It was before that," I said suddenly. "Something she
found herself. I saw her face. You came through the ivy curtain, as though you'd been standing for a time on the other
side, and she remembered something."

All Damaris' memories relating to the conservatory . . .
Warren had spoken of things at times which he ought not to
have known . . . "Had you been there before?" I asked
abruptly. "Before they went to Italy, before the accident?
Did you know Damaris' mother?"

It was a shot at random, but Warren went very still. After
a time he let his breath out in something like a shudder. "It
would explain," he said at last, slowly. "Her change of manner; perhaps—God help me—perhaps even the arsenic, if she
misinterpreted, if she thought . . ." He swallowed painfully.
"Yes, I knew her mother. I was a bright young thing, eager
and bushy-tailed, in love with a world which I could not
afford. I was apprenticed, you might say, to an art restorer;
I'd been sent up here to work with a local gallery, with an
eye to making acquisitions for the shop back home. One day
she came into the gallery."

"Damaris' mother?"

He nodded. "I was high on a ladder, making surreptitious
notes for my real employer on a certain picture—it was listed
in the gallery catalogue as a minor work, but I had reason to
believe it might be a major find. A voice hailed me. She was
standing below, looking up at me. She ordered me to come

down at once so she herself could climb up and view the picture. She was wearing white, as she often did, and never a mark on it even after she'd clambered up that dusty ladder. She made me give her my hand to steady her as she came down."

"What was she like?" I said softly. "Make me see her."

"Isabella?" Warren's voice changed, warmed. "Golden. There's a phrase from the old myths that seemed to fit her—'daughter of the sun.' Her dark eyes had that same golden light. She had the same power her sister has, to kindle warmth, but she was—very kind. I found that, that first day. I was right about the picture, she said; it was very valuable; she would make her husband buy it. I would have the commission, and I was not to tell my employers back at home. She took an interest in my career, she was able to steer several small sales my way. She was a—very great lady, and I was grateful. Nothing more. I would not have dared. And if Damaris believes otherwise, she is terribly mistaken."

"The day of the accident—you were there? Is that what she remembers?"

"It must be. *She* sent for me." It was clear that he meant Isabella. "She knew of a business transaction, she said, which would be to my advantage. I must come discreetly and let no one see, for it would not do for her to be known to favor one craftsman above another. I came when she bid me, but I could hear at once that there were others in the room. There was an argument going on, so I withdrew behind the ivy till we should be alone. Then all at once there was a scream—"

He closed his eyes. "That is why, you see," he went on in a dry voice, "I can understand what Damaris has been going through, better than the others. I heard the accident happen. But she *saw*."

There was no sound in the room save for the coal fire crackling on the hearth. "There was a smell," he said slowly, "a smell like burning cloth. And a faint frying sound, even after the screams had stopped. I didn't have to see, I have pictured it in my mind's eye ever since . . . that lovely, lovely face . . . No one had seen me enter. I got out of there fast and spent the first moments being very sick indeed. Afterwards, discretion seemed the better part of valor. I went back to New York, plunged into my career, and prospered. Then this winter, the museum proposed to send me up to Boston— the marchesa had sought an expert to assist with the unveiling of the Culhaine Collection. I knew how Isabella had been scorned in Boston. It seemed—well, to be blunt, my ideas roughly coincided with the great Culhaine's. Working on the Collection seemed a way to perpetuate Isabella's memory and make the city that had snubbed her to eat crow. I was safely anonymous. No one knew me here. And so I came."

"And met Damaris."

Warren nodded. "And met Damaris, who is to her mother as the bud is to the rose. A bud being systematically blighted by those two damned proud fools. For her mother's sake, I was determined not to let that happen."

"Hence your proposal."

I did not mean to sound sardonic, but I must have, for Warren shot me a level look. "And for Damaris' sake, and definitely for my own. I do love her, Lavinia."

Yes, I could believe that, in a way. But I knew something more as well. Despite his protestations, his undoubted worship from afar, he had been and still was head over heels in love with Isabella Culhaine.

"And now what?"

"Now," Warren said firmly, "we must find some way to make Damaris safe from harm. I can't get to her; she'd not listen anyway, if what you say is true. Can't you return to New York and take her with you? Kidnap her if necessary."

"I can't go back to New York. I—have no family there, or property. I was employed there, but my job no more exists."

"I'm sorry, I thought . . . Anyway, the important thing is to get her out of that house, somewhere, somehow. You had better leave here now, Lavinia, before you're missed. We will think of something."

"Do you really think," I asked slowly, "that Damaris could have taken the poison herself, because of what she remembered?"

"There's another possibility, you know," Warren said, looking at me oddly. "Has it never crossed your mind? Damaris believes she is responsible for Isabella's death. And Ross adored his wife—adored her with a passion bordering on obsession."

So troubled was I at this thought that I was halfway home before I realized I had never asked Warren whether he had been the mysterious person Marina had been talking to in the conservatory.

Ross. I tried to blot out the suggestion Warren had made, but it insinuated itself like a worm in the apple of temptation. Insinuated, and would not go away.

I turned the corner blindly into Marlborough Street, battling against the storm. The lamps in the lavender windows all were lit, and I could see Ross in his library, standing motionless and remote before the fire. A Prince of Darkness? Yes. But Milton's poem was also about something more, about covenants made and broken. There, in the snow and cold, I faced in a kind of irrevocable illumination what I now long had known—good or evil, better or worse, without a word spoken, *whatever* he was, I was indissolubly covenanted to Ross Culhaine.

XVIII

It was quite the custom, in Boston as in New York, this making of New Year's calls. It meant an all-day open house, collations, the celebrating of old friendships and cementing of new ones; it meant, inevitably, manipulations and flirtations, the exploiting of slight acquaintance for social or business advantages. In the House of Culhaine it meant today a bitter and ironic masquerade. For Damaris' illness was not to be allowed to become known. "Those damned proud fools," Warren had said. I did not know whether to admire, or scorn, or weep.

What I did do was don my aubergine silk, and coil my hair with more than usual care, and go down to play my role of gracious guest. Damaris was much better, but she would not come down. She had demanded shrilly that her doors be locked, and refused to leave her room.

"Which is just as well, all things considered," Marina said. "In her disoriented condition, who knows what fantasies she might blurt out." She pressed her hand hard against her forehead for a moment, then moved on determinedly, attending to last-minute details. It was hard for me to adjust to the change which had come over Marina the past few weeks. Or was it just that earlier I had been bemused by glamour? She was thinner, and the lines of her face now seemed sharp. Moreover she looked, for the first time, quite fully Ross's age. I had always assumed she was the younger of the sisters, but I began to realize this might not be so. The most noticeable change was the pain which had been in her eyes of late. She might be the dark sister of the legend, as I now well believed, but she was genuinely and deeply anguished at Damaris' illness.

Her ability to play the role of femme fatale was unimpaired, however, and I could not but admire the grace and charm with which she moved among her guests. "So kind of you to come . . . So nice to see you . . . No, our debutante is not down today; she has never been well, you know, and these New England winters—so debilitating . . . Devastated, of course, but I would not allow her to attempt it. Such a social whirl it's been, one's first season, disastrous to a frail constitution . . . One must exert control. . . ." Artfully, skillfully painting the portrait of a social butterfly much in demand, while upstairs Damaris, webbed in by God-knows-what mental nightmares, shuddered behind locked doors and tight-drawn curtains. I had learned as much from Maggie.

"Such a state she's in, miss. Taken a fancy the New Year's bringing in some dreadful thing. Made the nurse promise not to unlock the door till every guest had gone. She wouldn't even see her aunt, and the marchesa was that undone."

In the late afternoon Warren Sloane arrived, wearing his insouciance like a mask. He pulled me off into the alcove. "I figured this was a good day to storm the citadel, among all the other guests. Hopkins gave me a curdling glance, but he daredn't stop me. Lavinia, you've got to get me in to see Damaris."

"Not a chance. She won't speak to me; she wouldn't even see Marina."

"How is she?"

"Better, Maggie says. At least . . ."

"Better in body but not in mind? Don't flinch like that, we've got to face it squarely. It would take the constitution of an ox to come unwarped through the things Damaris has endured, and her strength is in her spirit only."

He did not finish, but we both were thinking the same thing. If something happened to break her spirit, what was left? Something *had* happened. Damaris seemed to have remembered, or discovered, a connection between her lover and her mother, a connection crystallized in the memory of Isabella's dreadful death.

"God, Vinnie. *God.* If she thought—and if it made her—if it's pushed her finally over the edge—"

"Steady."

Warren smiled raggedly. "It is the port talking. It is very good, and I have had too much. I needed it. I am speaking like a melodramatic fool, but I swear to you, Vinnie, if what we think is true, Romeo at his loved ones' deaths shall be as nothing to me. The Sloanes are not noble, but they shall nobly do."

"You *have* had too much port," I said firmly. "Go home, Warren. As things are, you can do nothing other than make them worse."

"I salute you for your intuition, and I take my leave. I shall linger only to make felicitations to our honored hostess." He departed, somewhat unsteadily, toward Marina, while I watched with some alarm. Marina was adroit, however; she had him off from the others in a moment, pouring him coffee, serving him herself. I saw him talking earnestly to her; she smiled, shrugged, nodded, and eased him unobtrusively over to Hopkins, who saw him out the door. I remember feeling grateful in a way for that New Year's masquerade, grateful that the guests and the necessity for my own pretending did not allow me time to think. I expected that once I was alone, upstairs, my inexorable brain would not let me sleep, but I was wrong, probably because I too, in a mild way, had partaken of the port. I slept soundly, though my sleep was peopled by tiny tapestried figures moving through a formal dance.

I came down to breakfast the next morning to find Ross and Marina both at table, determinedly matter-of-fact. Business as usual, it seemed, was to be the theme for the new year. There was talk of booking passage on a ship to Italy, as soon as Damaris was pronounced well enough to travel. As for the Renaissance Fête—"I'll call on Madame Cabot in a few days and tell her it's indefinitely postponed, that we're going abroad for the balance of the winter for Damaris' health. She will not like it, but there is little she can do." Marina was being uncharacteristically plain-spoken. "The servants will know the truth, of course, I daresay hers already do, but they won't talk. Thank fortune for the class loyalty that exists below the stairs."

"And your Mr. Sloane?" Ross inquired coldly.

"He is not *my* Mr. Sloane." Marina frowned. "That is more difficult, certainly. But I doubt he would jeopardize his own professional opportunities by injudicious gossip. *Caro,* could you not agree to a loan of just part of the Collection to his New York museum before it's packed away?"

"No." Ross was emphatic. "I shall make that perfectly clear to Sloane today. He *is* coming?"

"Yes, indeed. He said he wants to complete the last details of that value certification for your approval. Considering his proclivity for early-morning impressing of employers, I am surprised he is not here already."

The morning passed; I engaged myself in the absorption of mending tapestries in the sewing room, and when I came down to luncheon, Warren still had not appeared. That seemed odd; knowing how anxious Warren had been to gain admittance to the house, I had expected him to leap at this opportunity. I began to wonder what he had meant by his grandiose parting remarks the previous afternoon. "Nobly do"—what?

We were just finishing our sweet when Hopkins appeared in the dining room door, looking what was for him considerably disturbed.

"A person to see you, sir. A police person. He requires to see all of the household at your earliest convenience."

Ross frowned. My own mind leaped in two widely divergent paths. The stolen objects—had one of them been found and traced to the Culhaine Collection? I felt quite certain Ross had never reported the thefts to the police; he would, he had said, handle it himself. Or had Dr. Martinson been having second thoughts about the arsenic being self-administered? Marina had gone deathly pale, and I saw Ross steady her elbow with his hand to steer her out the door. She murmured something to him faintly, about scandal, and he bent to answer. At the small intimacy, a knife twisted in my own heart. I steeled myself against it.

Hopkins had left the "police person" in the hall, obviously uncertain where to place him in the social hierarchy. He proved to be a heavyset, matter-of-fact New Englander. "Sorry to bother you, sir, ladies. Been some trouble this morning which we expect you can help clear up. Are these all the members of the household who were present yesterday, Mr. Culhaine?"

"My daughter," Ross said curtly. "She is an invalid, has not been out of her bed for several days. I scarcely think you need disturb her, officer."

"As you say. I should like your permission to interview the servants afterwards, however." His manner made it clear that the phrasing of a request was merely a formality.

"Can we get on with this? Let us step into the drawing

room, where the ladies can sit down." Ross's tone was pointed, but the officer ignored it and settled himself four-square on one of the larger of the drawing-room chairs. He took out a notebook and contemplated several entries, moistening each page with his finger before turning it, a habit I always have detested.

"You have an employee here by the name of Warren Sloane?"

"Scarcely an employee," Ross answered frigidly. "He is on leave of absence from the firm that engages him, a museum in New York. He has been doing some inventory and evaluation work for me, yes, but on a free-lance basis. May I ask what concern that is of the Boston police?"

"A good deal of concern, as it happens," the officer responded bluntly. "Mr. Sloane is dead."

It was Marina who gasped, but my own heart pounded, my eyes ached with unshed tears. Ross became very cold and still. "It seems impossible," he said calmly. "He was here yesterday, and seemed extremely well."

"So we understand."

He is playing cat and mouse with us, I thought.

"Do you intend to tell us how and why he died?" So Ross thought so, too.

The cat eyes in the broad face were watching, watching, but the tone was affable. "Some time last night, it seems. His landlady sent in a call for us this morning, when she couldn't arouse him. The cause of death, from the preliminary report, was arsenic."

I did not cry out. My corset held my backbone rigid but my fingernails dug into my palms under the cover of my spreading skirt.

Ross's eyebrow raised. So coolly; a consummate actor. "Are you seriously suggesting, officer, that anyone should have cause to murder Mr. Sloane?"

The word was out now, open, not to be taken back. I saw

Marina's eyes close tightly, convulsively, as though pain had struck her.

Then relief, absurd, ironic. The policeman shaking his head, saying mildly, "Not at all. We have good reason to presume the death was self-inflicted."

Suicide. Was that what Warren had meant? *"Romeo at his loved ones' death shall be as nothing."* Romeo had died by a swift-acting poison.

"His landlady said he had been here yesterday. We understand someone from here visited him a day or so ago. We hoped you could confirm his motives, as we have reconstructed them."

"Of course, officer. My brother-in-law and I shall be glad to offer any help we can." Marina was summoning her reserves of strength, being gracious. "I saw at once when he was here yesterday that the poor young man did seem disturbed."

The walls of the Culhaines were closing, shutting all links to trouble out. Ross was nodding, saying, "He has seemed unstable. I have reasons to be, shall we say, suspicious of his business dealings? Also, he seemed to be developing highly unsuitable attachments . . . He had been, I may say, consuming a good deal too much spirits yesterday. My daughter declined to see him. Yes, I can see where in that irrational condition—"

"No!"

The voice came from the stairs, and it was Damaris' voice. She clung to the railing, her nightgown and negligee trailing like gravecloths, her eyes wild and her hair disheveled. She looked like an overwrought, operatic Ophelia, and she shocked us all so thoroughly that for one terrible moment I almost laughed.

"Warren did not kill himself. He would not! *Never!*" I had not known Damaris was given to eavesdropping. She clutched her nightclothes together with one trembling hand

and her voice grew shrill. "I know what killed him. If you do not tell them, Papa, then I will!"

"Now, what—" the officer began, but Ross cut in coldly, saying, "Perhaps you had better listen to her yourself."

"Yes, listen! Oh, God, if I had only listened . . . I thought I could escape it, but I was wrong." Suddenly, shockingly, Damaris began to laugh. "The curse of the Culhaines! Anyone, anything that we love is doomed. Just ask my father! Our love can kill, and I loved him, oh, I did love him . . ."

I moved towards her instinctively, and so did Ross, but she thrust us off, screaming, "*No!*", making the sign of the evil eye against us. It was to Marina that she ran, and Marina gathered tight with a look on her face that shook me to my roots. I had never thought her capable of such possessive love, such pity, and such fear.

"You see, you must see—" Marina's voice was shaking. "The poor *bambina*, she is not responsible—"

The policeman nodded heavily, and closed his book. A few of the masks in the House of Culhaine at last were off.

"I won't trouble you further. It explains a great deal," he said cryptically, nodding towards Damaris, who had subsided to a sort of animal moaning. "I may have to come back to you later about some business details, but I'll not disturb the ladies." He bowed, and went, and we were left together.

"*Carissimo*, we must go, go quickly!" Marina flung back her head, staring at Ross over Damaris' hair. "The police, I do not trust them. They will return. They will pry and poke, and they will find out *she* has admitted having arsenic. Oh, *caro*, I am afraid!"

"We must not allow ourselves to become hysterical," Ross said. I looked at him and saw that Damaris' words had struck him like a stone. "No one is suggesting Damaris had anything to do with this."

"But they will! They will start to think, this fellow liked himself too much to kill himself, and they will say it is not *he* who was insane. They will find out about the arsenic, and more, and they will guess at everything! Everything we have labored so to do will be for nothing! *Caro*, I beg of you! We must go away so there will be no more deaths!"

"*Silenzio!*" Ross said sharply, and followed with staccato Italian. Marina paled, but her hysteria stilled. Ross's voice returned to that flat, emotionless tone. "Right now we must get the child upstairs to bed. You had better do it, since she will not let us near her. Perhaps it would be wise to send for Dr. Martinson."

"He knows too much already. I will take care of her," Marina said quietly. She eased Damaris towards the stairs, murmuring to her softly, holding her closely as Damaris cowered to her. I turned away and closed my eyes.

"I had best begin checking into Sloane's relations," Ross said at last, "whether he had any family in New York, what we can do to assist with funeral arrangements. The fellow was working for us, after all."

Noblesse oblige. I heard his footsteps, less brisk than usual, recede into the library, and the doors swung closed.

I wished I had something to occupy my time. There were the tapestries; I climbed the stairs doggedly to the sewing room and set about my mending, but it was not a good decision. The tapestries made pictures of Warren swim before me, and the implications of all that had just been said were heavy in my thoughts.

XIX

Boston is a city rife with provincial gossip, and by nightfall, innuendos and speculations were springing up like rank weeds in the columns of the evening paper. Warren's frequent visits to the Marlborough Street house, his attentions to Damaris on Christmas Eve and at the ball had been noticed and were enlarged upon. I thanked fortune that Damaris was too ill to read them. For Damaris lay upstairs in her hothouse bedroom, tossing and turning in a delirium of nightmare.

The morning papers sprang the sensation of the mysterious female visitor to Warren's rooms, and a chill ran up my own spine. I was very glad I was alone at the breakfast table when I read them. At present, apparently, the scandalmongers assumed that caller was Damaris, for they did not know that she had been too ill. I pressed my hands together hard beneath the tablecloth, where the too-alert Sarah could not see them, and wondered what I ought to do.

In midafternoon Hopkins announced that the "police person" had come again and wished to see us all. Apparently he had first been interviewing the servants below-stairs, for I caught a glimpse of Sarah, looking overexcited, and Maggie, looking grim. The officer was already established, seated, in the library when we arrived, a distinction whose significance Ross caught at once. He went round pointedly and sat down himself in his doge's chair behind his desk.

"Well, officer? I thought you said you would not disturb the ladies here again."

"Sorry, but the picture has changed since yesterday." The man was affably implacable.

"In what way?"

"For one thing, you said Sloane was doing work for you, but you did not explain why you had kept him on after you knew he had been systematically pilfering from you." The inspector's left hand had been in his pocket; now he reached out and placed something on the desk. A tiny silver box.

Ross's eyebrow lifted. "What makes you think I knew about any thefts?"

"I think you did. You've employed a detective to shadow him since shortly before your daughter's ball."

A faint ejaculation came from Marina.

"You said for *one* thing . . . ?" Ross said evenly.

"For another, you also neglected to tell us that you had made arrangements through Sloane to donate a sizable portion of your collection to the art museum in New York."

If he was looking for a reaction from Ross, he got it, but in silence. Almost at once the iron mask was up, and his voice was cold. "I don't know where you have picked up that piece of misinformation, but it is utter balderdash. Wishful thinking, or injudicious bragging on Sloane's part, I have no doubt, but nothing more."

"I am afraid there is. We have legal papers, signed by Sloane as witness, bearing what purports to be your signature."

"Then they are forgeries." The muscle was working in Ross's cheek, but he maintained his level calm. "I knew about the counterfeit art objects, yes. Perhaps in your eyes I was remiss in not reporting them. But in my own, sir, retrieving the originals was more important than serving your ideas of justice. I felt I had my best chance of so doing by keeping him here, under my own surveillance." He nodded towards me. "Miss Stanton, who I might point out is a recognized authority, can confirm that I carefully catalogued the counterfeits some months ago, and made note of all substitutions since."

"And that is the only reason you kept the fellow on?" What was he suggesting, blackmail? My mind flashed back to that overheard conversation in the conservatory.

Ross was silent for some time. "The man was a protégé of my wife's," he said at last. "For her sake, I wished to make very sure of my ground before any accusations were made, and to keep them private."

I caught a glimpse of Marina's face; no doubting it, she had received a shock.

"You were not concerned about his attentions to your daughter?"

"My daughter, I fear, is going to have to become accustomed to fortune hunters courting her for her wealth." How coldly he said it. "In this case, I saw no need to disillusion her. Nothing would come of it; she has not been well and we are returning to Italy shortly for her health."

"Not so unwell as to prevent her visiting Sloane's rooms in a blizzard some few days past."

"It was not Damaris," I heard my own voice saying. I had not made any conscious decision so to speak, yet even as I was doing so I knew that this was right. I, at least, had come to an end of playing games. I straightened and looked the inspector directly in the eye. "As you no doubt know, I received a note from Mr. Sloane that afternoon, asking me to come. He is a business associate, and we had rather become friends."

"To the extent of visiting unchaperoned at his lodgings?"

My body was commencing to shake. I willed it still. "I am a businesswoman, Inspector. Many things are perfectly proper for an independent gentlewoman pursuing a profession which would be quite unsuitable for a young girl such as Miss Culhaine."

"Your meeting with Sloane that day was purely business?"

"I did not say that. He was concerned about Damaris. She had been ill, and he had not been allowed to see her. He was extremely worried."

"About what? Her health, or possible exposure of his thefts?"

"Precisely what are you suggesting, Inspector?" Ross cut in sharply.

The inspector turned a bland face. "Only that his attempts to infatuate your daughter provided him with a temporary defense against charges of nefarious activity, since you did not wish to disillusion her and he doubtless knew it. With her ill, and—er, unable to comprehend what was going on," he delicately skated around blunt mention of her mental state, "you might not hesitate to expose him. Especially if, as you say, the contracts with the museum in New York were forged. To a man of his, ah, sensibilities, suicide could indeed seem preferable to the consequences of his acts." The inspector apparently had no high opinion of a man who spent his time in the pursuit of works of art.

"Will that be all, then?" Ross inquired frigidly.

"Except for coming down to Headquarters tomorrow, if you will, to sign a statement and identify the property which we've reclaimed. We'll have an expert meanwhile examining the signatures you say are forged. I imagine there will be no great difficulty to prove the point. Oh, yes." He consulted his notes. "I understand you have requested the body be released to you if there are no next of kin. That will be quite in order. And thank *you*, miss." He bowed to me. "Coming forward frankly with an admission cannot but have caused you personal discomfort."

I nodded distantly, feeling very conscious I had not come off well in the encounter.

The interview worked its way to a close with perfunctory comments. Mortuary arrangements were made. So Warren would be buried at Culhaine expense, his death tidily labeled and filed, and there were none to mourn except myself, who was not quite a friend, and Damaris, who was not quite more and who did not even know. Something was wrong somewhere. I pressed my fingers against my temples and closed my eyes.

The inspector went, shown out by Hopkins, who shut the door behind him with an air of distant satisfaction. The walls of the Culhaines were rising again, impenetrable, inviolable. My head began to ache intolerably.

"I must go back to Damaris," Marina said half-inaudibly, and hurried off. I waited only until I was sure I would not be going with her, then rose to follow. A too-familiar starburst exploded in my inner vision as I stood.

"Lavinia." Ross spoke to stop me, and I cursed my headache for slowing me so that I seemed to heed.

"I want to thank you—for what you did just now. For Damaris' sake."

"You could have told as much. Surely your detective must have reported back about my visit."

"Yes. But I would not have spoken."

"The gentleman, protecting my tarnished reputation?" I laughed, too shrilly. The throbbing behind my eyelids drummed like thunder. "I did not, you see, heed your earlier advice."

"So I notice. And though worse for you, it may in the long run prove better for us all. Why did he really want to talk to you, Lavinia?"

The ticking of the clock in the corner sounded unnaturally loud.

"Was he trying to find out about the thefts, or about the arsenic?" Ross's voice went on inexorably. "Did he say anything about my wife?"

Unbidden, the picture Warren had conjured of Isabella's death leaped up in my mind's eyes, and I pressed my hands before my face. Thank God the inspector had said nothing to call it back. Whoever it was said truth was easier than falsehood, had been wrong; they were both traps. Something was wrong, something was terribly wrong, the pieces of the puzzle lay just beyond my edge of thought and suddenly I did not want to find them. Suddenly I knew what I had to do, ought to have done long before. The pressure of pain diminished as if by magic.

"I want to tell you," my voice came as from a great distance, "that I am leaving. At once, as soon as I can pack. There is no more good I can do here."

"Lavinia!" Ross strode over and caught me by the shoulders before I could jerk away. "This is ridiculous. You are overwrought. Where will you go?"

"I don't know. It doesn't matter. If I am worth the salary you are paying me, I will find some work."

"Damaris needs you, now more than ever."

"You know she will not even let me near her. In any event, you are going back to Italy."

"I had hoped you would come with us."

"No!" I shook my head, but he held me tightly.

"Lavinia, be sensible! I know you are upset, you were fond of Sloane, but stop acting on emotions and use your brains! I have a responsibility—"

"To whom? To Damaris?" My voice came without my own volition, and without volition, too, my hand swept up, thrusting my mother's ring before his eyes. "Or are you trying to buy peace from me for the wrong you did my father? Did you kill him when you stole the collar?"

It happened so quickly. His hands dropped and I was free,

so suddenly that I almost fell. I caught myself and fled, up the stairs and into my own room, gagging and choking, my stays digging into me painfully with my gasping breath. Like a mad thing, I dragged out carpetbags and trunk, swept clothes off hangers. I would be gone, gone to New York before nightfall, if I had to sleep the night in Washington Square. And somewhere, someday, there would be an end to dreams of a Prince of Darkness.

"Lavinia." In my haste I had not locked the door and he had not knocked, had come in unbidden, knowing that otherwise he would not gain entrance. "Lavinia, look at me."

His voice was very quiet, with not even that edge of threat it often held. I turned. He was standing just inside the open door, the Culhaine Collar dangling from his hand. As I stared, mesmerized, he held it out.

"I have come to apologize. And to explain, if you will let me. Take it, Lavinia. It is rightly yours."

I could not move. He shrugged and, with a sigh, dropped it on the bed. The rubies sparkled in the late light and Leo, stirring among the pillows, pounced upon them. Ross's mouth twisted.

"He's dazzled. Just as I was. Lavinia, will you permit me to sit down? This has been an extremely trying day."

At my nod he dropped into the high-backed chair beside the fire and I sat opposite him, rigidly, on the edge of the chaise. He looked very tired.

"I should like to tell you an old story, if you will allow me. It will be, I think, a relief to have done with it at last. You have stumbled onto part of it already, I have known that for some time from your changed manner. I have known, from the time that Eustace died, that one day I should tell you. What I did not know was that in the interim I would come to love you." His eyes were ironic. "Love. I had never expected to hear myself use that word again. As my daughter said, for us it has been a curse."

"Who was my father?" I said tautly.

He did not answer me directly. "I told you how as a lad I shipped out to sea. With a man's ambition, but a child's head filled with visions of adventure and romance." He laughed shortly. "It took not three days out to disabuse me. A ship can be a cruel autocracy, and only one man aboard was human enough to feel for a frightened boy. His name was Andrew Stanton, a renegade Scottish Covenanter and the unlikeliest man who ever became first mate. By the time we put into our second port, he had also become my friend."

"You left him to die." I had not meant to say that; the words came of themselves from my dry throat. Ross shot me a look.

"You've heard about the fire? I'm not surprised. This town is rife with rumors about the origin of the Culhaine Collection. Surely you can't believe—Yes, you can, can't you? he said slowly. "I swear to you, Lavinia, by—by the collar, which may have more weight with you than Culhaine honor, I was not responsible, directly or indirectly, for your father's death."

I did not speak, and after a moment he went on. "Andrew had won the collar one night in Genoa, at cards. He didn't recognize its historic worth, but he knew it must have value, and he was jubilant. You see, he had married shortly before our ship had sailed, but his wife and he had parted on bad terms after a great quarrel. His Marianna did not want him to sail again. She was afraid, but he was determined to ship out the last time, to seek a nest egg on which to start his life on land. He knew what it was to have a family and no money; that's why he was so understanding of me. He used to dream aloud to me, of striding home and laying the collar before his bride. It had a ruby drop then," he nodded towards my finger, "and he shipped that home, as token of what was to come, but he was afraid to trust the collar unguarded on the seas. Then one night, when we were halfway around the world, there was a fire."

He stopped. "Have you ever seen pictures of Japan, Lavinia? Small houses, crowded together like paper, and heathen temples with great carved beams . . . It was one of our last shore leaves before sailing home, and we'd gone off exploring; Andrew never cared much for the usual sailor's pastimes, his thoughts were on people, strange places, and on books. We went wandering together through the byways and got caught up in some kind of festival. The people were adorning all the shrines with flowers and paper banners, and with candles—everywhere candles. We couldn't speak a word of Japanese but Andrew made friends quickly. He was like that, and somehow we were invited to a feast. When it all ended, it was very late, and very dark. We'd journeyed far off the main roads into twisting alleys, and Andrew said we'd never find our way back to the port till dawn. We'd best bed down till then, and so we did, in a Buddhist shrine. The last thing I remembered before I fell asleep were the paper banners fluttering softly, and the candle flames."

We were both silent, caught in the picture. "You can guess what happened, can't you? he said at last. "Flames, tight-packed houses, all the paper . . . We woke into an Inferno raging. Andrew grabbed me and tried to guide me out, but before we could go far, there was a great crack like the gates of Hell and the whole carved ceiling fell upon us. Andrew was pinned, back broken, by the ceiling beam. He screamed at me to run, to save myself, but I would not leave him. I kept tugging at the beam, but I could not budge it, and after a while I knew it was no use. When I spoke to him, he no longer answered. It was then I saw the collar, spilling out of his pocket, its jewels glittering in the infernal light. It was so beautiful—I could not bear to leave it there to melt. I grabbed it, and I ran, dodging this way and that through rat-tunnels of flaming beams, and out at last into the streets. There was no one there to help; they had all fled."

On the bed, Leo had given up his game and fallen asleep in the golden circle like a brooding idol.

"Over and over since then," Ross said slowly, "I have reviewed it in my mind. And I have had to accept that no, I was not wrong to run. Otherwise we would both have died, and for what use? I could not budge the beam, could get no help. Was Andrew still alive? I do not know, but he had the mercy of unconsciousness."

"The—collar?" I said painfully.

"Ah, yes, the collar. When I reached the port, the ship was gone . . . I had been burned myself in the fire, and some village people nursed me, and meanwhile the captain had heard of the catastrophe and assumed we both were dead. I signed on with the next ship that came along, but it was outward bound, and it was a year before I again reached home. For some time I kept the collar hidden, for I was young, and it could easily have been taken from me. But a year and hardship works many changes in a youth, and when I'd grown strong enough to risk the dangers, I used the collar for collateral. It was then its true value became known to me, and it opened up my eyes. There were many opportunities along the waterfront for a shrewd trader who knew value and could hold his liquor. Soon I had amassed a fortune and went sailing home to lay it at my mother's feet in triumph."

I knew, I knew what happened then.

"Lavinia," Ross said musingly, in a different voice. "Do you know that is an ancient Latin name? I was struck by it, when I first heard it. At first I gave no thought to Andrew's family, I was consumed by my own grief and revenge. But later, after I married and brought my bride to Boston, I thought of my dear friend's bride. I made inquiries, I hired detectives, but it was some time before I found her, and when I did it was to no avail. Your mother, Lavinia, was a very stubborn woman."

I nodded; yes, I knew that.

"She was still angry over Andrew's sailing off; she took it into her head it was his hunting for a fortune that brought about his death. She would not wear the ruby, and she would not take the collar. She would have no part in any money gained through his last journey. I had to find a way to aid without her knowledge, so I turned to my friend Eustace Robinson. He was a bachelor, he needed a housekeeper, and moreover he was a born romanticist who was entranced by my story and glad to help. He did not guess, no more than I, now, what would be the outcome; he too fell in love with the woman he sought to help, as you must know. He was old, he was willing to accept that there could be no future in that love, and he fell gracefully into the role of adopted uncle.

"Marianna was not a fool. She discovered in time that he was not Andrew's uncle, but by then both you and she were fond of him and she no longer let stubborn pride stand in the way. One thing she insisted: you were not to know. You adored your 'Uncle Eustace' and she was afraid of what the shock of learning he was not your uncle might do to you. After she died we abided by her wishes, but when you came of age Eustace wrote that he felt you had a right to learn the truth. He himself would take no action; it was my story, he said, and he would leave it up to me. I think he dreaded the thought of losing you as his niece. Then he, too, died. And I—I thought, if I had you here, I could find a way to let the truth out easily. I did not know each day that passed would make it harder."

He rose, went to the bed and brought back the collar, which he dropped into my lap. "It is yours by right. And believe me when I say I am glad to give it back where it belongs. It has brought me nothing but sorrow, and my daughter will not touch it."

I looked at it, glowing with somber power. "I am like my mother. I cannot take it as blood-debt."

"Then will you take it in another way? I will not ask you

yet to marry me. Too much has happened. I don't even know if you believe in me. I will ask you this. Give us time, time to start again as we should have in the beginning with the whole slate clean. And come with us to Italy, for Damaris' sake, if not for mine."

I walked to the window, my hand against my head. "I don't know—you are right, too much has happened. I don't know what I believe in any more. Since—Uncle Eustace died, I haven't even known who I was, till now."

"Who your father was," Ross corrected. "Who *you* are is your own character, that ancient Roman integrity of yours. It has nothing whatever to do with position or with birth."

"Damaris said that to me once. Damaris—she would not want me staying, she no longer trusts me."

"She will when she is better."

"She asked me if I poisoned her."

"She will know differently one day; she really knows it now."

I looked at him. "How can you be so sure?"

"Because I know my daughter," Ross said quietly. "You do, also, if you can let yourself accept it. I hope you will, she needs you desperately."

"Even though she runs from me?"

"She runs from you for the very reason that she needs you—because you are strong, and know her. And because you're the only person who can love her in spite of everything. Marina and I have tried, but apparently we have never quite been able to forgive, and somehow she has known that when we have not."

"What in God's name are you talking about?"

"Isabella. Have you never really guessed the truth, Lavinia? Damaris killed her mother."

XX

For a moment I could only stare. "It was an accident." My mouth was dry.

Ross shook his head. "That is what we told the servants. Marina was there. She saw. They were in the conservatory, she and my wife. Isabella was leaving for a drive and Marina detained her. They had some petty quarrel, as sisters will. Marina has never forgiven herself. If it had not been for that, Isabella would have been gone before Damaris found her."

He stopped, and I saw a muscle twitch in his temple, but after a moment he went on in the quiet detached tone of which he had made himself a master. "Damaris was in one of her hysteric fits. You've seen them; voice high and erratic, breath coming in gasps. A kitten I had given her had died, and for some reason she connected the death with Isabella, who hated cats. There were words. Isabella was late for an engagement, and she wouldn't listen. Marina says Damaris fairly flew at her to make her stay. My wife was wearing white as she liked to do—it made her resemble the portrait—and Damaris' hands were soiled. She made a move to hold the child away. Before Marina could guess the intention, let alone prevent it, Damaris seized a cup of acid standing on the work table, where the jewelry was being cleaned, and flung it full in her mother's face."

A convulsive sound escaped me and involuntarily my hands went up to my own face.

"Marina, with great presence of mind," Ross went on, "snatched up the tea she had been drinking and threw it on her sister's burns. But it was no use. Mercifully, perhaps, Isabella died almost at once."

"And—Damaris?"

"She fled," Ross said, "as soon as the act was done. In the excitement, no one thought of her. We found her later, in her mother's room, unconscious on the floor before the Tapestry of the Two Sisters. She had attempted to destroy it with a knife. She suffered brain fever for some period of time, and when she regained consciousness at last, she had no recollection at all of anything that had occurred. It seemed—kindest —to let her remain in ignorance, so we spread the story of an accident. While we were in Italy she seemed all right, or I should never have brought her home. But apparently all this time, as Marina feared, the memory has lain dormant in her poor brain, forcing her to inflict bizarre punishments on herself in expiation."

This cannot be Damaris we are speaking of, my mind cried out.

"And—her accusations, her suspicions?"

"She may well believe them. Her mind may have blocked out all memory of her own deeds."

"It seems so—incredible." I turned unseeingly towards the window, resting my head against the lavender panes. "All these months . . . Everything . . ." My thoughts raced backwards. The dual roles she had been playing, the pressures of the social battleground, the strain of trying to maintain a precarious control when she must have felt her mind was slipping—"No wonder her health snapped." I stopped, struck. "And Warren—oh, Ross, you don't believe—"

"I know nothing," Ross said firmly, "other than that it is a very great relief the authorities are convinced of suicide. Lavinia, you are trembling. Come by the fire."

I was shaking, and I could not stop. I let him lead me back to the chaise and set me on it. He lifted my feet and tucked the afghan round me. "Steady." His hands closed over mine and at his touch, curiously, my pulse grew quiet. "You need warming. If I ring for brandy, will you drink it?"

"*No*—not brandy." A common memory flared between us, driving our eyes apart. I felt myself flushing. Ross's hold on my wrists tightened.

"I said a great many things one ought not to say that night, but I will not apologize or regret. Do you know why? Because I knew even then that it was right. Do not waste time searching for a decorous façade, you sensed it too."

I well knew what the rules of the social game required—pretended ignorance, or a sly coquetry. But I had come to an end of games. I bowed my head, and it seemed the most natural thing in the world for him to take me in his arms.

How long we would have remained thus, immobile, like John Donne's couple, I do not know, had not that same sensation as in the closed bedroom not suddenly pressed upon me. Someone was watching. I straightened, gasping slightly, and he released me, but I could see nothing, sense nothing, save a palpable though invisible presence beyond the door, which was ajar. Ross looked at me.

"You are frightened."

"No. Only confused, and troubled, and very, very tired."

"I will leave you, then." He rose. "Lavinia. That was the name of Aeneas' second wife, after he had roamed the world an exile and a wanderer, and found at last in Italy his one true home. How strangely ironic and appropriate. I will not pressure you on our personal relationship. We can wait for a time. But come with us to Italy, Lavinia."

"Do you think that it would help—"

Ross lifted his shoulders. "How can anyone say? I can only tell you that if you do come it will give me very great joy." He lifted my hands, looked at them a moment, then bent and kissed them and was gone.

Maggie came up, later, to say Mr. Culhaine had suggested I might like to have my dinner served that evening in my room. "Since you're feeling weary, miss. Himself is dining at his club, and the marchesa don't want to leave Miss Damaris."

He had discerned my need to be alone; perhaps he shared it. I acquiesced gratefully to the suggestion, and I let Maggie serve me breakfast in bed next morning, too. It seemed a shame to put her stout old body to the effort of laboring up the stairs with a laden tray, but I had a feeling she was glad of any tasks that could distract her mind. I am afraid, though, that I was not kindly disposed to hear her chatter, and contrived to work her off as quickly as I could.

The day was grey and leaden, conducive to melancholy thoughts. In the afternoon we had the sad duty of attending the funeral Ross had arranged, and though I dreaded it I was glad I had disciplined myself to go, for aside from a few seemingly unmoved business acquaintances, we were the only mourners. How Warren would have hated it, I thought. He had liked cheerfulness and gaiety. Although he had not been cheerful, those last two days. He could not have been, not if he had—

Warren. It seemed impossible that he was dead. Any moment I half expected to see him strolling up the aisle, whistling a ribald tune, casting a mocking eyebrow towards the clergyman's solemnity and measured tones. I had a sudden image of him the night of Damaris' ball, whirling her round the floor in the patterns of the dance, her face glowing up at him with eyes like stars. Now he was dead and Damaris prostrate and senseless, Damaris who in either of two incredible and painful ways had been responsible . . .

I would not think of it. I would think of flowers. Warren had loved flowers and here they were, here from the Culhaine conservatory in arrangements he would have much admired. Ross, for all his dislike of Warren, had expended thought and care to do him honor. Tuberoses were here, and hyacinths, and silver-leaved geraniums and violets, the flowers with which he had decked the halls for Damaris' ball.

Flowers for the hall . . . I frowned. Something nagged at the edge of memory, but it as quickly passed.

The funeral over, we drove back to Marlborough Street. Marina left us at once to return to Damaris' side, and Ross and I took tea together in the library, scarcely speaking. We dined with the omnipresent servants standing by and I returned to my room early. The lamps were lit but dimly. I did not turn them high but sat for some hours musing by the fire.

When I had risen at last and prepared for bed, I extinguished the lamps and stood for a moment looking down into Marlborough Street, its frozen snow a crust of silver in the moonglow. I opened the window a crack and a draft eddied through the curtains, releasing a wave of scent from the flowers someone, Maggie probably, had placed on my bedside table. What luxury, this having hothouse flowers all year round. How easy for a man as rich as Ross Culhaine to arrange for that wealth of flowers at the funeral, all that had saved it from bleakness and oppression. For the rest of my life, the scent of tuberoses would be for me the distilled essence of this Boston winter.

Tuberoses . . . the memory that had nagged me at the funeral came back, more clearly. I climbed into bed, pulled the coverlet up to my chin, and lay there in the darkness, thinking hard.

Tuberoses—there had been tuberoses at Damaris' ball, and there weren't supposed to be. When she first sensed them, Damaris had frowned and gone quite giddy. Tuberoses affected Damaris strangely, Marina said. Isabella had died among the tuberoses—was that why? Marina had grown quite angry at Warren's using them, and Warren had smiled and said he introduced them as an undercurrent. There had been a clash of swords between them.

Warren had made other changes in Damaris' floral decorations too. I strained to concentrate, employing all my training to visualize, first, the sketches Damaris had so glowingly shown me and, then, the actual decorations as Marina had finally permitted them to stand. Silver-leaved geraniums, as at the funeral. Hollyhocks, and peonies, and cherry blossoms —I remembered wondering where on earth Warren had managed to procure them. They had had an artless charm, all luminous white.

And gold. Everywhere, scattered among the virginal flowers, blooms of gold, glowing like the burnished metal of the collar. Tulips and marigolds and roses all blooming together. And lilies, many lilies. And tuberoses, the tuberoses that intoxicated, and lush, enervating conservatory air.

Damaris had told me that the floral decorations for her ball would tell a story, that Warren was planning to employ the old Language of the Flowers of the medieval tapestries, and the suggestion had bewitched her.

Damaris, lying ill, had thrust from her the flowers Warren sent. Maggie's voice came back to me: "Got it into her head the flowers are messengers whispering evil things!"

Damaris had said something about an old book downstairs that gave the Language of the Flowers. Not quite sure why I was doing so, I swung my feet out of bed to the cold floor. Shivering slightly, I took a taper to the fire and lit my bedside candle. My bedroom door opened for me without a sound. The house was coal-dark, for family and servants had long since been abed. But it would be the work of only moments to run down to the library and scan the shelves—Ross's books were admirably arranged. I reached for the banister, stumbled, missed, and pitched forward into a well of nothingness, the fallen candle describing flaming arcs beside me as I fell.

I must have screamed, I cannot recall. I must have also lost consciousness, but only briefly. Within minutes, light was flaring in the stairwell overhead and Ross was running down to me with Marina, clutching a billowing negligee, behind him. The servants clustered sleepily at the railing high above, and Maggie almost immediately came puffing down.

"I'm all right." I struggled upward, then winced in pain, and Ross held me firmly.

"Don't try to rise. Not till we are sure there are no bones broken. Lavinia, what happened?"

"I don't know; I stumbled. I must have tripped on something . . ."

"That cat," Marina said, and shuddered. "A wonder it hasn't happened to one of us before. Nasty, twisting things, always twining round one's ankles." And sure enough, here was Leo, insinuating himself between us to prove I was his property, lavishing upon me uncharacteristic kisses.

Maggie, arms akimbo, snorted. "Cat would never hurt her, he loves Miss Vinnie. There's a spirit loose in this house, sir, and well you'd know it if you hadn't put by all the teachings of your bringing-up. And you'll not be putting the blame on my poor lamb, either, for I've looked in on her and she's well asleep."

"Cease your gibberish," Marina said harshly. "You might better have stayed with Miss Damaris. She ought not to be alone if she awakens. I must go to her."

It was the first night since Damaris' night nurse had been

dispensed with. "And a bad thing, too," Ross said grimly, "when we might have used her. Lavinia, will you permit me?" He ran his hands with deft sureness down my body, probing the bones. "You seem all right, just bruised. Maggie, will you assist me?"

They insisted on carrying me upstairs between them and settling me again in bed. Leo leaped up beside me quickly, and Ross sat down on the other side, after sending Maggie down for brandy. He stayed with me until I fell asleep.

I awoke the next day my body one great ache, more bruised and shaken than I had imagined. Indeed, so dazed was I that I could not recall at first what had occurred. I lay, blessedly immobile, among the featherbed and pillows, until Maggie arrived, gossipy and solicitous, with a breakfast tray. Leo, evincing great interest in the cream jug, permitted Maggie to scratch his ear.

"Talking about the poor beast something fierce, they are," she said darkly. "As though he'd try to break your neck on purpose! Probably not his fault at all, like as not, and so I told them!"

"What do you mean, Maggie?"

Maggie retreated at once behind a wall of class distinctions. "Not for me to say, miss, I'm sure. There's those that know what's going on hereabouts, and those that won't admit it. The master says you're to stay abed till the doctor gets here to visit Miss Damaris, and he's to have a look at you as well."

"How is she, Maggie?"

"That better, miss." Maggie waxed voluble again. "That terrible fever of the brain's gone down. I stood outside the door yesterday and heard her talking natural as ever to the marchesa. If you ask me, that mixture they've been giving her did more harm than good, but no matter now. I heard the doctor say to discontinue it today. The marchesa, she don't want to. I've a good mind to see the bottle gets knocked over, quite by accident, when I go to fetch her tray."

"Maggie!"

She looked at me inscrutably. "I don't hold with doping a person, Miss Vinnie, and that's a fact. It's not what the good Lord intended for us."

I had no wish to see the doctor, save as a means of getting information of Damaris, but I was well content to lie abed. Dr. Martinson did come to see me in the afternoon, and pronounced me only badly bruised, as I had thought. "Stay in bed today, and don't do anything strenuous for a few more days," was his verdict. "You must have a strong constitution, Miss Stanton, and you can thank your stars your fall was stopped by the banister before you reached the hall. That floor's solid marble, and it would have been a miracle if you'd escaped with your neck unbroken."

It was an echo of what Maggie had said earlier, and a chill touched me. When he was gone, I lay still, staring up at the shirred silk of the bed canopy, and thinking. I was trying to reconstruct the sequence of events.

Why had I been out in the hall at that unlikely hour? Odd that the shock had knocked all thought of that clear from my mind. I had been on my way downstairs, to get something, to get a book. I had remembered something somehow alarming about flowers, and I had been going downstairs to get a book. I strained my mind, trying to particularize the moments with all my senses. I had gotten out of bed, and it had been dark, it had been dark and cold, for I had not stopped to don slippers or a robe. I remembered the texture of the bedroom carpet beneath my feet, and the parquet of the hall. I remembered the scent of tuberoses on the window draught, and the faint smell of tallow from my flickering candle. It had traced a flaming cartwheel in the darkness as I fell, burning itself out at last harmlessly on the marble floor. I remembered the faint odor of lemon oil on the banister as I reached for it, and missed, and—my breath quickened—something more.

Something I had scarcely had time to notice, and had afterwards forgotten. That unmistakable, invisible sense of presence.

Someone had been with me in the black room of the hall. Leo? Marina said it was Leo caused my fall. And suddenly I knew what it was that had nagged me, what sensory impression I had not remembered because it had not been there.

I had tripped over, or trodden on, Leo many times over in the past. I knew well the feel of his silken fur against my ankles. I knew even better his flashing claws and shrieks of rage. Leo loved me, but he would have screamed his indignation if I had tripped on him, and he had not. Because he had not been there.

Leo had not been there. But someone had. Was it imagination or remembrance that made me feel all at once the thrust of a hand against my shoulder. Thrusting me forward into nothingness, down and down to a marble floor.

"Probably not his fault at all . . . As though he'd try to break your neck on purpose . . ." Had Maggie, ever so faintly, emphasized the pronouns? Implying someone else indeed had done so? I knew Maggie's oblique way of implying warning.

"You'll not be putting the blame on my poor lamb, either," Maggie had said.

Damaris.

Damaris, who was supposed to have killed her mother. Damaris, whom Ross and I had skittered away from blaming for Warren's death. Damaris, who knew not what she did. But Maggie said she talked "as natural as ever" yesterday.

Something was terribly wrong, and I did not know what. But two things I was very sure of, and I clung to them as to an anchor in a whirling sea. Damaris would not have tried to kill me, not if her mind was clear. And even more—my mind reached back—she would not have poisoned Leo. She had gasped something about it, that terrible night; she had feared the blame would be put upon her and she knew she had not done it. Not to Leo. Her mother, herself, and Warren—perhaps. But not to Leonardo, and not to me.

I pulled hard on the bellpull by my bed, and when Sarah appeared I bade her send Maggie to me.

"Maggie," I said to her when she arrived. "I want you to look for something for me in the library. It will be a book, an old book. I do not know its name, but it tells all about the meanings of different kinds of flowers. It ought to be on the shelves left of the fireplace by the window, but it may have been moved, or hidden. And Maggie, you are not to let anyone know you're looking for it."

Our eyes locked. Yes, she understood.

"Maggie—Miss Damaris' medicine?"

"The bottle got broken, miss. Since the doctor's been here. So she can't be kept on it, no matter how the marchesa thinks the doctor was wrong to discontinue, for he'll not send her more."

At dinner time, when Maggie brought up my tray, she produced a slim volume from her apron pocket. "Here 'tis, miss. It had strayed behind some others, but I found it."

"No one saw you?"

Maggie's look gave me to know that she was not so foolish.

I noticed that my fingers were actually trembling as I commenced to turn the pages of the little book. It took some time for me to find what I was seeking, as its alphabetical scheme was according to meaning, not to name of flower. In many cases, too, the blooms were given old, now-uncommon names, and I was forced to resort continually to my dictionary. But as my list of jotted notes lengthened beneath my pen, I became filled with a growing excitement.

> *white violet—innocence*
> *ivy—friendship*
> *fern—sincerity*

white lilac—purity
hyacinth—constancy

All quite chaste and appropriate for a debutante. It was when I reached the flowers unexpectedly inserted that the darker shadows came.

silver-leaved geranium—recall
a rose surmounting two buds—secrecy
white hollyhock—female ambition

Had that been the slap to which Marina had reacted?

White cherry—deception. I was right; the flowers *were* the key. My eyes raced on. *White peony—shame.* And gold—the gold that Warren had said was a tribute to Marina. *Yellow acacia—secret love; yellow tulip—hopeless love; marigold— jealousy. Yellow lilies—falsehood.*

Marina. Marina, the dark sister of the legend. Snatches of conversation came back to me: my own, "That sounded like a threat." And Warren, laughing, saying, "I know even more about her. Do not ask what. . . . Do not allow yourself to be drawn in." The flowers had been a threat . . . of what? Had Marina known about the thefts, issued an ultimatum that afternoon in the conservatory? Had Warren been using the floral decorations as a means to turn the tables?

Tuberoses—dangerous pleasures.

His game had proved dangerous indeed to Warren Sloane . . . I jerked upright, frightened at what my brain was thinking. But there was no holding it back now from its relentless chase. If what I was beginning to believe was true, there had been no suicide, no suicide attempts. There was a deadly game, and it had to do with a death that had been no accident, in the conservatory long ago. Warren had known about it, and he had died. Damaris knew, and she had almost died.

I had to see Damaris. Oh, yes, I could make her tell me; I

had a power over her. That was why she had kept me from her, wasn't it?

I waited until long past midnight, when the house was so still that every faint sound from the furnace was a shriek. Then I crept from my bed and extracted a long slender hatpin from my best bonnet. In my years of training under Eustace Robinson I had learned many skills never taught at Miss Milbrook's Select Female Academy. I went to the connecting door between my room and Damaris' dressing room, and quite deliberately I picked the lock.

XXI

A dim light burned on the marble table in Damaris' room and a sweet cloying scent struck me as I entered, composed of too much potpourri and too little fresh air. A scent of cinnamon . . . I had forgotten how Damaris kept cinnamon sticks among her letter paper. A sense of déjà vu assailed me, and a rush of the poignant, protective love I had felt long ago for a frail little child at boarding school, lonely and afraid. I felt, quite suddenly, a revulsion toward what I was about to do. Then another, prickling awareness followed, that sense of presence.

Damaris was watching me from among the chiffon draperies of her palaquin, watching me with dark somber eyes. I turned directly to her and for several seconds we did not speak. When at last she broke the silence her voice was quiet, level, with no trace of hysteric illness. "I have been waiting for you. I knew you'd come."

"How did you know?"

"Maggie's my friend," Damaris said obliquely. "Maggie keeps no secrets from me. She was right about the medicine, wasn't she? I thought there was something wrong, it made things queerer. Queerer instead of clearer!" She giggled, then sobered. "You know now, don't you? In a way, I wanted you to, but I couldn't tell you. You know, Vinnie."

I nodded. "You must tell me the rest now, all of it."

"I can't."

"You must. There've been—too many deaths. You must tell me. Then you'll no longer have to be afraid."

Damaris shook her head, wearily childish. "It doesn't matter any more. Not after Warren . . ."

"Do you want me to die, Damaris? I almost did, you know. Did they tell you?" That brought a reaction; her pupils dilated with alarm. I pressed my advantage. "Or Leo? You love Leo, don't you? Why did you say it wasn't your fault when he was poisoned?"

"He drank my milk," Damaris said dully. "It was on my bedside table. I reached for it, but Leo leaped up first. He drank it all. He thought he was so clever, and so did I."

"You'd never have poisoned Leo deliberately, would you?"

Damaris shook her head. "Aunt says I knew the milk was poisoned, but forgot it." Her voice was growing thin. "I forget so many things . . ."

"That's why I'm here, to help you to remember. It's why you sent for me, wasn't it, because you knew I could? Because you needed to know? Damaris, look at me. Tell me about your mother."

"I can't."

"You can; you will. What was she like?"

"Beautiful . . . like the sun . . ."

"And good?"

"Everyone said so." Damaris began to murmur the lines of the song. " '. . . pure in garb and heart . . . the other skilled in subtle art/And she wore lilies in her hair.' Golden lilies. Gold for falsehood. And I didn't know."

"You loved your mother, didn't you?" She nodded. "And Aunt Marina?"

"Yes, but Mama . . . No one else mattered, ever, if she was there."

"And then you were sent away to school, and you were unhappy, but you wouldn't cry—it was because you were a Culhaine, wasn't it, and Culhaines had pride?"

"I wanted to make my father proud of me," Damaris said, "the way he was of her. I peeked over the banister and saw them once, when they were ready to go out. She was so beautiful . . . The way he looked at her . . ." Her breath caught.

"You went away to school, and you came home, one weekend at the end of winter. What happened then, Damaris?" The rasping sound was starting in her breathing, and I hurried on. "It was cold then, wasn't it? Bitter cold, with snow, as it is now. But in the conservatory it was warm. Warm and moist and fragrant. The work table was up, your Aunt Marina was helping to clean corrosion off some of the pieces in the Collection. They were spread out on the table, weren't they?" She nodded. "Pendants and sleeve ornaments, and *enseignes*; bronze, and gold . . ."

"And diamonds," Damaris' little voice said dreamily. "Like little bits of frozen ice, winking . . . and rubies. Rubies like drops of blood." She commenced to tremble. I grasped her thin hands and held them tightly.

"And tuberoses. Hundreds of tuberoses, everywhere . . . You can see them, can't you? Damaris! Don't look away! Your mother was in the conservatory, dressed all in white, with your Aunt Marina." I searched frantically for every sensory clue I had been given. "You ran in, you ran in and you were angry. Why were you angry, Damaris?"

"My kitten was dead." She was shaking now. "A dear little kitten Papa had given me, and Mama hated cats. She said if it leapt on her bed one more time . . . Her maid had laid out her new *tailleur*, white albatross rimmed with swansdown, and there were cat hairs on it. She—she picked up Mignon and—and threw her—against the fireplace—" Damaris pulled her hands from me and pressed them hard against her head on either side. "Its neck was broken. Maggie told me—"

"And so you ran downstairs to find your mother." I grabbed her hands and forced them down again. "Don't shut it out! *Look* at it, and tell me—it's the only way you'll ever be free of it, you know that. What do you see?"

"Stephanotis. Stephanotis and ivy, hanging from the rafters, like a curtain." Damaris was leaning forward, staring into the past beyond my shoulder. "Mama—Mama was standing by the table in her white and swansdown, wearing orchids . . . those little greenish ones, with the brown throats. She had the collar in her hand."

"Go on! What did you do, Damaris? You were out of breath, did you feel faint? Did you hold onto the planting boxes, or grab the table?" Perhaps she had done so, and the acid had splashed on Isabella by accident.

"I stumbled." Damaris frowned. "I tripped and stumbled . . . something was in the path. A—a carpetbag." Her eyes widened and her breath racheted. "That was it, then . . . I knew, I knew . . . !"

"Knew what?"

"Nothing. It doesn't matter."

"Then what happened?"

The color all had left Damaris' face, and the pain in her chest was rising, I knew, but I would not let her go. Indeed, I think at that moment she could not have stopped. The words spilled from her with the force of nightmare. "I shouted at her that I knew—about the kitten. And Mama—*laughed*. She had a laugh like chiming bells and she was so happy that day, so excited . . . She said that Maggie was a lying fool who hated her, and I ought not to listen. I moved towards her, and she—backed from me. I hated her then. If she hadn't laughed . . . She said it was an accident, she hadn't done it, but the kitten my father had given me was dead and she laughed, she didn't care—" Damaris was gasping now, clutching my fingers tightly. "The pains were starting, and I would not let them shame me. I reached out . . . for the table . . . and I touched something . . . a cup. I picked it up . . . and threw it at my mother's face . . ."

"Did you know what was in it?"

"*No!*" Her whisper was a scream. "I just knew I had to stop her, stop her mouth from laughing. And I did . . . and there has been no laughter since . . ."

She fell forward, her face hidden in my skirts, rigid with pain, and I gathered her tight in my arms and held her, crooning to her and quieting her with the force of my own will until her shuddering ceased. I had been right; her Furies, invoked in words and faced, had been defanged, and she was able at last to sleep. They were my Furies now.

When I felt certain she was relaxed and still, with no dreams to haunt her, I went back to my own room, leaving a dim lamp burning at her bedside. I stood in the darkness of the luxurious green and purple room, staring out the window at the night street, and the Furies stood waiting at my shoulder.

I had it now, the riddle I had sought, the riddle of Isabella's death. I could accept that, festering in her unconscious, it had pushed Damaris into an abyss of self-persecution. Damaris had not meant to cause her mother's death. But would she accept that truth—or, what mattered more, would it make a difference? Isabella still was dead. And Warren . . .

Something still was wrong, was not explained. Warren's death. My fall. To keep us from learning—what?

Flowers. Flowers and the collar. These were the notes that had run like a dark motif beneath the pattern. I had almost died seeking to solve the riddle of the flowers. Isabella had died among the flowers, the collar in her hand. Messages in flowers, told in old tapestries. A tapestry long hidden, slashed by Damaris' hand, which no one knew I found.

It was the one place where I had not looked for clues, thinking that because I had found one secret there, it held no more. The tapestry was still locked in my trunk, hidden beneath the out-of-season clothes. It suddenly exerted upon me a kind of curious fascination to which I was both eager and loath to yield. Not here, where at any moment Damaris might wake and find me with it. In the darkness, silently, I knelt beside the trunk and with fingers suddenly clumsy brought out the key, inserted it and turned it, lifted the lid, wincing at its creak. I dug down and down beneath the piles of clothes, ghost-whispering silks and the stiff laces and embroideries of summer muslins. My probing fingertips encountered it at last, were pricked by the needle I had left that other night thrust into it in my haste and shock.

I drew it out, a thick and somber bundle, so like old rags and nondescript, its splendours hidden like its secrets in the patterning inside. I pressed it to me, hiding it against my body beneath the flowing cashmere of my robe. Then barefoot, soundlessly, without a candle, I eased my door open, slid into the hall, closed the door behind me. A step at a time, my senses all alert, I eased my way slowly, oh, so slowly, to the staircase and mounted with the caution of an Indian scout to the upper hall. Here on this level no one slept, here I could make my way into the sewing room, and shut and lock the door, and by the light of match and candle secreted in my pocket, could unfold the tapestry and its secrets to my Pandora's eyes. I did so, and tonight no formless presence walked behind me.

My senses were so heightened by all that had gone before that when I was at last in the sanctuary of the empty little room I felt light-headed. I gazed almost blankly at the tapestry, and its jewellike colors glowed back at me like Argo's hundred eyes. I knew not where to start, save in the flowers, and they were everywhere . . . all the flowers of Damaris' ball, and more.

Damaris' ball . . . I had had such a sense then of all of us—myself, Marina, Damaris, Ross and Warren—as figures in a tapestry or an old pavane, moving inexorably through some dark pattern. Had I pursued that pattern then, would the recent past have taken less dark turnings?

Pattern . . . my breath quickened. I had been gazing, without much reward, at the individual flowers of the carpet. What was that old saying about not seeing the forest for the trees? I turned my gaze, with steadily rising excitement, toward the pictured groupings. Here they all were, the two ladies, servants, gentlemen and craftsmen, moving in a progressive series like children's illustrated papers through the "Pavane for Two Sisters."

> There were two sisters, dark and fair,
> The one was skilled in subtle art,
> The other pure in garb and heart,
> And she wore lilies in her hair.
>
> Still through the dark pavane they move,
> A dark pavane of death and love.
>
> One sister loved with virgin truth
> A stranger gallant, strong and sure.
> The other, with her wiles impure,
> Stole off the heart of that same youth.
>
> One sister wore with brazen pride
> The favor once to t'other shown;
> And she, forsaken, mourned alone,
> Till in her bosom love had died.
>
> A man of craft came passing by,
> He saw a woman seemed so fair
> A-wearing lilies in her hair,
> And oh, she caught the craftsman's eye.

Alas for faithful love once scorned.
And for false love that seemeth true;
For failing old and choosing new,
Death came upon a grey-eyed morn.

"Oh sister, you have loved well,
I die of love that is not true,
But who chose better, I or you,
Is secret time alone will tell."

Here they were, indeed ، . . . My heart pounded in my breast, and I could hear Damaris' Cassandra voice ringing in my ears, and when I came at last to the wedding scene, the scene in which I had recognized my mother's ring in the design of the golden collar, I almost fainted. Why, why had I not pressed on, that other night, instead of shrinking back in grief and fear? If I had done so, there might have been no tragedies . . . and a house of masks would have fallen.

Two sisters, dark and fair—not in appearance, but in character. Isabella and Marina, a man of craft and a stranger. An innocent girl who loved a stranger until he was stolen off by her deceitful sister who was in turn, in time, seduced by a man of craft. Here it was, all here, in the tapestry's wedding portrait, the beautiful bride, proud in the golden collar, the sister standing by. Both of them wearing lilies in their hair. But the white lilies of purity were worn by the bare-throated waiting sister. The bride, triumphant in her gold and rubies, wore falsehood's yellow.

The devious sister, the second love, concealing black treachery beneath an angel's smile. Not Marina. Isabella.

XXII

There were two sisters, dark and fair,
The one was skilled in subtle art,
The other pure in garb and heart . . .

The pieces fell in place.

One sister loved with virgin truth / A stranger gallant . . .
Marina, the younger, who had never married. Ross, not the
man of craft and guile, but the lonely youth he once had
been . . . the haunted youth I had sensed beneath the Lucifer
mask, to whom my heart irrevocably had gone out, as Marina's must have then. Ross, not the faithless seducer as I had
feared, but the wronged stranger.

I who cared so much about knowing true identity, who
prided myself on my scorn for hypocrisy, I had been taken in
as the world had, by the masks which people wore. Damaris

wasn't. Damaris, for all her seeming to live in a fantasy world, had an uncanny knack for seeing true; I ought to have remembered that.

I—through my own insecurities?—had been misled by Marina's present glamour into assuming her the sister with the wiles impure. *But no one else mattered, ever*, Damaris had said, *if Isabella was there*. The pictures conjured by my racing brain crowded before my eyes. A Marina younger and, yes, much like Damaris, with that sort of evanescent beauty which only the advent of love could bring to life. Marina would have been drawn to that battered boy from Boston, just as I. The daughter of an old-world ducal family . . . what balm it must have been to that boy's proud, crushed spirit. Just as Damaris' love had been to Warren. And Ross, like Warren, had been kind, responding to a young girl's kindness. And the young girl had dreamed dreams.

And then—Isabella. Isabella like the sun. Coming between the needs of lost girl, lost youth, with charm and deliberate guile. As Damaris had accused me of doing with herself and Warren . . . My breath quickened. Oh, I had been right in my precognition of patterns repeating, interlocking, as in a dark pavane. Our lives seemed like the tapestry's mirror image, a coincidence that would have been derided had any modern novelist tried to use it.

One sister wore with brazen pride/The favor once to t'other shown. Ross would have told Marina of his mother, shown her the collar. But it was Isabella who had worn it, proudly, as her wedding-right. Damaris would not touch that collar. It had been in Isabella's hands at the moment that she died.

What else had Damaris said? Some picture lurked beyond the edge of memory and I frowned, straining. I closed my eyes and I could see the conservatory, hear Damaris' halting words as a narration, and the scent of overpowering sweetness was in my nostrils. Damaris running in, the thin little girl I had known at school, clutching her breast, overexcited, stumbling. Stumbling on a carpetbag . . .

Damaris' eyes, widening: "That was it, then ... I knew ...!"

Warren: "*She* sent for me . . . I must come discreetly." Warren, waiting behind the ivy curtain.

Damaris, again: "She was happy that day, so excited." In her white and swansdown, wearing orchids. Angry because of cat hairs on her gown. Then in the conservatory, arguing with Marina. And laughing, holding the golden collar. With a carpetbag at her feet.

Isabella was going away, with Warren, taking the golden collar which she considered hers by right. The collar which Ross so loved, not for Isabella's sake, but for his mother's.

It was all in the song, wasn't it? I opened my eyes, feeling a trembling and weakness spreading through my bones, and gazed down at the torn tapestry clutched tightly in my fingers.

A man of craft came passing by / He saw a woman seemed so fair . . . and oh, she caught his eye. Warren had adored Isabella. He had seen her as the world saw her, a beautiful madonna. *La belle dame sans merci.* Only Damaris had seen her true, and none of us had understood.

How much did Damaris really know, and how much of the song had flowed from the wellspring of her unconscious? Flowed like the prophecies of the oracles of old, enigmatic, ambiguous, and yet all there, awaiting only the interpretation by one who clearly saw. No wonder something had impelled Damaris to destroy the tapestry with its revealing, damning flowers. In the House of Culhaine, the legend of Isabella must be preserved or its walls would tumble like a house of cards. If Isabella were not pure, all that for which its inhabitants had lived for years was nothing.

Alas, then, for Marina's faithful silent love, love that stepped aside in favor of her sister, that the beloved might have what his heart desired. Alas for Isabella's false love that seemed so true; for failing Ross and choosing new, death had come to her on a grey-eyed morn. Death from the hands of a daughter pushed past bearing, stumbling over a carpetbag and knowing, knowing more than she could endure and face, striking out blindly. Athena, the grey-eyed goddess of wisdom . . . I had been wrong in thinking the patterns of these interlocking characters were Renaissance; they went back further, much further into the wellsprings of old Rome.

"Lavinia was the name of Aeneas' second wife, after he had roamed the world an exile and a wanderer, and found at last his one true home."

I pressed my hands to my temples. I must not allow myself to think in that direction now.

The legend of la Bianca. Isabella, for so she had been thought to be. Ross, Marina, Damaris, Warren, all bound together by her spiderweb of fascination, by their obsessive loves. All of them needing to believe in her perfection. Only Damaris, long ago, in a flare of awareness stumbling upon the truth and burying it deep in her unconscious.

I had compared Damaris once to Princess Aurora, the sleeping beauty slumbering in her enchanted wood. It was Isabella's spiderweb which had been sleeping, and she, even dead, its poisonous enchantress, slumbering like the long-buried tapestry in the closed-up house. It was the Culhaines' return to Boston which had stirred the spiderweb again to life; that, and my arrival, probing, prodding, using my power over Damaris to stir the coals of memory in the belief that truth could heal. Oh, I had been a catalyst in more ways than one.

Damaris, beginning to remember. Damaris, beginning to die. It was after the opening of this house where Isabella died that the arsenic attempts began. At whose hands? Ross, Marina, Warren, Damaris herself—all of them had needed to have her not remember. She almost had, she almost died— but she did not die. It was the man of craft who'd died.

With the sensation of a glimmer of light breaking through darkness, I was beginning to understand. Then I felt it, that other sensation. The sense of presence. I turned, rising slowly, and saw Marina standing in the doorway.

This is, I thought curiously, the first time I have really seen Marina. I had had glimpses before, in her ravaged face ever since that first night Damaris almost died, but I had misinterpreted, misunderstood. Through my own jealousy, my mind acknowledged humbly.

Marina was in her dressing gown, with her golden hair hanging down her back. A few streaks of grey showed, and the new lines around her eyes, and they tugged at my heart. She was still young, really, and she looked quite old. But also, oddly, as if she had found a kind of peace. She stood there, leaning against the door frame, regarding me quietly through those fine dark eyes.

"You know, don't you?" she said at last. "I knew you would, in time. Perhaps it's just as well. Now you can help me."

"Help you?"

"Ross must not know. You understand that, don't you? He has been hurt so much. Isabella's love was a—a sanctification to him. To destroy his belief in it would be too cruel."

How odd; Ross was the strongest man I had ever known, yet all of us felt this compulsion to mother him. Marina was right, I could not hurt him with this truth.

Marina, watching me, nodded, and I knew that she had read my mind. "I can trust you. You are in love with him. You need not be nice about pretending. You need not be tactful with me, either. For a long time, perhaps always, he has seen me only as Isabella's little sister. Any other—occurrences—were out of need, not love."

I was beginning to see where Damaris had gotten her unflinching ability to face the truth.

"It was Warren, wasn't it?" I said.

"Warren and Isabella. Yes." Marina went over to the old sewing rocker across from me, dropped into it, and, leaning back, closed her eyes. I realized she was very tired. After a moment she opened her eyes, gazed at the ceiling and yawned slightly. "How curious. It is almost a relief to talk of it. I have kept it to myself so long."

"You knew—from the beginning?"

"Not then, no. I thought she truly loved him." It was clear that by *him* she meant Ross Culhaine. How could she help it, I thought. "I was very young. And I—all that mattered to me was that he be happy. And he was, at first; I saw it, and I was—satisfied. But then . . ." Marina paused and shrugged.

"There was a statue in the garden of our home in Garda." Her voice had gone flat. "Diana, the untouched huntress. My sister was like that, I began to realize slowly. It was the hunt that mattered, not the quarry. Always the hunt, always the charm thrown out like a spider's snare, and then the victim possessed, discarded and forgotten. She could not help herself. But he—he worshipped her. So many dreams of his had burst, it must not happen again. And so I set myself to guard against it."

"You covered for her—hunts."

Marina nodded.

"When she died," my thoughts were working slowly, "you were alone with her for a time. You hid the carpetbag so Ross would never know she'd meant to leave him. That was why you quarreled with her that day, wasn't it? You knew that she was going off with Warren Sloane."

"Not that it was he!" Marina turned on me with a flash of her old fire. "*Madre dio*, you think I would have let him in this door when we returned? He came with a letter of introduction from New York, he spoke of her. I thought he was one of her puppydogs, pouncing on the fringes, nothing more. I thought I saw a way . . . Ross had insisted on returning here, and I was afraid, I did not know how much Damaris had seen that day, what she might remember, back in this house." An almost ruthless Etruscan smile tugged at her mouth. "I thought if I put pressure on Ross for an exhibition, sooner or later he would rebel. Sooner or later we would go back to Italy, to happiness, and we would be safe. For Damaris, too, it was so bad to be here, you have seen it. *He* cannot care for her, not since she caused her mother's death, but even that hate has limits."

"And the poison." My mouth felt dry. "It was Ross."

Her eyes widened. "How can you think it! He would never kill her!"

"But she wasn't meant to die, was she? Only to suffer. Or—or to not remember."

Marina looked at me sharply, nodded slowly. "You are very clever. Yes, that was it. Only it was not Ross, but Warren." She was beginning to tremble slightly, and she stopped and held her chin steady with her hand. "He told me, after a time, after he had begun to work on the Collection—about Isabella. He said that she had stolen for him, from the Collection, and he showed me two silver boxes, the real and the counterfeit, side by side. He said I must help him the same way, help him substitute the counterfeits, or he would tell Ross the truth about Isabella. He said that there was nothing I could do, that if I accused him of the thefts he would put the blame all on my sister. It had been her idea, he said; they were her gifts to him and he was innocent. There is a considerable market these days for stolen art, it seems, but it was not the money that mattered to him, I think. He hated Ross, he believed he had made Isabella's life unhappy and he wanted him to suffer for her death."

"And you *helped* him?"

"What could I do? The Collection, the thing that mattered most to Ross, after her—to learn that she had betrayed it, betrayed him . . . It did not matter so much whether the things were real," Marina said with Machiavellian practicality, "so long as he believed in them. And her."

"It was Warren with you, in the conservatory," I said slowly. "He used to come in and out some secret door there, didn't he, the way he must have come the day Isabella died. After the ball you told him you wouldn't help him any more."

Marina shot a glance at me. "You heard us? I feared as much." She looked at her hand with the yellow diamond, then let it fall. "I hadn't known, when it started . . . it was like walking in quicksand," she said softly. "At first, I told myself I could just stall for time—Ross would give in, we would go back to Italy. But time went by. Warren was growing greedy—and more confident. When I saw how he changed the flowers at the ball, I knew . . . there would be no end. He wanted me to make Ross give a part of the Collection to that New York museum. He wanted Damaris." She closed her eyes and shuddered.

"And the poison?" I said brutally.

"It wasn't meant to hurt her! Only to keep her unable to remember . . . if she remembered everything about Isabella's death she would tell her father, and Warren would have no more means of blackmail. And Ross would know the truth . . . I could not have that. So I—let him do it."

I shook my head, realization coming slowly. "It wasn't Warren. It had to be someone in the house, someone who could tamper with the milk and sugar, and also put the poison in my ring to make me a suspect. Someone whom Damaris would believe to be her mother in the night. It was you, wasn't it, Marina?"

Our eyes locked, and a faint sigh whispered through her. "I would do anything," she said at last, quietly, "to keep Ross from being hurt. Anything." Her voice was ˆt, but its intensity was frightening. I had to look away. ·

"You could have killed her." Odd, how my vc ˙ could sound so calm, unstressed; so commonplace. .

"I did not wish to! You saw that, didn't you? There was a different note in her voice. She's weeping, I thought. The discipline, the stern control of the old tradition, but inside—ah, that was different, a story I knew in my own blood and bone. Only one outward sign betrayed her, a thumb compulsively prodding the canary diamond round and round on her thin finger, and it moved me.

"Damaris," Marina said, and sighed. "Poor blighted child. Born under an unlucky star—Isabella never wanted children; I think Damaris knew. That was why, at the time, it seemed poetic justice . . . but I did not want her to suffer. You must believe that. And the more she remembered—the feelings of guilt, deep buried in her memory, but growing, as long as she was here. Destroying her sanity. And then Sloane, *daring*, trying to use her as he had used her mother . . . If she were ill, she could not marry. It was the only way I could think of to protect her, from her memories, and from him."

"She could have died."

Marina shuddered. "I was desperate. I did not know how much was safe, and I misjudged . . . I knew then, when we just barely saved her, that it had been a mistake to think I could buy time. I did what I ought to have done at the beginning. On New Year's Day, when that beastly little ferret came here, I—how do you say it? I called his game. I told him Damaris had remembered, that she knew about him and Isabella and would tell her father. I told him Ross had proof he was responsible for the thefts, and he would use it. And as for me—" Her head came up with that curious cruel smile and her old pride flared. "I was a lone, wronged woman, a marchesa. He was a thief, a parasite, a seducer. If he tried to implicate me in the thefts, no court in the world would believe his story over mine. He knew then that his game—was over. Had he been a Culhaine or an Orsini, he would have packed his bags in the night and gone elsewhere to carve a fortune. But he was a spineless rat, and he feared prison. He took the coward's way."

We both were silent, Marina staring at her yellow diamond, lost in somber thought. "So that is it," she said at last. The—what is it Damaris calls it?—the pavane is ended. That's all the mystery."

That was the whole story. No murder, no attempted murders. Only tragic accidents caused by desperation, and an old scandal that could destroy the lives of persons whom I deeply loved. Dangerous, desperate games played on the dark edges of legality, of morality. And yet—

"Tell me." Marina lifted her eyes to mine and held them. "If it had been you, would you have done differently?" And it was my glance that fell.

I knew then that my own game had ended too. For if I had come to Boston to find out who I was, I now had learned. What was it Ross had said of me? An ancient Roman code. Those towering archaic figures had known a fierce integrity which—like mine, like Marina's—was personal, not conforming to law or custom. They could, if a cause demanded it, be ruthless. And never again would I, looking on desperate acts, be able to pass a facile judgment, for I knew now that we walked in common sandals.

I knew too that I was bound to the House of Culhaine now by another bond. A covenant of silence. I would not betray Marina's confidences because I could not do that to Ross or to Damaris, and she knew it.

It was I at last who broke the stillness. "It's late. We'd best retire. If we both have no rest, it will be remarked upon tomorrow."

"It is more apt, I fear, to seem now commonplace." Marina's voice, I was glad to see, was returning to a wry normality. "I feel sometimes of late as if we were living in one of those appalling households in old plays."

Like the House of Atreus. I nodded. The tale had run its course now, and perhaps at last the Furies were appeased.

Marina rose. "You are right, it is late. We will speak more of this, if you wish, another time." We both knew we would not. "I'll see you to your room. And I shall take the tapestry, shall I not, and return it to its place? Better it is shut away where it can tell no tales."

We put out the candle and made our way downstairs together in the silent dark. In my own room, with the door shut, Marina turned up the lamp, and it threw out a cheerful yellow glow that banished shadows. "That is better. We have had too much dark of late. Now shall we not have a cup of tea together, and calm our nerves? You have a little spirit-kettle, do you not?" Marina herself prepared it, measuring tea leaves into my porcelain pot, allowing them to steep the proper number of minutes, pouring the tea out, adding sugar. "There is no milk up here, I fear, but you must take sugar. It will give you strength." She stirred it carefully and brought it to me.

"Aren't you joining me?"

"In a moment. First I want to see you comfortably in bed." She smoothed the bed covers, plumped up the pillows, and handed me the cup.

A light flared across the room over Marina's shoulder, a faint aureole of light surrounding a candle flame. Damaris stood in the doorway between our rooms, and I knew at once with a sinking heart that her grasp on reality again had slipped. I pushed her too far, I thought sickly. She looked like a mad Ophelia, her candle wavering, saying in a high, childlike voice, "Don't drink that, Vinnie."

Marina swung round, uttering a faint ejaculation in Italian, and made to move towards her, and at once Damaris' head went down and her arm came up to shield her face in the familiar horn-fingered gesture of warding off the evil eye. "No! Don't come near me! She won't rest, Vinnie, even though I killed her." She thought Marina was her mother, back from the dead, and was trying to protect me from her. "She tried to punish me, but I've escaped her always, thanks to you, so now she tries to hurt me by hurting you. You mustn't let her!" Damaris' breath was coming in harsh labored sobs and I saw her contort with pain. I feared the effect upon her of another collapse in her weak condition. It seemed best to humor her. "I'm all right, dear," I called. "Your mother won't hurt me, she has no reason to. But if you like, I will not drink my tea. You see?" I set the cup on the table by the bed.

Quick as a flash, Damaris darted in and seized it. She lurched forward and the candle in her other hand dipped crazily, almost touching Marina's unbound hair. Instinctively she recoiled and at once, with a strength I did not know she had, Damaris grabbed my wrist and jerked me behind her so forcibly that I fell upon the bed. She had now interposed herself between me and her aunt, and for the first time, seeing that wavering flame and the look on Marina's face, I felt afraid. Ever so faintly, Damaris seemed to be backing her aunt across the room. Then Marina straightened, and her eyes narrowed and changed.

"That is enough, Damaris," she said in a quiet, even tone. My neck felt cold. "You will do as I say and be a good girl so you will not be punished. Give me the cup."

She moved towards Damaris, who stopped uncertainly. I seized the moment; reaching from behind, I slid the dangerous candle out of Damaris' unresisting hand. At the same instant, Damaris' other hand came up. She flung the cup of scalding tea full in Marina's face.

The shock caught Marina off guard, and for a second we all stood there frozen as in a tapestry tableau. Damaris' voice came from her eerily, high and astonished, like the voice of some long-dead child.

"Look! That's how it was before when I flung the cup! Brown rivulets running down your white dress, Mama. It *wasn't* acid in my cup, you see? It was the tea. It wasn't I that killed you!"

XXIII

For a moment the significance of Damaris' words escaped me.
But not Marina. The expression on her face dissolved and
blurred. Like a lovely picture eaten away by acid. Acid, used
by Marina in the old days as a cleansing agent. Acid she had
known was there, on the table where she was working when
Isabella had come to meet her lover, come to wipe out in an
instant that illusory Happy Family which Marina had been
maintaining, with what cost of personal sanity and sacrifice,
for her own lost love. Acid flung not by Damaris but afterwards, as Damaris had fled in hysteria and panic. Afterwards,
from the second cup, in what everyone had thought was an
attempt to wash clean the burns.

Flung by Marina, not Damaris. And no accident.

I understood at last, and Marina knew it. In the ravaged
face those still-lovely eyes met mine with recognition, with a
grudging concession of respect and, yes, with a kind of triumph. Marina's hand swept up and the knuckles pressed

against her mouth, so that she seemed to be biting on diamond to steel her nerve. It took a few seconds for me to realize what was happening, then I swung round on Damaris and shook her by the shoulders roughly.

"Get your father! Quickly!" I saw reality snap back into her eyes, and released her, and she plummeted out.

Why had it never occurred to me that Marina too had a poison ring? Warren had told me he had seen another recently, and where else so likely? It explained so much. I had a sudden vision of Marina and Warren together on New Year's Day, just before he left, and another piece of the puzzle clicked into place.

All of this happened in an instant, even as I was running towards Marina, catching her as already her body contracted and she lurched forward. Arsenic, or the belladonna I suspected had been in Damaris' medicine? Or had she provided herself with some other, quicker-acting poison, just in case? At the moment nothing mattered except that I was down on the flowered carpet where the wet drops trickled like blood from the upturned cup, holding Marina's rigid body in its tea-stained nightdress as it stiffened and contorted. Then Ross was there, with Damaris pressing at his shoulder. Before he could even speak, Marina sensed his presence. Her anguished eyes opened and implored me, and I had to bend my head low to catch her whisper.

"Tell him—did it all for jealousy. He'll—believe that. Don't—tell truth." She meant about Isabella's infidelity, not her end. Even now, dying, she was using her death to protect the illusion to which she'd given her life.

Ross was beside me. "I'll take her. Get Maggie, and the doctor—quickly!"

"No." Damaris' voice, low-pitched, came swift and hard. She was shaking, but her eyes had a terrible sanity. "She killed my mother. And Warren. And herself, to keep truth silent. This is how she wants to end it. Let her!"

"We can't not send for help!"

"Then send! But not yet, not till it will be too late. Whatever she did—it was for love—let her finish it. It's the best gift we can give her."

Damaris was right, and Ross and I both knew it. And so once again we took the law into our hands, and who is there can prove that we were wrong?

I straightened, yielding my burden to Ross's arms, and looked at Damaris. She turned to me, a still and immeasurably stoic little figure. "It is not you and me she would want. Come with me, Vinnie." And I followed her in silence through the dressing room into her own room, where she shut and locked the door and leaned against it. She was trembling violently, but I dared not intrude on her dignity to touch her until at last she sought refuge in my arms. When, presently, much later, she stirred and straightened, I knew that whatever horrors of drugs and memory had possessed her mind and body the past months—years—they now were gone forever. Truth, however terrible, was easier to bear.

"She tried to kill me." Damaris moved, shakily, to the satin chair and sat down before the fire. I knew her mind, like mine, was moving rapidly, fitting the last pieces together in the pattern. "I think a part of my mind guessed it all along, but would not accept it. I thought it *ought* to be my mother . . . because of what I'd done."

"What you *believed* you'd done."

Damaris nodded. "I must have known all along, mustn't I, to have written as I did? The Two Sisters. So much alike, two sides of the same coin. I was starting to remember, to understand . . . Coming home here, meeting Warren. Loving him . . . it must have driven her mad with fear."

"And my coming, making you remember, poking and prying—"

"*And* my father." Damaris looked at me. Oh, yes, she knew. "She lost my father once," Damaris said dreamily, "and it was disastrous. I think she would have done anything to keep from losing him again. Even kill us both."

"She said she did not want to kill you." Oddly enough, I believed that, and I saw that Damaris did as well.

"Do you remember Christmas Eve, Lavinia? She was so kind to me. She gave me *pannetone*, and the family miniature. I think she was trying to give me a good death." We both were silent.

"Why?" I asked at last. "Why did you say you'd taken the arsenic yourself? If you'd spoken then—" She knew what I meant: Warren might not have died.

"But I *was* taking arsenic." Damaris smiled without humor at my start of shock. "Oh, months ago, when I first guessed I was being poisoned, I read up . . . I found that arsenic poisoning matched my symptoms, and I found too that the best protection from it was immunization from small steady doses. So that is what I did."

I was speechless.

"Later," Damaris said, "when I started thinking, I realized it had to be one of them. Aunt. Papa. Warren. I didn't want them hurt."

"You accused me."

"It seemed the best way to drive you off," she said simply. "For your own sake. I'd learned, you know, the price one pays for being loved by a Culhaine."

I shook my head, bewildered. "But later, when you began to know . . . you shut me out. You allied yourself with Marina."

Damaris shrugged. "Warren was dead." And with him, I thought, illusions she had not known she had. "Besides, I think I felt dying would be just retribution. I still believed, you know, that I'd killed my mother."

She pressed her hands together tightly, then raised them to her lips. For a minute she looked like one of those old portraits of medieval ladies bowed in prayer. Then she turned and smiled. "And now, Lavinia? Will you come with us to Italy?"

"I—don't know."

"I hope you will. We will go to Garda, and we will exorcise our ghosts. We will go to the belvedere beside the lake, where Papa went as a young man to find a life, and we will begin, the three of us, to weave a different pattern." She rose. "It is time, now. I will rouse the footman and send him for the doctor. I will do it well, and probably I shall make myself ill, so help me, Vinnie." She ran her fingers through her hair, and disarranged her wrapper, and opened the hall door. And the next moment I heard her frantic voice, her labored breathing as she screamed for help.

It was well-played, the charade we staged that night, and none will ever know. The servants stumbled down, frightened and horror-struck as they had been on other nights—nights which are behind us now forever. The doctor came, and by that time Damaris had indeed worked herself into a state, and I took care of her while Dr. Martinson made futile efforts with Marina. I got Damaris into bed, and sat beside her, talking steadily, relentlessly, trying to blot from both our ears the sounds from the room next door. Damaris wouldn't let me give her a sleeping-draught, but when she was at last asleep and I could leave her, I bathed my face at her washstand and went quietly downstairs. I did not go to the conservatory, which for so long had been my refuge. I opened the door of Ross's library, as if it were my right, and went inside to sit, for however long I might have to wait, beside the smoldering fire.

I did something else, too. I took from my pocket, where I had thrust it in the moment when I followed Damaris from my room, the golden collar. I looked at it, and I laid it round my shoulders where its weight settled as if by long custom. I was still in my nightdress, but it did not matter.

It was long hours before Ross came down, and when he

did it was to go round the desk and stand gazing out the window where a faint light was rising, turning the lavender panes to rose. "She's gone," he said at last. "She—died in my arms, the way she would have wanted." He said it without bravado, simply stating a fact, and he sounded tired to death. "At the end, she thought we were back in Italy, beside the lake where we first met. She'd forgotten everything that came between. I'm glad."

"And the doctor?"

"Knows nothing. Oh, he knows she swallowed poison, of course, but not the reason. He's been murmuring sympathetically about delicate female sensibilities that cannot stand strain. Little does he understand these Orsini women!" Ross was silent for a moment. "She tried to kill you. And Damaris. She did kill Warren. You guessed that, didn't you?"

"Not until the last. Suicide didn't seem in character for Warren, but then Marina told me a reason that made sense. Then, after Damaris remembered—when I knew it had been Marina, the other time—I recalled seeing her fix a cup of coffee for him on New Year's Day. She had been wearing her ring then, too, of course."

"She always wore it. She must have carried poison in it ever since the—episodes began . . ." He stopped, his head back, pressed his hands against his face, then dropped them. "Obsessions, illusions. How terrible they are, how dangerous . . . I lived the first half of my life trying to measure up to an illusion I could not fill, then cursed myself for failing. I've spent the second half trying to perpetuate the illusion of la Bianca, long after I knew the gold was dross. I told myself I was doing it for others' sakes, not wanting to face it was for my own false pride. And what has come of it? Three deaths: my wife, her sister, that poor ambitious fool who after all was not so different from myself. A daughter almost dead, and near crushed beneath a load of unnecessary guilt. And you . . ." He swung round. "Marina talked to you, didn't she, before Damaris came? She would have, thinking it was safe. What did she tell you?"

And I told him, breaking for the second time a vow of silence. I did it because I guessed what Marina had not, could not have borne to know: that Ross had long since lost his illusions about Isabella. And more, because of what I at last have come to see—that often the cruelest thing you can do to another person is to protect them from the truth. When I had finished at last, we sat in a long silence.

Ross shook his head slightly, then dropped it in his hands. "Poor soul," he said. I did not know if he meant Marina or Isabella. Perhaps both. "So much anguish, so much suffering, done to protect a dream from fading. A dream already dead. And one word from me would have prevented all." He said, an echo of my thoughts, "Truth is less dangerous than deception, however loving. At least it's final."

"You must not blame yourself."

Ross smiled crookedly. "No. That would only perpetuate the circle, wouldn't it? Guilt, and self-punishment, and retribution. And for what? It will not cancel half a line, nor all our tears wash out a word of it. At least we've put an end to that. The Furies will pursue the House of Culhaine no more, and I am glad, for my daughter's sake." He straightened with a look of rueful wonder. "I'd not need to worry about it, would I, anyway? Damaris was—remarkable. There, too, I have been suffering from illusions."

"Damaris is an Orsini, too, after all. *And* a Culhaine."

"So I begin to see. I wonder how much she knows."

"I should say, all of it. Unlike the rest of us, she lives with few illusions."

He shot me a look. "Including in Sloane? Yes—I begin to see." He said again, "Remarkable . . . And now?"

"Now?"

"Now you, Lavinia, *quo vadis?*" I did not answer, and after a moment he straightened and looked at me again. The rose-violet light was filling the room as the dawn was rising, and it was the first time, I think, that he perceived the collar. He recognized its significance at once; he rose, and made a slight movement towards me, quickly checked. He went instead to the window and drew the curtain back, and the light came flooding in.

"I could not ask you before to marry me. I was—too much imprisoned. Today I feel, for the first time in my life perhaps, truly free. I think, I have thought for some time now, that you feel the same. So it is as equal to equal that I ask you now, shall we pledge together?"

I sought for words to answer. "If you need me—"

He would have none of my face-saving pride. He swung on me. "I am asking you to marry me out of love, not need. You had a sample last night of how dangerous obsessive needs can be. An identity that is based on one's own need of another, or vice versa, is one of the most destructive forces on this earth. Your life is your identity, Lavinia, as my life is mine; we can stand on it, stand alone if need be. And, therefore, are free to stand together."

"With no ghosts?"

"Of course with ghosts," Ross said roughly. "Our ghosts are part of what we are. But they need not be chains. That, if anything, is what these days should teach us. We are strong enough to carry them with us—towards each other."

He did come towards me then, but quietly. "Lavinia. Aeneas' gift of grace, do you remember? After he left behind him the flames of his lost world, and walked into the new. Carrying his past, his present and his future with him, and standing tall."

Yes, I thought. Those ancient Romans understood.

I turned slightly, and my eyes fell on Damaris' little harp. I picked it up, more to occupy my trembling hands than for any purpose, and one wire gave out a plaintive *pling*.

It was the note with which Damaris had always started her

pavane. The recognition struck Ross and me at once, and our eyes met, in memory and shared pain. Ross lifted the little instrument from my fingers.

"Damaris will want to take this with her to Italy. But I doubt if she will sing that song again." No, it was not likely. The pattern was complete; the pavane was over.

"Now," said Ross firmly, "we will write new songs."

We will go to Italy, Ross and I. And Damaris, and old Maggie, whose fierce love for her "lamb" will triumph over her distrust of foreign ways. I will walk in the Florentine palaces, and glide down the Grand Canal by moonlight in my husband's arms. We will go to Garda, and the hot sun Damaris spoke of so longingly will bring its healing, and we will sit in the belvedere beside the lake, and peace will come, and the mountains will drip sweet wine.

If this were a novel, that is how our story would end. But this is life, and we are strong, Ross and I. Yes, and Damaris, too. The house on Marlborough Street holds no terrors now. And so we will come back again to Boston. The Irish lace will hang with pride at our lavender windows. And it is here in Boston, the Lord Culhaine beside me, that I will wear in the golden collar the Medici ring.